ALSO BY JESMYN WARD

The Fire This Time:
A New Generation Speaks about Race
(editor)

Men We Reaped: A Memoir

Salvage the Bones: A Novel

Where the Line Bleeds: A Novel

SING, UNBURIED, SING

A Novel

JESMYN WARD

SCRIBNER

New York   London   Toronto   Sydney   New Delhi

SCRIBNER

An Imprint of Simon & Schuster, Inc.

1230 Avenue of the Americas

New York, NY 10020

First Scribner hardcover edition September 2017

SCRIBNER and design are registered trademarks of The Gale Group, Inc., used under license by Simon & Schuster, Inc., the publisher of this work.

For information about special discounts for bulk purchases, please contact Simon & Schuster Special Sales at 1-866-506-1949 or business@simonandschuster.com.

The Simon & Schuster Speakers Bureau can bring authors to your live event. For more information or to book an event contact the Simon & Schuster Speakers Bureau at 1-866-248-3049 or visit our website at www.simonspeakers.com.

Interior design by Kyle Kabel

Manufactured in the United States of America

3   5   7   9   10   8   6   4

ISBN 978-1-5011-2606-2

ISBN 978-1-5011-2609-3 (ebook)

For my mother, Norine Elizabeth Dedeaux,
who loved me before I took my first breath.
Every second of my life, she shows me so.

Who are we looking for, who are we looking for?
It's Equiano we're looking for.
Has he gone to the stream? Let him come back.
Has he gone to the farm? Let him return.
It's Equiano we're looking for.

—Kwa chant about the disappearance
of Equiano, an African boy

The memory is a living thing—it too is in transit. But during its moment, all that is remembered joins, and lives—the old and the young, the past and the present, the living and the dead.

—from *One Writer's Beginnings*,
by Eudora Welty

The Gulf shines, dull as lead. The coast of Texas
glints like a metal rim. I have no home
as long as summer bubbling to its head

boils for that day when in the Lord God's name
the coals of fire are heaped upon the head
of all whose gospel is the whip and flame,

age after age, the uninstructing dead.

—from "The Gulf," by Derek Walcott

SING,
UNBURIED,
SING

Chapter 1
Jojo

I like to think I know what death is. I like to think that it's something I could look at straight. When Pop tell me he need my help and I see that black knife slid into the belt of his pants, I follow Pop out the house, try to keep my back straight, my shoulders even as a hanger; that's how Pop walks. I try to look like this is normal and boring so Pop will think I've earned these thirteen years, so Pop will know I'm ready to pull what needs to be pulled, separate innards from muscle, organs from cavities. I want Pop to know I can get bloody. Today's my birthday.

I grab the door so it don't slam, ease it into the jamb. I don't want Mam or Kayla to wake up with none of us in the house. Better for them to sleep. Better for my little sister, Kayla, to sleep, because on nights when Leonie's out working, she wake up every hour, sit straight up in the bed, and scream. Better for Grandma Mam to sleep, because the chemo done dried her up and hollowed her out the way the sun and the air do water oaks. Pop weaves in and out of the trees, straight and slim and brown as a young pine tree. He spits in the dry red dirt, and the wind makes the

1

trees wave. It's cold. This spring is stubborn; most days, it won't make way for warmth. The chill stays like water in a bad-draining tub. I left my hoodie on the floor in Leonie's room, where I sleep, and my T-shirt is thin, but I don't rub my arms. If I let the cold goad me, I know when I see the goat, I'll flinch or frown when Pop cuts the throat. And Pop, being Pop, will see.

"Better to leave the baby asleep," Pop says.

Pop built our house himself, narrow in the front and long, close to the road so he could leave the rest of the property wooded. He put his pigpen and his goat yard and the chicken coop in small clearings in the trees. We have to walk past the pigpen to get to the goats. The dirt is black and muddy with shit, and ever since Pop whipped me when I was six for running around the pen with no shoes on, I've never been barefoot out here again. *You could get worms*, Pop had said. Later that night, he told me stories about him and his sisters and brothers when they were young, playing barefoot because all they had was one pair of shoes each and them for church. They all got worms, and when they used the outhouse, they pulled worms out of their butts. I don't tell Pop, but that was more effective than the whipping.

Pop picks the unlucky goat, ties a rope around its head like a noose, leads it out the pen. The others bleat and rush him, butting his legs, licking his pants.

"Get! Get!" Pop says, and kicks them away. I think the goats understand each other; I can see it in the aggressive butts of their heads, in the way they bite Pop's pants and yank. I think they know what that loose rope tied around the goat's neck means. The white goat with black splashes on his fur dances from side to side, resisting, like he catches a whiff of what he is walking toward. Pop pulls him past the pigs, who rush the fence and grunt at Pop, wanting food, and down the trail toward the shed, which is closer to the house. Leaves slap my shoulders, and they scratch me dry, leaving thin white lines scrawled on my arms.

"Why you ain't got more of this cleared out, Pop?"

"Ain't enough space," Pop says. "And don't nobody need to see what I got back here."

"You can hear the animals up front. From the road."

"And if anybody come back here trying to mess with my animals, I can hear them coming through these trees."

"You think any of the animals would let themselves get took?"

"No. Goats is mean and pigs is smarter than you think. And they vicious, too. One of them pigs'll take a bite out of anybody they ain't used to eating from."

Pop and I enter the shed. Pop ties the goat to a post he's driven into the floor, and it barks at him.

"Who you know got all they animals out in the open?" Pop says. And Pop is right. Nobody in Bois has their animals out in the open in fields, or in the front of their property.

The goat shakes its head from side to side, pulls back. Tries to shrug the rope. Pop straddles it, puts his arm under the jaw.

"The big Joseph," I say. I want to look out the shed when I say it, over my shoulder at the cold, bright green day, but I make myself stare at Pop, at the goat with its neck being raised to die. Pop snorts. I hadn't wanted to say his name. Big Joseph is my White grandpa, Pop my Black one. I've lived with Pop since I was born; I've seen my White grandpa twice. Big Joseph is round and tall and looks nothing like Pop. He don't even look like Michael, my father, who is lean and smudged with tattoos. He picked them up like souvenirs from wannabe artists in Bois and out on the water when he worked offshore and in prison.

"Well, there you go," Pop says.

Pop wrestles the goat like it's a man, and the goat's knees buckle. It falls face forward in the dirt, turns its head to the side so it's looking up at me with its cheek rubbing the dusty earth and bloody floor of the shed. It shows me its soft eye, but I don't look away, don't blink. Pop slits. The goat makes a sound of surprise, a bleat swallowed by a gurgle, and then there's blood and mud everywhere. The goat's legs go rubbery and loose, and Pop isn't struggling anymore. All at once, he stands up and ties a rope around the goat's ankles, lifting the body to a hook hanging from the rafters. That eye: still wet. Looking at me like I was the one who cut its neck, like I was the one bleeding it out, turning its whole face red with blood.

"You ready?" Pop asks. He glances at me then, quickly. I nod. I'm frowning, my face drawn tight. I try to relax as Pop cuts the goat along the legs, giving the goat pant seams, shirt seams, lines all over.

"Grab this here," Pop says. He points at a line on the goat's stomach, so I dig my fingers in and grab. It's still warm, and it's wet. *Don't slip*, I say to myself. *Don't slip.*

"Pull," Pop says.

I pull. The goat is inside out. Slime and smell every-where, something musty and sharp, like a man who ain't took a bath in some days. The skin peels off like a banana. It surprises me every time, how easy it comes away once you pull. Pop yanking hard on the other side, and then he's cutting and snapping the hide off at the feet. I pull the skin down the animal's leg to the foot, but I can't get it off like Pop, so he cuts and snaps.

"Other side," Pop says. I grab the seam near the heart. The goat's even warmer here, and I wonder if his panicked heart beat so fast it made his chest hotter, but then I look at Pop, who's already snapping the skin off the end of the goat's foot, and I know my wondering's made me slow. I don't want him to read my slowness as fear, as weakness, as me not being old enough to look at death like a man should, so I grip and yank. Pop snaps the skin off at the animal's foot, and then the animal sways from the ceiling, all pink and muscle, catching what little light there is, glistening in the dark. All that's left of the goat is the hairy face, and somehow this is even worse than the moment before Pop cut its throat.

"Get the bucket," Pop says, so I get the metal tub from one of the shelves at the back of the shed, and I pull it under the animal. I pick up the skin, which is already turning stiff, and I dump it into the tub. Four sheets of it.

Pop slices down the center of the stomach, and the innards slide out and into the tub. He's slicing and the smell overwhelms like a faceful of pig shit. It smells like foragers, dead and rotting out in the thick woods, when the only sign of them is the stink and the buzzards rising and settling and circling. It stinks like possums or armadillos smashed half flat on the road, rotting in asphalt and heat. But worse. This smell is worse; it's the smell of death, the rot coming from something just alive, something hot with blood and life. I grimace, wanting to make Kayla's stink face, the face she makes when she's angry or impatient; to everyone else, it looks like she's smelled something nasty: her green eyes squinting, her nose a mushroom, her twelve tiny toddler teeth showing through her open mouth. I want to make that face because something about scrunching up my nose and squeezing the smell away might lessen it, might cut off that stink of death. I know it's the stomach and intestines, but all I can see is Kayla's stink face and the soft eye of the goat and then I can't hold myself still and watch no more, then I'm out the door of the shed and I'm throwing up in the grass outside. My face is so hot, but my arms are cold.

Pop steps out of the shed, and he got a slab of ribs in his fist. I wipe my mouth and look at him, but he's not looking at me, he's looking at the house, nodding toward it.

"Thought I heard the baby cry. You should go check on them."

I put my hands in my pockets.

"You don't need my help?"

Pop shakes his head.

"I got it," he says, but then he looks at me for the first time and his eyes ain't hard no more. "You go ahead." And then he turns and goes back to the shed.

Pop must have misheard, because Kayla ain't awake. She's lying on the floor in her drawers and her yellow T-shirt, her head to the side, her arms out like she's trying to hug the air, her legs wide. A fly is on her knee, and I brush it away, hoping it hasn't been on her the whole time I've been out in the shed with Pop. They feed on rot. Back when I was younger, back when I still called Leonie *Mama*, she told me flies eat shit. That was when there was more good than bad, when she'd push me on the swing Pop hung from one of the pecan trees in the front yard, or when she'd sit next to me on the sofa and watch TV with me, rubbing my head. Before she was more gone than here. Before she started snorting crushed pills. Before all the little mean things she told me gathered and gathered and lodged like grit in a skinned knee. Back then I still called Michael *Pop*. That was when he lived with us before he moved back in with Big Joseph. Before the police took him away three years ago, before Kayla was born.

Each time Leonie told me something mean, Mam would tell her to leave me alone. *I was just playing with him*, Leonie would say, and each time she smiled wide, brushed her hand across her forehead to smooth her short, streaked hair. *I pick colors that make my skin pop*, she told Mam. *Make this dark shine.* And then: *Michael love it.*

I pull the blanket up over Kayla's stomach and lie next to her on the floor. Her little foot is warm in my hand. Still asleep, she kicks off the cover and grabs at my arm, pulling it up to her stomach, so I hold her before settling again. Her mouth opens and I wave at the circling fly, and Kayla lets off a little snore.

*   *   *

When I walk back out to the shed, Pop's already cleaned up the mess. He's buried the foul-smelling intestines in the woods, and wrapped the meat we'll eat months later in plastic and put it in the small deep-freezer wedged in a corner. He shuts the door to the shed, and when we walk past the pens I can't help avoiding the goats, who rush the wooden fence and bleat. I know they are asking after their friend, the one I helped kill. The one who Pop carries pieces of now: the tender liver for Mam, which he will sear barely so the blood won't run down her mouth when he sends me in to feed it to her; the haunches for me, which he will boil for hours and then smoke and barbecue to celebrate my birthday. A few of the goats wander off to lick at the grass. Two of the males skitter into each other, and then one head-butts the other, and they are fighting. When one of the males limps off and the winner, a dirty white color, begins bullying a small gray female, trying to mount her, I pull my arms into my sleeves. The female kicks at the male and bleats. Pop stops next to me and waves the fresh meat in the air to keep flies from it. The male bites at the female's ear, and the female makes a sound like a growl and snaps back.

"Is it always like that?" I ask Pop. I've seen horses rearing and mounting each other, seen pigs rutting in the mud, heard wildcats at night shrieking and snarling as they make kittens.

Pop shakes his head and lifts the choice meats toward me. He half smiles, and the side of his mouth that shows teeth is knife-sharp, and then the smile is gone.

"No," he says. "Not always. Sometimes it's this, too."

The female head-butts the neck of the male, screeching. The male skitters back. I believe Pop. I do. Because I see him with Mam. But I see Leonie and Michael as clearly as if they were in front of me, in the last big fight they had before Michael left us and moved back in with Big Joseph, right before he went to jail: Michael threw his jerseys and his camouflage pants and his Jordans into big black garbage bags, and then hauled his stuff outside. He hugged me before he left, and when he leaned in close to my face all I could see were his eyes, green as the pines, and the way his face turned red in splotches: his cheeks, his mouth, the edges of his nose, where the veins were little scarlet streams under the skin. He put his arms around my back and patted once, twice, but those pats were so light, they didn't feel like hugs, even though something in his face was pulled tight, wrong, like underneath his skin he was crisscrossed with tape. Like he would cry. Leonie was pregnant with Kayla then, and already had Kayla's name picked out and scrawled with nail polish on her car seat, which had been my car seat. Leonie was getting bigger; her stomach looked like she had a Nerf basketball shoved under her shirt. She followed Michael out on the porch where I stood, still feeling those two little pats on my back, soft as a weak wind, and Leonie grabbed him by the collar and pulled and slapped him on the side of the head, so hard it sounded loud and wet. He turned and grabbed her by her arms, and they were yelling and breathing hard and pushing and pulling each other across the porch. They were so close to each other, their hips and chests and faces, that they were one, scuttling, clumsy like a hermit crab over sand. And then they were leaning in close to each other, speaking, but their words sounded like moans.

"I know," Michael said.

"You ain't never known," Leonie said.

"Why you push me like this?"

"You go where you want," Leonie said, and then she was crying and they were kissing, and they only moved apart when Big Joseph pulled onto the dirt driveway and stopped, just so his truck was out of the street and in the yard. He didn't lay on the horn or wave or nothing, just sat there, waiting for Michael. And then Leonie walked away from him and slammed the door and disappeared back into the house, and Michael looked down at his feet. He'd forgot to put shoes on, and his toes were red. He breathed hard and grabbed his bags, and the tattoos on his white back moved: the dragon on his shoulder, the scythe down his arm. A grim reaper between his shoulder blades. My name, *Joseph*, at the root of his neck in between ink prints of my baby feet.

"I'll be back," he said, and then he jumped down off the porch, shaking his head and hauling his garbage bags over his shoulder, and walked over to the truck, where his daddy, Big Joseph, the man who ain't never once said my name, waited. Part of me wanted to give him the bird when he pulled out of the driveway, but more of me was scared that Michael would jump back out of the truck and whip me, so I didn't. Back then I didn't realize how Michael noticed and didn't notice, how sometimes he saw me and then, whole days and weeks, he didn't. How, in that moment, I didn't matter. Michael hadn't looked back after he jumped off the porch, hadn't even looked up after he threw his bags into the bed of the pickup truck and got into the front seat. He seemed like he was still concentrating on his red, naked feet. Pop says a man should look another man in the face, so I stood there, looking at Big Joseph putting the truck in reverse, at Michael looking down at his lap, until they pulled out of the driveway and went down the street. And then I spat the way Pop does, and jumped off the porch and ran around to the animals in their secret rooms in the back woods.

"Come on, son," Pop says. When he begins walking toward the house, I follow, trying to leave the memory of Leonie and Michael fighting outside, floating like fog in the damp, chilly day. But it follows, even as I follow the trail of tender organ blood Pop has left in the dirt, a trail that signals love as clearly as the bread crumbs Hansel spread in the wood.

The smell of the liver searing in the pan is heavy in the back of my throat, even through the bacon grease Pop dribbled on it first. When Pop plates it, the liver smells, but the gravy he made to slather on it pools in a little heart around the meat, and I wonder if Pop did that on purpose. I carry it to Mam's doorway, but she's still asleep, so I bring the food back to the kitchen, where Pop drapes a paper towel over it to keep it warm, and then I watch him chop up the meat and seasoning, garlic and celery and bell pepper and onion, which makes my eyes sting, and set it to boil.

If Mam and Pop were there on the day of Leonie and Michael's fight, they would have stopped it. *The boy don't need to see that*, Pop would say. Or *You don't want your child to think that's how you treat another person*, Mam might've said. But they weren't there. It's not often I can say that. They weren't there because they'd found out that Mam was sick with cancer, and so Pop was taking her back and forth to the doctor. It was the first time I could remember they were depending on Leonie to look after me. After Michael left with Big Joseph, it felt weird to sit across the table from Leonie and make a fried potato sandwich while she stared off into space and crossed her legs and kicked her feet, let cigarette smoke seep out of her lips and wreathe her head like a veil, even though Mam and Pop hated when she smoked in the house. To be alone with her. She ashed her cigarettes and put them out in an empty Coke she had been drinking, and when I bit into the sandwich, she said:

"That looks disgusting."

She'd wiped her tears from her fight with Michael, but I could still see tracks across her face, dried glossy, from where they'd fallen.

"Pop eat them like this."

"You got to do everything Pop do?"

I shook my head because it seemed like what she expected from me. But I liked most of the things Pop did, liked the way he stood when he spoke, like the way he combed his hair back straight from his face and slicked it down so he looked like an Indian in the books we read in school on the Choctaw and Creek, liked the way he let me sit in his lap and drive his tractor around the back, liked the way he ate, even, fast and neat, liked the stories he told me before I went to sleep. When I was nine, Pop was good at everything.

"You sure act like it."

Instead of answering, I swallowed hard. The potatoes were salty and thick, the mayonnaise and ketchup spread too thin, so the potatoes stuck in my throat a little bit.

"Even that sounds gross," Leonie said. She dropped her cigarette into the can and pushed it across the table to me where I stood eating. "Throw that away."

She walked out the kitchen into the living room and picked up one of Michael's baseball caps that he'd left on the sofa, before pulling it low over her face.

"I'll be back," she said.

Sandwich in hand, I trotted after her. The door slammed and I pushed through it. *You going to leave me here by myself?* I wanted to ask her, but the sandwich was a ball in my throat, lodged on the panic bubbling up from my stomach; I'd never been home alone.

"Mama and Pop be home soon," she said as she slammed her car door. She drove a low maroon Chevy Malibu that Pop and Mam had bought her when she'd graduated from high school. Leonie pulled out the driveway, one hand out the window to catch the air or wave, I couldn't tell which, and she was gone.

Something about being alone in the too-quiet house scared me, so I sat on the porch for a minute, but then I heard a man singing, singing in a high voice that sounded all wrong, singing the same words over and over. "Oh Stag-o-lee, why can't you be true?" It was Stag, Pop's oldest brother, with a long walking stick in hand. His clothes looked hard and oily, and he swung that stick like an axe. Whenever I saw him, I couldn't never make out any sense to anything he said; it was like he was speaking a foreign language, even though I knew he was speaking English: he walked all over Bois Sauvage every day, singing, swinging a stick. Walked upright like Pop, proud like Pop. Had the same nose Pop had. But everything else about him was nothing like Pop, was like Pop had been wrung out like a wet rag and then dried up in the wrong shape. That was Stag. I'd asked Mam once what was wrong with him, why he always smelled like armadillo, and she had frowned and said: *He sick in the head, Jojo.* And then: *Don't ask Pop about this.*

I didn't want him to see me, so I jumped off and ran around the back to the woods. There was comfort in that, in hearing the pigs snuffle and the goats tear and eat, in seeing the chickens peck and scratch. I didn't feel so small or alone. I squatted in the grass, watching them, thinking I could almost hear them talk to me, that I could hear them communicate. Sometimes when I looked at the fat pig with splashed black spots on his side, he'd grunt and flap his ears, and I'd think he meant to say: *Scratch here, boy.* When the goats licked my hand and head-butted me while nibbling at my fingers and bleated, I heard: *The salt is so sharp and good—more salt.* When the horse Pop keeps bowed his head and shimmied and bucked so that his sides gleamed like wet red Mississippi mud, I understood: *I could leap over your head, boy, and oh I would run and run and you would never see anything more than that. I could make you shake.* But it scared me to understand them, to hear them. Because Stag did that, too; Stag stood in the middle of the street sometimes and had whole conversations with Casper, the shaggy black neighborhood dog.

But it was impossible to not hear the animals, because I looked at them and understood, instantly, and it was like looking at a sentence and understanding the words, all of it coming to me at once. So after Leonie left, I sat in the backyard for a while and listened to the pigs and the horses and old Stag's singing sinking to silence like a whipping and dropping wind. I moved from pen to pen, watching the sun and estimating how long Leonie'd been gone, how long Mam and Pop were gone, how soon I could expect them to come back so I could go inside the house. I was walking with my head tilted up, listening for the growl of tires, so I didn't see the jagged lid of the can rising from the earth, didn't see it when I put my foot on it, stepped down in the instinct of walking. It sank deep. I screamed and dropped, holding my leg, and I knew the animals understood me then, too: *Let me go, great tooth! Spare me!*

Instead, it burned and bled, and I sat on the ground in the horse's clearing and cried and tasted ketchup and acid at the back of my throat and grabbed my ankle. I was too scared to pull the lid out, then I heard a car door slam shut and nothing else until Pop's voice called and I answered and he found me sitting on the ground, sniffing with my breath hitching and not caring my face was wet. Pop came to my side and touched me on the leg like he does our horse when he's checking the shoe. In a quick second, he pulled it out, and I hollered. It was the first time I thought Pop didn't do something good.

When Leonie came home that night, she didn't say nothing. I don't think she noticed my foot until Pop shouted at her, over and over again, *Goddamnit, Leonie!* I drowsed with pain medicine, itchy with antibiotics, my foot all wrapped in white, bound tight, and watched Pop slap the wall to punctuate: *Leonie!* She flinched, stepped away from him, and then said in a small voice: *You was shucking oysters down at the docks when you was his age, Mam changing diapers.* And then: *He old enough.* She said: *You all right, huh, Jojo?* And I looked at her and said: *No, Leonie.* It was a new thing, to look at her rubbing hands and her crooked teeth in her chattering mouth and not hear *Mama* in my head, but her name: *Leonie.* When I said it, she laughed, the sound erupting from her insides like a hard shovel cleaved it from her. Pop looked like he wanted to slap her face, but then he changed, and he snorted like he does when his crop don't take or when one of his sows bears a half-dead litter: disappointed. He sat with me on one of the two sofas in the living room. That was the first night he let Mam sleep in the bed by herself. I slept on the love seat, and he slept on the sofa, where, after Mam got sicker and sicker, he stayed.

The goat smells like beef when it boils. It even looks like it, too, dark and stringy in the pot. Pop pokes it with a spoon, testing the tenderness, and cocks the lid crooked so that steam billows in the air.

"Pop, you going to tell me about you and Stag again?" I ask.

"About what?" Pop asks.

"Parchman," I say. Pop folds his arms. Leans over to smell the goat.

"Ain't I told it to you before?" he asks.

I shrug. Sometimes I think I look like Stag around my nose and mouth. Stag and Pop. I want to hear about the ways they are different. The ways we are all different. "Yeah, but I want to hear it anyway," I say.

This is what Pop does when we are alone, sitting up late at night in the living room or out in the yard or woods. He tells me stories. Stories about eating cattails after his daddy been out gathering them from the marsh. Stories about how his mama and her people used to collect Spanish moss to stuff their mattresses. Sometimes he'll tell me the same story three, even four times. Hearing him tell them makes me feel like his voice is a hand he's reached out to me, like he's rubbing my back and I can duck whatever makes me feel like I'll never be able to stand as tall as Pop, never be as sure. It makes me sweat and stick to the chair in the kitchen, which has gotten so hot from the boiling goat on the stove that the windows have fogged up, and the whole world is shrunk to this room with me and Pop.

"Please," I say. Pop beats the meat he still has left to add to the boil, making it soft and tender, and clears his throat. I put my elbows on the table and listen:

Me and Stag, we got the same papa. My other brothers and sisters got different daddies because my papa died young. Think he was in his early forties. I don't know how old he was because he ain't know how old he was. Said his maman and daddy avoided them census takers, never answered their questions right, changed the number of kids they had, never registered none of they births.

Said them people came around sniffing out that information to control them, to cage them like livestock. So they never did any of that official stuff, held to the old ways. Papa taught us some of that before he died: some hunting and tracking, some animal work, some things about balance, things about life. I listened. I always listened. But Stag ain't never listen. Even when we was little, Stag was too busy running with the dogs or going to the swimming hole to sit and listen. And when he got older, he was off to the juke joint. Papa said he was too handsome, said he'd been born pretty as a woman, and that's why he got into so much trouble. Because people like pretty things, and things came to him too easy. Maman say hush when Papa say that, say Stag just feel things too much, is all. Say that make it hard for him to sit and think. I ain't tell them this, but I thought both of them was wrong. I think Stag felt dead inside, and that's why he couldn't sit still and listen, why he had to climb the highest cliff when we went swimming at the river and jump off headfirst into the water. That's why Stag went to the juke joint damn near every weekend when he got eighteen, nineteen, drinking, why he walked with a knife in each shoe and one up each sleeve, why he cut and came home cut so often—he needed that to feel more alive. And he could have kept it up if that navy man ain't came up in there, one in a group of White men from up north stationed out on Ship Island. Wanted to have a good time with the coloreds, I guess, but bumped into Stag at the bar, and they had words, and then the man broke a bottle over Stag's head, and then Stag cut him, not enough to kill him, but enough to hurt him, to make him slow so Stag could run, but his friends beat up Stag before he could get a clean break. I was at the house alone when Stag got here, Maman up the road taking care of her sister and Papa out in the fields. When all them White men came to get Stag, they tied both of us and took us up the road. You boys is going to learn what it means to work, they said. To do right by the law of God and man, they said. You boys is going to Parchman.

I was fifteen. But I wasn't the youngest noway, Pop says. *That was Richie.*

Kayla wakes up all at once, rolling over and pushing up and smiling. Her hair is everywhere, tangled as the sticker vines that hang from pine trees. Her eyes are green as Michael's, her hair caught somewhere between Leonie's and Michael's with a hint of hay color to it.

"Jojo?" she asks. That's what she always says, even when Leonie is next to her in the bed. That's the reason I can't sleep on the love seat with Pop in the living room anymore; when Kayla was a baby, she got so used to me coming in the middle of the night with her bottle. So I sleep on the floor next to Leonie's bed, and most nights Kayla ends up on my pallet with me, since Leonie's mostly gone. There's something gummy on the side of Kayla's mouth. I lick the hem of my shirt and wipe her cheek, and she shakes my hand off and crawls onto my lap: she's a short three-year-old, so when she curls into me, her feet don't even hang over my lap. She smells like hay baked in the sun, warm milk, and baby powder.

"You thirsty?" I ask.

"Yeah," she whispers.

When she's done, Kayla drops her sippy cup on the floor.

"Sing," she says.

"What you want me to sing?" I ask, even though she never tells me. Like I love to hear Pop tell stories, she loves to hear me sing. " 'Wheels on the Bus'?" I say. I remember that one from Head Start: sometimes the local nuns would visit the school, acoustic guitars slung over their backs like hunting rifles, and play for us. So I sing it low enough that I won't wake Mam, my voice dipping and cracking and grating, but Kayla swings her arms and marches around the room anyway. When Pop leaves the boiling pot and comes into the living room, I can hardly breathe and my arms are burning. I'm singing "Twinkle Twinkle Little Star," another Head Start hit, and throwing Kayla up in the air, almost to the high ceiling, before catching her. If she was a squealer, I wouldn't do it, because then she would definitely wake Mam. But as the smell of onions and garlic, bell pepper, and celery cooked in butter clouds the air, Kayla rises and falls, her arms and legs flung out, her eyes shining, her mouth open in a smile so wide it looks like she could be screaming.

"More," she pants. "More," she grunts when I catch her to toss her again.

Pop shakes his head, but I keep throwing, because I know, by the way he wipes his hands on the dish towels and leans in the wood doorjamb he planed and nailed to make the archway, he doesn't disapprove. He built the ceilings high on purpose, twelve feet, because Mam asked him to, said that the more room in the house from floor to roof, the cooler it would be. He knows I won't hurt her.

"Pop," I huff when Kayla lands more on my chest than in my arms. "You'll tell me the rest before you take the meat out to the smoker?"

"The baby," Pop says.

I catch Kayla and spin her around. She pouts when I put

her down and pull a Fisher-Price play set that used to be mine from under the sofa. I blow off the dust and push it toward her. There's a cow and two chickens in the set, and one of the red barn doors is broken, but she still sinks to the floor and lies on her chest to make the plastic animals hop.

"See, Jojo?" Kayla asks, and bounces the goat. "Baa, baa," she says.

"She all right," I say. "She ain't paying no attention to us."

Pop sits on the floor behind Kayla and flicks the remaining door.

"It's sticky," he says. And then he looks up at the dimpled ceiling and sighs into a sentence, and then another. He is telling the story again.

Richie, he was called. Real name was Richard, and he wasn't nothing but twelve years old. He was in for three years for stealing food: salted meat. Lot of folks was in there for stealing food because everybody was poor and starving, and even though White people couldn't get your work for free, they did everything they could to avoid hiring you and paying you for it. Richie was the youngest boy I ever saw up in Parchman. There was a couple thousand men separated into work farms over all them acres. Damn near fifty thousand acres. Parchman the kind of place that fool you into thinking it ain't no prison, ain't going to be so bad when you first see it, because ain't no walls. Back in the day, it was just fifteen camps, each one surrounded by a barbed-wire fence. Wasn't no brick; wasn't no stone. Us inmates was called gunmen because we worked under the trusty shooters, who was inmates theyselves, but who the warden gave guns to oversee the rest of us. The trusty shooters was the type of men that be the first one to speak when they walk into a room. The kind that draws attention to hisself,

*talks big about the beating and stabbing and killing they did to
get up in a place like that because it makes them feel bigger to be
seen. Makes them feel like real men to see fear.*

When I first got to Parchman, I worked in the fields, planting
and weeding and harvesting crops. Parchman was a working
farm right off. *You see them open fields we worked in, the way
you could look right through that barbed wire, the way you could
grab it and get a toehold here, a bloody handhold there, the way
they cut them trees flat so that land is empty and open to the ends
of the earth, and you think,* I can get out of here if I set my
mind to it. I can follow the right stars south and all the way
on home. *But the reason you think that is because you don't
see the trusty shooters. You don't know the sergeant. You don't
know the sergeant come from a long line of men bred to treat you
like a plowing horse, like a hunting dog—and bred to think he
can make you like it. That the sergeant come from a long line of
overseers. You don't know them trusty shooters done been sent
to Parchman for worse than getting into a fight at a juke joint.
Just know the trusty shooters, the inmate guards, was sent there
because they like to kill, and because they done it in all kind of
nasty ways, not just to other men, but to women and—*

Me and Stag was put in separate camps. Stag got convicted
of assault, I got convicted of harboring a fugitive. I'd worked,
but never like that. Never sunup to sundown in no cotton field.
Never in that kind of heat. It's different up there. The heat. Ain't
no water to catch the wind and cool you off, so the heat settles
and bakes. Like a wet oven. Soon enough my hands thickened
up and my feet crusted and bled and I understood that when
I was on that line in them fields I had to not think about it.
I ain't think about Papa or Stag or the sergeant or the trusty

shooters or the dogs, barking and slobbering at the mouth at the edge of the fields, daydreaming of tearing into a heel, a neck. I forgot it all and bent and stood and bent and stood and only thought of my mother. Her long neck, her steady hands, the way she braided her hair forward to cover her crooked hairline. The dream of her was the glow of a spent fire on a cold night: warm and welcoming. It was the only way I could untether my spirit from myself, let it fly high as a kite in them fields. I had to, or being in jail for them five years woulda made me drop in that dirt and die.

Richie ain't had near that time. It's hard enough for a man of fifteen, but for a boy? A boy of twelve? Richie got there a month and some weeks after I got there. He walked into that camp crying, but crying with no sound, no sobbing. Just tears leaking down his face, glazing it with water. He had a big head shaped like an onion, the kind of head seemed too big for his body: a body all bones and skin. His ears set straight away from his head like leaves coming off a branch, and his eyes was big in his face. He ain't blink. He was fast: walked fast, his feet not shuffling, not like most when they first come to camp, but high-stepping, knees in the air, like a horse. They undid his hands and led him to the shack, to his bunk, and he lay down in the dark next to me and I knew he was still crying because his little shoulders had curved in like a bird's wings when it's landed but they still fluttering, but he still ain't make no noise. Them night guards at the doors to the shack go on a break, things can happen to a boy of twelve in the dark if he a crybaby.

When he woke up in the dark morning, his face was dry. He followed me out to the latrines and to breakfast, and sat down next to me in the dirt.

"*Mighty young to be in here. How old you is? Eight?*" *I asked him.*

He looked insulted. Frowned and his mouth fell open.

"*How biscuits taste nasty?*" *he asked, and hid his mouth behind his hand. I thought he was going to spit the bread out, but he swallowed and said: "I'm twelve."*

"*Still mighty young to be in here.*"

"*I stole.*" *He shrugged.* "*I was good at it. I been stealing since I was eight. I got nine little brothers and sisters always crying for food. And crying sick. Say they backs hurt; say they mouths sore. Got red rashes all over they hands and they feet. So thick on they face you can't hardly see they skin.*"

I knew the sickness he was talking about. We called it "red flame." Heard tell some doctor had claimed most that had it was poor, eating nothing but meat, meal, and molasses. I could've told him those was the lucky ones that ate that way: in the Delta, I'd heard stories of people cooking dirt patties. He was proud of himself when he told me what he'd done, even though he got caught; I could tell in the way he leaned forward, in the way he watched me after he finished talking, like he was waiting for my approval. I knew I couldn't get rid of him then, especially because he was following me around and sleeping in the bunk next to me. Because he looked at me like I could give him something nobody else could. The sun was coming up through the trees, lighting the sky like a new fire, and I was already feeling it in my shoulders, my back, my arms. I chewed something baked into the bread, something crunchy. I swallowed quick—best not to think about it.

"*What's your name, boy?*"

"*Richard. Everybody call me Richie for short. Like it's a*

joke." He looked at me with his eyebrows raised and a little smile on his face, so small it was only his mouth opening to show his teeth, white and crowding. I didn't get the joke, so he slumped and explained with his spoon. "'Cause I be stealing. So I'm rich?"

I looked down at my hands. Crumb-clean and still felt like I hadn't eaten.

"It's a joke," he said. So I gave Richie what he wanted. He was just a boy. I laughed.

Sometimes I think I understand everything else more than I'll ever understand Leonie. She's at the front door, paper grocery bags obscuring her, hitching the screen and kicking it open, and then edging through the door. Kayla scoots toward me when the door bangs shut; she snatches up her juice cup and sucks before kneading my ear. The little pinch and roll of her fingers almost hurts, but it's her habit, so I swing her up in my arms and let her knead. Mam says she does it for comfort because she never breast-fed. *Poor Kayla*, Mam sighed every time. Leonie hated when Mam and Pop began calling her Kayla like me. *She has a name*, Leonie said, *and it's her daddy's. She look like a Kayla*, Mam said, but Leonie never called her that.

"Hey, Michaela baby," Leonie says.

It's not until I'm standing in the door of the kitchen and see Leonie pulling a small white box out of one of the bags that I realize this is the first year Mam won't be making me a cake for my birthday, and then I feel guilty for realizing it so late in the day. Pop would make the meal,

but I should have known that Mam couldn't. She's too sick
with the cancer that came and left and returned, steady
as the rising and sinking of the marsh water in the bayou
with the moon.

"I got you a cake," Leonie says, as if I'm too dumb to
know what the box contains. She knows I'm not stupid. She
said it herself once, when a teacher called her in to school
to talk about my behavior, to tell Leonie: *He never speaks
in class, but he's still not paying attention.* The teacher said it
in front of all the children, who were still sitting in their
seats waiting to be dismissed for the buses. She assigned
me to the frontmost desk in the classroom, the desk nearest
the teacher's, where every five minutes, she'd say, *Are you
paying attention,* which inevitably interrupted whatever
work I was doing and made it impossible to focus. I was
ten then, and had already begun to see things that other
kids didn't, like the way my teacher bit her fingernails raw,
like the way she sometimes wore so much eye makeup
to hide bruising from someone hitting her; I knew what
that looked like because both Michael's and Leonie's faces
sometimes looked that way after fights. It made me wonder if my teacher had her own Michael. On the day of the
conference, Leonie hissed: *He ain't stupid. Jojo, let's go.* And
I winced at the way she used *ain't* and the way she leaned
in to the teacher without even knowing it, and the teacher
blinked and stepped away from the latent violence coiled
in Leonie's arm, running from her shoulder down to her
elbow and to her fist.

Mam always made me red velvet birthday cake. She
began when I was one. When I was four, I knew it well

enough to ask for it: said *red cake* and pointed at the picture on the box on the shelf in the grocery store. The cake that Leonie brought is small, about the size of both of my fists together. Blue and pink pastel sprinkles litter the top of the cake, and on the side, two little blue shoes. Leonie sniffs, coughs into her bony forearm, and then pulls out a half gallon of the cheapest ice cream, the kind with a texture like cold gum.

"They didn't have no more birthday cakes. The shoes is blue, so it fits."

It's not until she says it that I realize Leonie got her thirteen-year-old son a baby shower cake. I laugh but don't feel nothing warm, no joy in me when I do it. A laugh that ain't a laugh, and it's so hard Kayla looks around and then at me like I've betrayed her. She starts crying.

Usually, the singing is my favorite part of my birthday, because the candles make everything look gold, and they shine in Mam's and Pop's faces and make them look young as Leonie and Michael. Whenever they sing to me, they smile. I think it's Kayla's favorite part, too, because she sings stutteringly along. Kayla's making me hold her, because she cried and pushed at Leonie's collarbone and reached for me until Leonie frowned and held her out to me, said: "Here." But this year, the song is not my favorite part of my birthday because instead of being in the kitchen, we're all crowded into Mam's room, and Leonie's holding the cake like she held Kayla earlier, out and away from her chest, like she going to drop it. Mam's awake but doesn't really look awake, her eyes half open, unfocused, looking past me and Leonie and Kayla and Pop. Even though Mam's sweating, her skin looks pale and dry, like a muddy puddle dried to nothing after weeks of no rain in the summer. And there's a mosquito buzzing around my head, dipping into my ear, veering out, teasing to bite.

When the happy birthday song starts, it's only Leonie. She has a pretty voice, the kind of voice that sounds good singing low but sort of cracks on the high notes. Pop is not singing; he never sings. When I was younger, I didn't know because I'd have a whole family singing to me: Mam, Leonie, and Michael. But this year, when Mam can't sing because she's sick and Kayla makes up words to the melody and Michael's gone, I know Pop isn't singing because he's just moving his lips, lip-synching, and there's no noise coming out. Leonie's voice cracks on *dear Joseph*, and the light from the thirteen candles is orange. No one but Kayla looks young. Pop is standing too far out of the light. Mam's eyes have closed to slits in her chalky face, and Leonie's teeth look black at the seams. There's no happiness here.

"Happy birthday, Jojo," Pop says, but he's not looking at me when he says it. He's looking at Mam, at her hands loose and open at her sides. Palms up like something dead. I lean forward to blow out my candles, but the phone rings, and Leonie jumps, so the cake jumps with her. The flames waver and feel hotter under my chin. Pearls of wax drip onto the baby shoes. Leonie turns away from me with the cake, looking to the kitchen, to the phone on the counter.

"You going to let the boy blow out his candles, Leonie?" Pop asks.

"Might be Michael," Leonie says, and then there is no cake because Leonie's taken it with her to the kitchen, set it on the counter next to the black-corded phone. The flames are eating the wax. Kayla shrieks and throws her head back. So I follow Leonie into the kitchen, to my cake, and Kayla smiles. She's reaching for the fire. The mosquito that was in Mam's room has followed us, and he's buzzing around my head, talking about me like I'm a candle or a cake. *So warm and delicious.* I swat him away.

"Hello?" Leonie says.

I grab Kayla's arm and lean in to the flames. She struggles, transfixed.

"Yes."

I blow.

"Baby."

Half the candles gutter out.

"This week?"

The other half eating wax to the nub.

"You sure?"

I blow again, and the cake goes dark. The mosquito lands on my head. *So scrumptious,* he says, and bites. I swat him, and my palm comes away smeared with blood. Kayla reaches.

"We'll be there."

Kayla has a handful of frosting, and her nose is running. Her blond afro curls high. She sticks her fingers in her mouth, and I wipe.

"Easy, baby. Easy."

Michael is an animal on the other end of the telephone behind a fortress of concrete and bars, his voice traveling over miles of wire and listing, sun-bleached power poles. I know what he is saying, like the birds I hear honking and flying south in the winter, like any other animal. *I'm coming home.*

Chapter 2

Leonie

L ast night, after I hung up the phone with Michael, I called
Gloria and got another shift. Gloria owns the country
bar where I work up in the backwoods. It's a hole-in-the-
wall, slapped together with cinder blocks and plywood,
painted green. The first time I saw it, I was riding with
Michael upcountry to a river; we'd park under an over-
pass on the road that crossed the river and then walk until
we reached a good swimming spot. *What's that?* I asked,
and pointed. I figured it wasn't a house, even though it sat
low under the trees. There was too many cars parked in
the sandy grass. *That's the Cold Drink*, Michael said, and
he smelled like hard pears and his eyes were green as the
outside. *Like Barq's and Coke?* I said. *Yep.* He said his mama
went to school with the owner. I called his mama years later
after Michael went to jail, thanked God when it was her that
picked up the phone and not Big Joseph. He would have
hung up in my face rather than speak to me, the nigger his
son had babies with. I told Michael's mother I needed work,
and asked if she could put in a good word with the owner.
It was the fourth conversation we'd ever had. We spoke

first when Michael and I started dating, second time when Jojo was born, and third when Michaela was born. But still she said yes, and then she told me I should go up there, up to the Kill, upcountry, where Michael and his parents are from, where the bar is, and I should introduce myself to Gloria, so I did. Gloria hired me for a probationary period of three months. *You're a hard worker*, she said, laughing, when she told me she was keeping me on. She wore heavy eyeliner, and when she laughed, the skin at the sides of her eyes looked like an elaborate fan. *Even harder than Misty*, she said, *and she damn near lives here*. And then waved me back out front to the bar. I grabbed my tray of drinks, and three months turned into three years. After my second day at the Cold Drink, I knew why Misty worked so hard: she was high every night. Lortab, Oxycontin, coke, Ecstasy, meth.

Before I showed up for work at the Cold Drink last night, Misty must have had a good double, because after we mopped and cleaned and shut everything down, we went to her pink MEMA cottage she's had since Hurricane Katrina, and she pulled out an eight ball.

"So he's coming home?" Misty asked.

Misty was opening all the windows. She knows I like to hear outside when I get high. I know she doesn't like to get high alone, which is why she invited me over, and why she opens the windows even though the wet spring night seeps into the house like a fog.

"Yep."

"You must be happy."

The last window snapped up and locked into place, and I stared out of it as Misty sat at the table and began cutting and dividing. I shrugged. I'd felt so happy when I got the phone call, when I heard Michael's voice saying words I'd imagined him saying for months, for years, so happy that my insides felt like a full ditch ridden with a thousand tadpoles. But then when I left, Jojo looked up from where he sat with Pop in the living room watching some hunting show, and for a flash, the cast of his face, the way his features folded, looked like Michael after one of our worst fights. Disappointed. Grave at my leaving. And I couldn't shake it. His expression kept coming back to me through my shift, made me pull Bud Light instead of Budweiser, Michelob instead of Coors. And then Jojo's face stuck with me because I could tell he secretly thought I was going to surprise him with a gift, something else besides that hasty cake, some *thing* that wouldn't be gone in three days: a basketball, a book, a pair of high-top Nikes to add to his single pair of shoes.

I bent to the table. Sniffed. A clean burning shot through my bones, and then I forgot. The shoes I didn't buy, the melted cake, the phone call. The toddler sleeping in my bed at home while my son slept on the floor, just in case I'd come home and make him get on the floor when I stumbled in. Fuck it.

"Ecstatic." I said it slow. Sounded the syllables out. And that's when Given came back.

The kids at school teased Given about his name. One day he got into a fight about it on the bus, tumbling over the seats with a husky redhead boy who wore camo. Frustrated and swollen-lipped, he came home and asked Mama: *Why y'all give me this name? Given? It don't make no sense.* And Mama squatted down and rubbed his ears, and said: *Given because it rhymes with your papa's name: River. And Given because I was forty when I had you. Your papa was fifty. We thought we couldn't have no kids, but then you was Given to us.* He was three years older than me, and when him and Camo boy went flipping and swinging over the seat, I swung my book bag at Camo and hit him in the back of the head.

Last night, he smiled at me, this Given-not-Given, this Given that's been dead fifteen years now, this Given that came to me every time I snorted a line, every time I popped a pill. He sat in one of the two empty chairs at the table with us, and leaned forward and rested his elbows on the table. He was watching me, like always. He had Mama's face.

"That much, huh?" Misty sucked snot up her nose.

"Yep."

Given rubbed the dome of his shaved head, and I saw other differences between the living and this chemical figment. Given-not-Given didn't breathe right. He never breathed at all. He wore a black shirt, and it was a still, mosquito-ridden pool.

"What if Michael's different?" Misty said.

"He won't be," I said.

Misty threw a wadded-up paper towel she'd been using to clean the table.

"What you looking at?" she said.

"Nothing."

"Bullshit."

"Don't nobody sit and stare for that long on something

this clean without looking at something." Misty waved her hand at the coke and winked at me. She'd tattooed her boyfriend's initials on her ring finger, and for a second it looked like letters and then bugs and then letters again. Her boyfriend was Black, and this loving across color lines was one of the reasons we became friends so quickly. She often told me that as far as she was concerned, they were already married. Said she needed him because her mother didn't give a shit about her. Misty told me once that she got her period in fifth grade, when she was ten years old, and because she didn't realize what was happening to her, her body betraying her, she walked around half the day with a bloody spot spreading like an oil stain on the back of her pants. Her mother beat her in the parking lot of the school, she was so embarrassed. The principal called the cops. *Just one of the many ways I disappointed her*, Misty said.

"I was feeling it," I said.

"You know how I know you lie?"

"How?"

"You get dead still. People is always moving, all the time, when they speak, when they're quiet, even when they sleep. Looking off, looking at you, smiling, frowning, all of that. When you lie, you get dead still: blank face, arms limp. Like a fucking corpse. I ain't never seen nothing like it."

I shrugged. Given-not-Given shrugs. *She ain't lying*, he mouths.

"You ever see things?" I say. It's out my mouth before I have a chance to think it. But at that moment, she's my best friend. She's my only friend.

"What you mean?"

"When you on?" I waved my hand like she'd waved hers moments before. At the coke, which was now just a little sorry pile of dust on the table. Enough for two or three lines more.

"That's what it is? You seeing shit?"

"Just lines. Like neon lights or something. In the air."

"Nice try. You tried to twitch your hands and everything. Now, what you really seeing?"

I wanted to punch her in her face.

"I told you."

"Yeah, you lied again."

But I knew this was her cottage, and when it all came down to it, I'm Black and she's White, and if someone heard us tussling and decided to call the cops, I'd be the one going to jail. Not her. Best friend and all.

"Given," I said. More like a whisper than anything, and Given leaned forward to hear me. Slid his hand across the table, his big-knuckled, slim-boned hand, toward mine. Like he wanted to support me. Like he could be flesh and blood. Like he could grab my hand and lead me out of there. Like we could go home.

Misty looked like she ate something sour. She leaned forward and sniffed another line.

"I ain't a expert or nothing, but I'm pretty sure you ain't supposed to be seeing nothing on this shit."

She leaned back in her chair, grabbed her hair in a great sheaf, and tossed it over her back. *Bishop loves it,* she'd said of her boyfriend once. *Can't keep his hands out of it.* It was one of the things she did that she was never conscious of, playing with her hair, always unaware of the ease of it.

The way it caught all the light. The self-satisfied beauty of it. I hated her hair.

"Acid, yeah," she continued. "Maybe even meth. But this? No."

Given-not-Given frowned, mimicked her girly hair flip, and mouthed: *What the fuck does she know?* His left hand was still on the table. I could not reach out to it, even though everything in me wanted to do so, to feel his skin, his flesh, his dry, hard hands. When we were coming up, I couldn't count how many times he fought for us on the bus, in school, in the neighborhood when kids taunted me about how Pop looked like a scarecrow, how Mama was a witch. How I looked just like Pop: like a burnt stick, raggedly clothed. My stomach turned like an animal in its burrow, again and again, seeking comfort and warmth before sleep. I lit a cigarette.

"No shit," I said.

Jojo's birthday cake doesn't keep well: the next day, it tastes five days old instead of one. It tastes like paper paste, but I keep eating. I can't help it. My teeth chomp and grind, even though I don't have enough spit and my throat doesn't want to swallow. The coke done had me chewing like this since last night. Pop's talking to me, but all I can think about is my jaw.

"You don't have to take them kids nowhere," Pop says.

Most days, Pop is a younger man. Same way, most days, Jojo is stuck for me at five. I don't look at Pop and see the years bending and creasing him: I see him with white teeth and a straight back and eyes as black and bright as his hair. I told Mama once that I thought Pop dyed it, and she rolled her eyes at me and laughed, back when she could laugh. *That's just him*, she'd said. The cake is so sweet it's almost bitter.

"I do," I say.

I could just take Michaela, I know. It would be easier, but I know that once we get to the jail and Michael walks out, something in him would be disappointed if Jojo wasn't there. Already Jojo looks too much like me and Pop, with his brown skin and black eyes, with the way he walks, bouncing on the balls of his feet, everything about him upright. If Jojo weren't standing there with us, waiting for Michael, well, it wouldn't be right.

"What about school?"

"It's just two days, Pop."

"It's important, Leonie. Boy need his learning."

"He smart enough to miss two days."

Pop grimaces, and for the length of it I see the age in his face. The lines of it leading him inexorably down, like Mama. To infirmity, to bed, to the ground and the grave. This is coming down.

"I don't like the idea of you with them two kids by y'all self out on the road, Leonie."

"It's going to be a straight trip, Pop. North and back."

"You never know."

I clench my mouth, speak through my teeth. My jaw aches.

"We'll be fine."

Michael's been in jail three years now. Three years, two

months. And ten days. They gave him five with the possibility of early release. The possibility's real now. Present. My insides are shaking.

"You all right?" Pop asks. He's looking at me like he looks at one of his animals when something's wrong with it, the way he looks like when his horse limps and needs to be reshoed, or when one of his chickens starts acting funny and feral. He sees the error, and he's dead committed to fixing it. Armor the horse's tender hooves. Isolate the chicken. Wring its neck.

"Yeah," I say. My head feels filled with exhaust fumes: light and hot. "Fine."

Sometimes I think I know why I see Given-not-Given whenever I'm high. When I had my first period, Mama sat me down at the kitchen table while Pop was at work and she said: "I got something to tell you."

"What?" I said. Mama looked at me sharp. "Yes, ma'am," I said instead, swallowing my earlier words.

"When I was twelve, the midwife Marie-Therese came to the house to deliver my youngest sister. She was sitting a moment in the kitchen, directing me to boil water and unpacking her herbs, when she start pointing and asking me what I thought each of the bundles of dried plants did. And I looked at them, and knew, so I told her: *This one for helping the afterbirth come, this one for slowing the bleeding, this one for helping the pain, this one for bringing the milk down.* It was like someone was humming in my ear, telling me they purpose. Right there, she told me I had the seed of a gift.

With my mama panting in the other room, Marie-Therese took her time, put her hand on my heart, and prayed to the Mothers, to Mami Wata and to Mary, the Virgin Mother of God, that I would live long enough to see whatever it was I was meant to see."

Mama put her hand over her mouth like she'd told me something she shouldn't have, like she could cup her words and scoop them back inside, back down her throat to sink to nothing in her stomach.

"Do you?" I asked.

"See?"

I nodded.

"Yes," Mama said.

I wanted to ask her: *What you see?* But I didn't. I kept my mouth shut and waited for her to talk. I might have been scared of what she would tell me if I asked her what she saw when she looked at me. Dying young? Never finding love? Or if I lived, bent by hard work and hard living? Growing old with my mouth twisted bitter at the taste of what I'd been accorded in the feast of life: mustard greens and raw persimmons, sharp with unfulfilled promise and loss?

"You might have it," Mama said.

"Really?" I asked.

"I think it runs in the blood, like silt in river water. Builds up in bends and turns, over sunk trees." She waved her fingers. "Rises up over the water in generations. My mama ain't have it, but heard her talk one time that her sister, Tante Rosalie, did. That it skips from sister to child to cousin. To be seen. And used. Usually come around full-blown when you bleed for the first time."

Mama worried her lip with her fingernails and then tapped the kitchen table.

"Marie-Therese herself could hear. Could look at a woman and hear singing: If she was pregnant, could tell her when she going to have a baby, what sex the baby going to be. Could tell her if she going to see trouble and how she could avoid it. Could look at a man and tell him if the 'shine done ate up his liver, done cured his insides like sausage, could read it in the yellow of his eyes, the shake of his hands. And something else, she said. How she might hear a multitude of voices ringing from any living thing, and how she followed the loudest voices, 'cause these was the most likely. How the clearest voices sang over the jumble of the rest. She could hear sound come from one woman's face in the supply store: *Flip slice me across the face for dancing with Ced*. From the man that run the store who had a leg that sang: *The blood turns black and pools, the toes rot*. How a cow's belly said: *The calf is coming hooves first*. How she first heard the voices when she came to puberty. And when she explained it like that, I realized I had been hearing voices, too. When I was younger, my mama complained about her stomach, how she had ulcers. They was sounding to me, saying, *We eat, we eat, we eat*; I was confused and kept asking her if she was hungry. Marie-Therese trained me, taught me everything she knew, and when your pop and me got married, that was my job. I was busy birthing babies and doctoring folks and making gris-gris bags for protection." Mama rubbed her hands like she was washing them. "But it's slow now. Don't nobody but the old folks come to me for remedies."

"You could deliver a baby?" I asked. The other thing she'd said, about the gris-gris bags, sat unspoken on the table between us, as matter-of-fact as a butter dish or a sugar bowl. She blinked and smiled and shook her head, all of which meant one thing: *yes*. In that moment, Mama became more than my mother, more than the woman who made me say my rosary before I went to sleep with the words *Make sure you pray to the Mothers*. She'd been doing more than mothering when she put homemade ointments on me when I broke out in rashes or gave me special teas when I was sick. That half smile hinted at the secrets of her life, all those things she'd learned and said and seen and lived, the saints and spirits she spoke to when I was too young to understand her prayers. The half smile angled to a frown when Given walked in the door.

"Son, how many times I got to ask you to take off your muddy boots when you walk in the house?"

"Sorry, Ma." He grinned, bent to kiss her, and then stood and walked backward out the door. He was a shadow through the screen as he slipped out of his shoes by stepping on the toes. "Your brother can't even hear what I tell him, never mind what the world sings. But you might. If you start hearing things, you tell me," she said.

Given crouched down on the steps, beating his shoes on the wood, shaking out the mud.

"Leonie," Pop says.

I wish he would call me something else. When I was younger he would call me *girl*. When we were feeding the chickens: *Girl, I know you can throw that corn farther than that.* When we were weeding the vegetable garden and I complained about my back hurting: *You too young to know pain, girl, with that young back.* When I brought report cards home with more As and Bs than Cs: *You a smart one, girl.* He laughed when he said it, sometimes just smiled, and sometimes said it with a plain face, but it never felt like censure. Now he never calls me by anything but my name, and every time he says it, it sounds like a slap. I throw the rest of Jojo's birthday cake in the garbage before filling a glass with tap water and drinking it so I don't have to look at Pop. I can feel my jaw tick every time I gulp.

"I know you want to do right by that boy and go pick him up. You do know they'll put him on a bus, don't you?"

"He's my kids' daddy, Pop. I got to go get him."

"What about his mama and pappy? What if they want to go get him?"

I hadn't thought about that. I place the empty glass in the sink and leave it there. Pop will complain about me not washing my dishes, but he usually only fights with me about one thing at a time.

"If they were coming to get him, he would have told me that. But he didn't."

"You can wait for him to call again before you decide."

I catch myself massaging the back of my neck and stop. Everything hurts.

"No, I can't do that, Pop."

Pop steps away from me, looks up at the kitchen ceiling.

"You need to talk to your mama before you leave. Tell her you going."

"Is it that serious?"

Pop grips a kitchen chair and jerks it an inch or two, straightening it, then stills.

Given-not-Given stayed with me for the rest of the night at Misty's. He even followed me out to the car and climbed into the passenger seat, right through the door. When I pulled out of Misty's gravel driveway into the street, Given looked straight ahead. Halfway home, on one of those dark two-lane country roads, the asphalt worn so bare the grind of the car's tires made me think it wasn't paved, I swerved to avoid hitting a possum. It froze and arched its back in the headlights, and I could swear I heard it hissing. When my chest eased and didn't feel like a cushion studded with hot pins anymore, I looked back over to the passenger seat, and Given was gone.

"I have to go. We have to go."

"Why?" Pop says. It almost sounds soft. The worry he feels makes his voice an octave lower.

"Because we his family," I say. A line sizzles from my toes to my belly and up to the back of my head, a lick of what I felt last night. And then it goes, and I'm static, still, a depression. The corners of Pop's mouth pull tight, and he's a fish pulling against a hook, a line, something much bigger than him. And then it's gone, and he blinks at me and looks away.

"He got more than one, Leonie. The kids got more than one, too," Pop says, and then he's walking away from me, calling Jojo.

"Boy," he says. "Boy. Come here."

The back door slams.

"Where you at, boy?"

It sounds like a caress, like Pop's singing it.

"Michael's getting out tomorrow."

Mama pushes her palms down on the bed, shrugs her shoulders, and tries to raise her hips. She grimaces.

"He is, now?" Her voice is soft. Barely a breath.

"Yeah."

She lets herself fall back against the bed again.

"Where's your pop?"

"Out back with Jojo."

"I need him."

"I got to go to the store. I'll get him on my way out."

Mama scratches her scalp and lets out a breath. Her eyes close to seams.

"Who going get Michael?"

"Me."

"And who else?"

"The kids."

She's looking at me again. I wish I could feel that sizzling lick, but I've come all the way down, and I'm left with a nothing feeling. Hollow and dry. Bereft.

"Your friend ain't going with you?"

She's talking about Misty. Our men are in the same penitentiary, so we ride up around once every four months. I hadn't even thought to ask.

"I ain't asked her."

Growing up out here in the country taught me things. Taught me that after the first fat flush of life, time eats away at things: it rusts machinery, it matures animals to become hairless and featherless, and it withers plants. Once a year or so, I see it in Pop, how he got leaner and leaner with age, the tendons in him standing out, harder and more rigid, every year. His Indian cheekbones severe. But since Mama got sick, I learned pain can do that, too. Can eat a person until there's nothing but bone and skin and a thin layer of blood left. How it can eat your insides and swell you in wrong ways: Mama's feet look like water balloons set to burst under the cover.

"You should."

I think Mama's trying to roll on her side, because I can see the strain in her, but in the end all she does is roll her head to the side and look at the wall.

"Turn on the fan," she says, so I scoot Pop's chair back, and I switch on the box fan propped in the window. The air ululates through the room, and Mama turns back to face me.

"You wondering . . . ," she says, and stops. Her lips thin. That's the place I see it most. Her lips, which were always so full and soft, especially when I was a girl, when she kissed my temple. My elbow. My hand. Even sometimes, after I had a bath, my toes. Now they're nothing but differently colored skin in the sunken topography of her face.

". . . why I ain't fussing."

"A little," I say. She's looking at her toes.

"Pop stubborn. You stubborn."

Her breath stutters, and I realize it's a laugh. A weak laugh.

"Y'all always going to fuss," she says.

She closes her eyes again. Her hair is so threadbare, I can see her scalp: pale and blue-veined, hollowed and dimpled, imperfect as a potter's bowl.

"You full grown now," she says.

I sit, cross my arms. It makes my breasts stick out a little. I remember the horror of them coming in, budding like little rocks, when I was ten. How those fleshy knots felt like a betrayal. Like someone had lied to me about what life would be. Like Mama hadn't told me that I would grow up. Grow into her body. Grow into her.

"You love who you love. You do what you want."

Mama looks at me, only her eyes looking full in that moment, round as they ever were, almost hazel if I lean in close enough, water gathering at the edges. The only thing time hasn't eaten.

"You going to go," she says.

I know it now. I know my mother is following Given, the son who came too late and left too early. I know that my mother is dying.

Given played football with single-minded purpose his senior year, the fall before he died. Recruiters from local community and state colleges came every weekend to see his games. He was tall and well muscled, and his feet didn't touch the ground once he got the pigskin in his hand. Even though he was serious about football, he was still social when he wasn't at practice or on the field. Once he told Pop his teammates, White and Black, were like brothers to him. That it was like the team went to war every Friday night, came together and became something more, something greater than themselves. Pop looked down at his shoes and spat a brown stream in the dirt. Given said he was going up to the Kill to party with his White teammates, and Pop cautioned him against it: *They look at you and see difference, son. Don't matter what you see. It's about what they do*, Pop had said, and then spit the whole mess of chew out. Given had rolled his eyes, leaned into the hood of the '77 Nova they were fixing up for him to drive, and said: *All right, Pop.* Looked up at me and winked. I was just grateful Pop hadn't sent me inside, glad I could hand them tools and fetch them water and watch them work because I didn't want to go in the house just in case Mama decided to give me one of her plant lessons. *Herbs and medicine*, she'd told me when I turned seven, *I can teach you.* I was hoping somebody, Big Henry or one of the twins, would walk down the street, emerge whole out of the green, so we'd have somebody else to talk to.

Given ignored Pop. Late that winter, in February, he decided to go hunting with the White boys up in the Kill. He saved up his money and bought a fancy hunting bow and arrow. He had bet Michael's cousin that he could kill a buck with a bow before the boy could take one down with a rifle. Michael's cousin was a short boy with a wandering eye who wore cowboy boots and beer T-shirts like it was a uniform; he was the kind of boy who dated and hung out with high schoolers even though he was in his early thirties. Given practiced with Pop. Shot for hours in the backyard when he should have been doing homework. Started walking straight as Pop since he spent so long drawed up tight, every line on him as taut as the bow, until he could sink an arrow into the middle of a canvas tied between two pine trees fifty yards away. He won that bet one cold overcast winter sunrise, in part because he was so good, in part because everybody else, all the boys he played football with, tussled in the locker room with, sweated almost to breaking on the stadium field with, woke up drinking beer like orange juice that morning because they figured Given would lose.

I didn't know Michael yet; I'd seen him around school a few times, his blond hair thick and curly, always looking like it was on the verge of matting because it wasn't ever brushed. He had ashy elbows and hands and legs. Michael didn't go hunting that morning, because he didn't want to get up that early, but he heard about it once his uncle came to Big Joseph in the middle of the day, the cousin sobering up, a look on his face like he smelled something bad, something like a rat dead on poison driven inside the walls by the winter cold, and the uncle saying: *He shot the nigger. This fucking hothead shot the nigger for beating him.* And then, because Big Joseph had been sheriff for years: *What we going to do?* Michael's mama told them to call the police. Big Joseph ignored her and all of them went back up into the woods, an hour in, and found Given lying long and still in the pine needles, his blood a black puddle beneath him. Beer cans all around him from the boys throwing them and running once the cousin with the bad eye aimed and fired, once the shot rang out. How they scattered like roaches in the light. The uncle had slapped his son across the face, once and twice. *You fucking idiot,* he'd said. *This ain't the old days.* And then his cousin had put his arms up and mumbled: *He was supposed to lose, Pa.* A hundred yards off, the buck lay on his side, one arrow in his neck, another in his stomach, all of him cold and hard as my brother. Their blood congealing.

Hunting accident, Big Joseph told them once they got back to the house and sat around the table, phone in hand, before the cousin's daddy, short as his son but with synced eyes, called the police. *Hunting accident,* the uncle said, speaking on the phone with the light of the cold noon sun slicing through the curtains. *Hunting accident,* the lazy-eyed cousin said in court, his good eye fixed on Big Joseph, who sat behind the boy's lawyer, his face still and hard as a dinner plate. But his bad eye roving to Pop and me and Mama, all in a row behind the DA, a DA who agreed to a plea deal that sentenced the cousin to three years in Parchman and two years' probation. I wonder if Mama heard some humming from the cousin's bad eye, some feelings of remorse in its wandering, but she looked through him, tears leaking down her face the whole time.

A year after Given died, Mama planted a tree for him. *One every anniversary,* she said, pain cracking her voice. *If I live long enough, going to be a forest here,* she said, *a whispering forest. Talking about the wind and pollen and beetle rot.* She stopped and put the tree in the earth and started beating the soil around the roots. I heard her through her fists. *The woman that taught Marie-Therese—she could see. Old woman looked damn near White. Tante Vangie. She could see the dead. Marie-Therese ain't never had that talent. Me neither.* She dug her red fists into the dirt. *I dream about it. Dream I can see Given again, walking through the door in his boots. But then I wake up. And I don't.* She started to cry then. *And I know it's there. Right on the other side of that veil.* She knelt like that until her tears stopped running, and she sat up and wiped her face and smeared blood and dirt all over it.

Three years ago, I did a line and saw Given for the first time. It wasn't my first line, but Michael had just gone to jail. I had started doing it often; every other day, I was bending over a table, sifting powder into lines, inhaling. I knew I shouldn't have: I was pregnant. But I couldn't help wanting to feel the coke go up my nose, shoot straight to my brain, and burn up all the sorrow and despair I felt at Michael being gone. The first time Given showed up, I was at a party in the Kill, and my brother walked through there with no bullet holes in his chest or in his neck, whole and long-limbed, like always. But not smirking. He was shirtless and red about the neck and face like he'd been running, but his chest was still as stone. Still as he must have been after Michael's cousin shot him. I thought about Mama's little forest, the ten trees she'd planted in an ever-widening spiral on every death day. I ground my gums sore staring at Given. I ate him with my eyes. He tried to talk to me but I couldn't hear him, and he just got more and more frustrated. He sat on the table in front of me, right on the mirror with the coke on it. I couldn't put my face in it again without putting it in his lap, so we sat there staring at each other, me trying not to react so I wouldn't look crazy to my friends, who were singing along to country music, kissing sloppily in corners like teenagers, walking in zigzags with their arms linked out into the dark. Given looked at me like he did when we were little and I broke the new fishing pole Pop got him: murderous. When I came down, I almost ran out to my car. I was shaking so hard, I could hardly put my key in the ignition. Given climbed in next to me, sat in the passenger seat, and turned and looked at me with a face of stone. *I quit,* I said. *I swear I won't do it no more.* He rode with me to the house, and I left him sitting in the passenger seat as the sun softened and lit the edges of the sky, rising. I crept into Mama's bedroom and watched her sleep. Dusted her shrine: her rosary draped over her Virgin Mary statue in the corner, nestled among blue-gray candles, river rocks, three dried cattails, a single yam. When I saw Given-not-Given for the first time, I didn't tell my mama nothing.

A phone call to Michael's parents would tell me everything I need to know. I could just pick up the receiver, dial the number, and pray for Michael's mama to answer the phone. This would be our fifth conversation, and I'd say: *Hello Mrs. Ladner I don't know if you realize but Michael's getting out tomorrow and me and the kids and Misty is going to get him so y'all don't need to all right ma'am bye.* But I don't want Big Joseph to answer, to hang up on me after I sit on the line and breathe into the mouthpiece and don't say nothing while he says nothing. At least then I'd know if I call back, he'd let Mrs. Ladner pick up the phone to deal with whoever it is: prankster, bill collector, wrong number dialer, his son's Black babymama. But I don't want to deal with all that: to talk to Michael's mother in halting starts and stops, or to suffer Big Joseph's heavy silence. This is why I am riding upcountry to the Kill, my trunk packed with gallon jugs of water and baby wipes and bags of clothes and sleeping bags, to leave a note in their mailbox way down at the end of their driveway, a breathless note. What I would have said in a rush. No punctuation. The note signed: Leonie.

Michael had never spoken to me before. During lunch break at school one day, a year after Given died, Michael sat next to me on the grass, touched my arm, and said: *I'm sorry my cousin is a fucking idiot.* I thought that was it. That after Michael apologized, he'd walk away and never speak to me again. But he didn't. He asked me if I wanted to go fishing with him a few weeks later. I said yes, and walked out the front door. Wasn't no need to sneak out anymore, my parents wrapped up in their grief. Spider-bound: web-blind. The first time me and Michael went on a date, we went out to the pier off the beach with our poles, me with Given's held out in front of me like some sort of offering. We talked about our families, about his father. He said: *He old—a old head.* And I knew what he meant without him having to say more. *He would hate that I'm out here with you, that before the night's through, I'm going to kiss you.* Or, in fewer words: *He believes in niggers.* And I swallowed the fact of his father's bile and let it pass through me, because *the father was not the son,* I thought.

Because when I looked at Michael in the piecemeal dark underneath the gazebo at the end of the pier, I could see a shadow of Big Joseph in him; I could look at his long neck and arms, his lean, muscled torso, the fine shank of his rib cage, and see the way years would soften him to his daddy. How fat would wreathe him, and he would settle into his big frame the way a house settles into the earth underneath it. I had to remind myself: *They are not the same.* Michael leaned over our poles and his eyes changed color like the mountainous clouds in the sky before a big storm: darkest blue, water gray, old-summer green. He was just tall enough that when he hugged me, his chin rested on my head, and I was cupped under him. Like I belonged. Because I wanted Michael's mouth on me, because from the first moment I saw him walking across the grass to where I sat in the shadow of the school sign, he saw me. Saw past skin the color of unmilked coffee, eyes black, lips the color of plums, and *saw me.* Saw the walking wound I was, and came to be my balm.

Big Joseph and Michael's mother live at the top of a hill in a low country house, the siding white, the shutters green. It looks big. There are two trucks parked in the driveway, new pickup trucks that catch the sun and throw it back into the air, shooting sparks off the angles. One red truck, one white. Three horses roam around the segmented fields that abut the house, and a gaggle of hens scamper across the yard, under the trucks, to disappear around the back. I pull over to the side of the road, stop feet from their mailbox;

the grassy shoulder is not so wide here, bordered by a ditch at least hip-deep, so I have to get out of the car and walk, can't just pull up next to it and slide the note inside. It's been some days since we had rain. When I walk around to the box, the grass sounds with a dry crunch. There are no other cars on this road. They live way up in the Kill, nothing but houses and trailers in great spreading fields, off a dead-end road.

Just as I'm pulling the mailbox door down, I hear a buzz, which loudens to a humming, which loudens to a growl, and then a man is riding around the side of the house on a great lawn mower with a steel bolted deck, the kind that's so expensive it's as big as a tractor. It costs as much as my car. I slide the note into the mailbox. The man angles toward the north end of the pasture, turns left, and begins making his way toward the road. He must mean to cut the yard from top to bottom, riding in long, clean lines.

I reach for the handle, pull it open, and it shrieks, metal grinding against metal.

"Shit."

He looks up. I get into the car.

The lawn mower speeds up. I turn the key. The car stutters and stalls. I turn it back, look down at the dashboard like I could make it start if I just stared long enough. Maybe if I prayed.

"Shit. Shit. Shit."

I turn the key again. The engine groans and catches. The man, who I can see now is Big Joseph, has decided to abandon his plan of cutting the top of the yard first and is cutting diagonally across the yard, trying to reach me and the mailbox. And then he is pointing, and I see the sign nailed to a tree feet away from the mailbox. No Trespassing.

He accelerates.

"Goddamnit!"

I shift the car to drive, look back to check the street, and see a car advancing, a gray SUV. Fear rises to my shoulders, up my neck, a bubbling choke. I don't know what I'm afraid of. What can he do but curse me? What can he do? I'm not in his driveway. Doesn't the county own the sides of the road? But something about how fast he's gunning that lawn mower, the way he points to that tree, the way that tree, a Spanish oak, reaches up and out and over the road, a multitude of dark green leaves and almost black branches, the way he's coming at me, makes me see violence. I press the gas and swerve out into the street, the car behind me skids and its horn sounds, but I don't care. My transmission switches gears with a high whine. I sling the car around and go faster. The gray SUV has pulled into a driveway, but the driver is waving his arm out the window, and Big Joseph is passing under the tree, stopping at the mailbox I just abandoned, lumbering off his lawn mower, striding toward the box. He is taking something off the seat of the mower, a rifle that was strapped there, something he keeps for wild pigs that root in the forest, but not for them now. For me.

When I pass him, I stick my left arm out the window. Make a fist. Raise my middle finger. I see my brother in his last photo: one taken on his eighteenth birthday, leaning back on the kitchen counter while I hold his favorite sweet potato pecan cake up to his face so he can blow his candles out; his arms are crossed on his chest, his smile white in his dark face. We are all laughing. I accelerate so quickly my tires spin and burn rubber, throwing up clouds of smoke. I hope Big Joseph has an asthma attack. I hope he chokes on it.

Chapter 3

Jojo

Breakfast today was cold goat with gravy and rice: even though it's been two days since my birthday, the pot was still halfway full. When I woke up, it was to Leonie stepping over me. She had a bag over her shoulder and was grabbing Kayla. "Wake up," Leonie said, not looking at me, but frowning as Kayla whimpered to waking. I got up, brushed my teeth, threw on my basketball shorts and a T-shirt, and brought my bag out to the car. Leonie had a real bag, something made of cotton and canvas, although it was a little beat up, pulling loose at the edges. Mine was a plastic grocery bag. I never needed an overnight bag, so Leonie never got me one. This is our first trip north to the jail with her. I wanted to eat the goat hot, to heat it up in the small brown microwave, the one Pop say is leaking cancer in our food because the enamel on the inside is peeling off like paint. Pop won't heat anything in it, and Leonie won't give him half to replace it. When I started to put it in the microwave, Leonie walked by and said: "We ain't got time." So I put my birthday leftovers in a Styrofoam bowl; crept in the room to kiss sleeping Mam, who muttered *babies* and twitched in her sleep; and then went out to the car.

Pop was waiting for us. Looked like he had slept in his clothes, his starched khaki pants, his short-sleeved button-up shirt, all gray and brown, like him. He matched the sky, which hung low, a silver colander full to leak. It was drizzling. Leonie threw her bag in the backseat and marched back into the house. Misty was playing with the radio controls and the car was already running. Pop frowned at me, so I stopped and shuffled in front of him. Looked down at my feet. My basketball shoes were Michael's; an old pair an inch too big for me I found abandoned under Leonie's bed. I didn't care. They were Jordans, so I wore them anyway.

"Might rain bad up the road."

I nodded.

"You remember how to change a tire? Check the oil and coolant?"

I nodded again. Pop taught me all of that when I was ten.

"Good."

I wanted to tell Pop I didn't want to go, that I wanted me and Kayla to stay home, and I might have if he didn't look so mad, if his frown didn't seem carved into his mouth and brow, if Leonie hadn't walked out then with Kayla, who was rubbing her eyes and crying at being woken up in the gray light. It was 7 a.m. So I said what I could.

"It's okay, Pop."

His frown eased then, for a moment, long enough for him to say:

"Watch after them."

"I will."

Leonie rose from buckling Kayla into her seat in the back.

"Come on. We got to go."

I stepped in to Pop and hugged him. I couldn't remember the last time I had, but it seemed important to do it then, to fold my arms around him and touch my chest to his. To pat him once, twice, on his back with my fingertips and let him go. *He's my pop*, I thought. *He's my pop.*

He put his hands on my shoulders and squeezed, and then looked at my nose, my ears, my hair, and finally my eyes when I stepped back.

"You a man, you hear?" he said. I nodded. He squeezed again, his eyes on the forgotten shoes I wore, rubbery and silly next to his work boots, the ground worn sandy and grassy thin in the driveway from the beating it took from Leonie's car, the sky bearing down on us all, so all the animals I thought I could understand were quiet, subdued under the gathering spring rain. The only animal I saw in front of me was Pop, Pop with his straight shoulders and his tall back, his pleading eyes the only thing that spoke to me in that moment and told me what he said without words: *I love you, boy. I love you.*

It's raining now, the water coming down in sheets, beating against the car. Kayla sleeps, a deflated Capri Sun in one hand, a stub of a Cheeto in another, her face muddy orange. Her brown-blond afro matted to her head. Misty is humming to the song on the radio, her hair piled in a nest. Some of it escapes, a loose twig, to hang against her neck. Her hair turning dark with sweat. It's hot in the car, and I watch the skin all around her nape dampen and bead, and the beads run like the rainwater down the column of her neck to disappear in her shirt. The longer we ride, the hotter it gets, and Misty's shirt, which is cut wide and loose around the neckline, stretches out even more so that the top of her bra peeks through, and tall as I am, I realize I can see it from the backseat if I look diagonally across the car. It's electric blue. The windows begin to fog.

"Ain't it hot in here?" Misty's fanning herself with a piece of paper she's pulled out of Leonie's glove box. Looks like Leonie's forged car insurance papers. People pay Misty twenty dollars to make copies of cards and insert their names into the copies so if they get stopped by the county police, it looks like they have insurance.

"A little," Leonie says.

"You know I can't stand heat. It makes my allergies act up."

"This coming from somebody born and raised in Mississippi."

"Whatever."

"I'm just saying you in the wrong state for heat."

Misty's hair is dark at the root, blond everywhere else. She has freckles on her shoulders.

"Maybe I need to move to Alaska," Misty says.

We taking back roads all the way there. Leonie threw the atlas in my lap when I got in the backseat behind her, said: "Read it." She's marked the route with a pen; it scrawls north up a tangle of two-lane highways, smudged in places from Leonie's finger running up and down the state. The pen's marks are dark, so it's hard for me to read the route names, the letters and numbers shadowed. But I see the prison name, the place Pop was: Parchman. Sometimes I wonder who that parched man was, that man dying for water, that they named the town and the jail after. Wonder if he looked like Pop, straight up and down, brown skin tinged with red, or me, an in-between color, or Michael, the color of milk. Wonder what that man said before he died of a cracked throat.

"Me, too," Leonie says. Last night, she relaxed her hair in the kitchen and rinsed it out in the sink, so it's as straight and wispy as Misty's. Misty dyed the tips of Leonie's hair the same blond as hers a few weeks ago, so when Leonie stood over the sink and rinsed and hissed as the water ran over her scalp, over the chemical burns I'd see later, little scabs like dimes on her scalp, her hair looked like it didn't belong on her, limp and flowing an orange-blond down the drain. Now her hair is starting to puff and frizz.

"I like it," I say. They ignore me. I do. I like the heat. I like the way the highway cuts through the forests, curves over hills heading north, sure and rolling. I like the trees reaching out on both sides, the pines thicker and taller up here, spared the stormy beating the ones on the coast get that keeps them spindly and delicate. But that doesn't stop people from cutting them down to protect their houses during storms or to pad their wallets. So much could be happening in those trees.

"We got to stop," Leonie says.

"Why?"

"Gas," Leonie says. "I'm thirsty."

"Me, too," I say.

When we pull onto the gravel strip in front of the little gas station, Leonie hands me the same thirty dollars I saw Misty hand to her when she got in the car this morning and looks at me like she didn't hear me say I'm thirsty.

"Twenty-five for gas. Get me a Coke, and bring me my change."

"Can I have one?" I push. I can imagine the dark burning sweetness of it. I swallow and my throat seems to catch like Velcro. I think I know what the parched man felt.

"Bring me my change."

I don't want to go nowhere. I want to keep looking down Misty's shirt. Her bra flashes bright blue again, the kind of blue I've only seen in photographs, the color of deep water off in the Gulf of Mexico. The kind of blue in the pictures Michael took when he worked on the oil rig offshore, and the water was a living wet plain around him, making a great blue bowl with the sky.

The inside of the store is even dimmer than the dull glow of the spring outside. There's a woman sitting behind the counter, and she's prettier than Misty. Black curly fro, her lips pinkish purple from the AC, her mouth an upside-down U. She's my color, and thicker than Misty, too, and a whip of longing, like a cut power line set to sparking, jumps behind my ribs.

"Hey," she mumbles, and goes back to playing on her cell phone. Every wall is lined with metal shelves, and the metal shelves are lined with dust. I walk toward the dimmer back like I've been here before, like I know what I want and I know where it's at. Like a man would walk. Like Pop would. My eyes burn and find the display case of drinks in the front of the store. I stare at the glass, imagining how wet and fizzy a cold drink would be, swallowing against the parched closure of my throat: dry as a rocky river wash in drought. My spit is thick as paste. I look back at the clerk and she's watching me, so I take the biggest Coke and don't even try to slip another in my pocket. I walk toward the front.

"A dollar thirty," she says, and I have to lean toward her to hear because thunder booms, a great clacking split, and the sky dumps water on the tin roof of the building: a tumble of sound. I can't see down her shirt but it's what I think about when I'm standing out in the rain, the back of my shirt pulled over my head like it could protect me, but all of me wet, gas fumes thick with the smell of wet earth, rain running down to blind my eyes, to stream from my nose. It all makes me feel like I can't breathe. I remember just in time and tilt my head back, hold my breath, and let rain trickle down my throat. A thin knife of cool when I swallow. Once. Twice. Three times because the pump is so slow. The rain presses my eyes closed, kneads them. I think I hear a whisper of something, a whoosh of a word, but then it's gone as the tank pings and the nozzle goes slack. The car is close and warm, and Kayla is snoring.

"I could've got you a drink if you was that thirsty," Misty says. I shrug and Leonie starts the car. I peel off my shirt, heavy as a wet towel, and lay it on the floor before bending to root through my bag for another one. When I pull it on, I notice Misty looking at me in the mirror attached to the back of the passenger shade while she reapplies gloss, her lips going from dry pink to glossy peach; when she sees I see her looking, she winks. I shiver.

* * *

I was eleven when Mam had the talk with me. By that time, she'd gotten so sick she spent a few hours in the middle of each day in the bed, a thin sheet looped around her waist, sleeping and startling awake. She was like one of Pop's animals hiding in the barn or one of the lean-tos built on the side of the barn, secreted away from the heat. But this day she didn't sleep.

"Jojo," she called, and her voice was a fishing line thrown so weakly the wind catches it. But still, the lead weight settled in my chest, and I stopped mid-walk toward the back door, toward Pop, who was outside working, and walked into Mam's room.

"Mam?" I said.

"The baby?"

"Sleep."

Mam swallowed and it looked like it hurt, so I passed her water.

"Sit," she said, so I pulled the chair next to her bed close, happy that she was awake, and then she pulled a slim, wide book from her side and opened it up to the most embarrassing diagrams I'd ever seen, flaccid penises and ovaries like star fruit, and began to teach me human anatomy and sex. When she started talking about condoms, I wanted to crawl under her bed and die. My face and my neck and my back were still burning when she laid the book down on the side closest to the wall, thankfully away so I couldn't see it again.

"Look at me," she said.

There were lines, new since the cancer, running from her nose down to the edges of her mouth. She smiled half a smile.

"I embarrassed you," she said.

I nodded. The shame was choking me.

"You getting older. You needed to know. I gave your mama this talk." She looked past me, to the doorway at my back, and I twisted, expecting to see Pop, or Kayla stumble-walking and cranky from her too-short nap, but there was nothing except the light from the kitchen casting a glowing doormat. "Your uncle Given, too, and he was redder than you."

Not possible.

"Your pop don't know how to tell a story straight. You know that? He tell the beginning but don't tell the end. Or he leave out something important in the middle. Or he tell you the beginning without setting up how everything got there. He always been like that."

I nod.

"I used to have to piece the things he told me together to get the whole picture. Piece his paragraphs together like puzzles. It was worse when we just started courting. I knew he'd been away for some years, up in Parchman. I knew because I listened when I shouldn't have been. I was only five when he got arrested, but I heard about the brawl at the juke joint, and then him and his brother, Stag, disappearing. He went away and was gone for years, and when he came back, he moved into the house with his mama to take care of her, and worked. He was back for years before he started coming over, helping my daddy and mama with little things around the house. Doing chore after chore before he even introduced himself to me. I was nineteen, and he was twenty-nine. One day, me and him was sitting on my mama and daddy front porch and we heard Stag a ways off, coming up the road, singing, and River said: *There's things that move a man. Like currents of water inside. Things he can't help. Older I got, the more I found it true. What's in Stag is like water so black and deep you can't see the bottom.* Stag was laughing now. But then Pop said: *Parchman taught me the same in me, Philomène.* Some days later, I understood what he was trying to say, that getting grown means learning how to work that current: learning when to hold fast, when to drop anchor, when to let it sweep you up. And it could be something simple as sex, or it could be something as complicated as falling in love, or it could be like going to jail with your brother, thinking you going to protect him." The box fan hummed. "You understand what I'm telling you, Jojo?"

"Yes, Mam," I said. I didn't. Mam let me go and I wandered out to the yard and found Pop slopping the hogs. "Will you tell me again?" I asked him. "What happened, Pop? When you went to jail?" And he paused, a hitch in the smooth arc of the bucket, and he told me his story.

That twelve-year-old boy I told you about? Richie? They put him on the long line. From sunup to sundown we was out there in them fields, hoeing and picking and planting and pulling. A man get to a point like that, he can't think. Just feel. Feel like he want to stop moving. Feel his stomach burn and know he want to eat. Feel his head packed full of cotton and know he want to sleep. Feel his throat close and fire run up his arms

*and legs, his heart beat out his chest, and know he want to
run. But wasn't no running. We was gunmen, under the gun
of them damn trusty shooters. That was our whole world: the
long line. Men strung out across the fields, the trusty shooters
stalking the edge, the driver on his mule, the caller yelling to
the sun, throwing his working song out. Like a fishing net. Us
caught and struggling. Once, my grandmama told me a story
about her great-grandmama. She'd come across the ocean, been
kidnapped and sold. Said her great-grandmama told her that
in her village, they ate fear. Said it turned the food to sand in
they mouth. Said everyone knew about the death march to the
coast, that word had come down about the ships, about how
they packed men and women into them. Some heard it was
even worse for those who sailed off, sunk into the far. Because
that's what it looked like when the ship crossed the horizon:
like the ship sailed off and sunk, bit by bit, into the water. Her
grandmama said they never went out at night, and even in the
day, they stayed in the shadows of they houses. But still, they
came for her. Kidnapped her from her home in the middle of
the day. Brought her here, and she learned the boats didn't sink
to some watery place, sailed by white ghosts. She learned that
bad things happened on that ship, all the way until it docked.
That her skin grew around the chains. That her mouth shaped
to the muzzle. That she was made into an animal under the
hot, bright sky, the same sky the rest of her family was under,
somewhere far aways, in another world. I knew what that was,
to be made a animal. Until that boy came out on the line, until
I found myself thinking again. Worrying about him. Looking
out the corner of my eye at him lagging crooked like a ant
that's lost scent.*

* * *

It's not until an hour later, when I figure the shirt's as dry as it's going to get in the humid-close car, that I see it. A small bag, so small two could fit in the palm of my hand, secreted in the middle of my bundle of clothes. Like the dot of blood the size of a pin at the center of the yolk in an egg: life that would have been life, but not. It's smooth and warm, soft to my touch. Feels like leather, and it's tied together with a sinewy leather strip. I glance up. Misty's dozing in the front seat, her head falling forward and jerking upright only to list forward again. Leonie's got both hands on the wheel, her fingers tapping to the music on the radio; we're listening to country, which I hate. We've been in the car a little over two hours, so we lost the Black station from the coast at least an hour ago. Leonie smooths the hair at the nape of her neck with one hand, as if she could caress it into flatness, and then she taps again. I hunch over my lap, turning toward the door, making a small room with my body, a screen. I pull the strip. The knot gives, and I tease it open.

I find a white feather smaller than my pinkie finger, tipped with blue and a slash of black. Something that at first looks like a small chip of white candy, but when I pick it up and hold it close to my face, it's some kind of animal tooth, lined with black in the chewing grooves, sharp like a canine. Whatever animal it came from knew blood, knew how to tear knotty muscle. Then I see a small gray river rock, a little perfect dome. I swirl my pointer finger into the dark of the sack, searching, and pull out a piece of paper, rolled thin as a fingernail. In slanted, shaky script, in blue ink: *Keep this close.*

It's either Pop's or Mam's handwriting. I know this because I've seen it all my life, on Catholic wall calendars, on the inside of a kitchen cabinet next to the refrigerator where they tack a list of important names and phone numbers, starting with Leonie's. On permission slips and report cards when Leonie was too busy or absent to sign. And because Mam hasn't left her bed in weeks and can't hold a pen, I know it's Pop who wrote the note, Pop who gathered the feather, the tooth, the rock, who sewed the leather pouch, who says to me: *Keep this close.*

My knees rub the seat in front of me. I can't help it; I've gotten tall enough that the backseat of Leonie's hatchback is close and tight. Leonie glances in the rearview.

"Stop kicking the back of my seat."

I hold my palms, a warm open bowl, over the things that Pop has given me, which are in a tiny pile in my lap.

"I didn't mean to," I say.

"You should have said sorry," Leonie says.

I wonder if Pop ever did something like this for her when she made this trip before. If he snuck out in the morning when Leonie was sleeping, at 9 a.m. or 10 a.m., and secreted something in her car, some little collection of things he thought might be able to keep her safe, to watch for her when he couldn't, to protect her on her trips to north Mississippi. Some of my friends at school have people living up there, in Clarksdale or outside of Greenwood. What they say: *You think it's bad down here.* What they do: frown. What they mean: *Up there? In the Delta? It's worse.*

Up ahead, the trees by the side of the road begin to thin, and there are suddenly billboards. A picture of a new baby in the womb: a red-yellow tadpole, skin and blood so thin the light shines through it like a gummy candy. *Protect Life*, the sign says. I put the feather, the rock, and the tooth in the bag. Roll Pop's note so thin it could be a straw for a mouse, and put it in the bag before tying it shut and putting it into the small square pocket sewn into the waistband of my basketball shorts. Leonie is not looking at me anymore.

"Sorry," I say.

She grunts.

I think I know what my friends mean when they talk about north Mississippi.

Pop's told me some parts of Richie's story over and over again. I've heard the beginning at least too many times to count. There are parts in the middle, about the outlaw hero Kinnie Wagner and the evil Hogjaw, that I've only heard twice. I ain't never heard the end. Sometimes I'd try to write them down, but they were just bad poems, limping down the page: *Training a horse.* The next line. *Cut with the knees.* Sometimes I got fed up with Pop. At first, he told me the stories while we were awake at night in the living room. But after some months, he always seemed to tell me part of his Richie story when we were doing something else: eating red beans and rice, picking our teeth with toothpicks on the porch after lunch, sitting in front of the television in the living room watching westerns in the afternoon, when Pop would interrupt the cowboy on the screen to say this about Parchman: *It was murder. Mass murder.* When Pop told me about the small pouch he kept tied to one of his belt loops, it was cold outside, and he was splitting logs for the woodstove that heated the living room. We were out of gas for the weekend. Mam had all the covers in the house on her, crocheted blankets and quilts and flat and fitted sheets, and still she moaned: *My bones.* Her hands tucked up under her neck, wringing one against the other, the skin raspy and chafed white, even though I lotioned them every hour. *It's so cold.* Her teeth rattling like dice in her mouth.

"Everything got power."

He hit a log.

"My great-granddaddy taught me that."

The log split.

"Said there's spirit in everything. In the trees, in the moon, in the sun, in the animals. Said the sun is most important, gave it a name: Aba. But you need all of them, all of that spirit in everything, to have balance. So the crops will grow, the animals breed and get fat for food."

He put another log on the stump, and I breathed into my hands, wishing I had a hat for my ears.

"Explained it to me like this: if you got too much sun and not enough rain, crops will wither. If you got too much rain, they rot in the ground."

He swung again.

"You need a balance of spirit. A body, he told me, is the same way."

The logs fell.

"Like this. I'm strong. I can split this wood. But maybe if I had some of the boar's strength, a little bit of wild pig's tusk at my side, something to give me a little bit of that animal's spirit, then maybe, just maybe," he huffed, "I'm better at this. Maybe it come a little easier to me. Maybe I'm stronger."

He split another.

"But never more than I could handle. The boar share so much, and I take so much. No waste. Waste rots. Too much either way breaks the balance." He rested his axe on the ground. "Get me another log."

I returned from the pile, put the wood on the stump, balanced it just so. Snatched my hand away as Pop brought the axe down, clean through the center of it.

"Or a woodpecker could share something, too. A feather, for aim."

My finger stung from the nearness of that blade, how close Pop come to my hand.

"That's what you keep in your pouch?" I asked. I'd noticed his small pouch when I was four or five, and I'd asked him what he kept in it. He never told me.

Pop smiled.

"Not that," he said. "But close."

When that next log split, I looked up at Pop and shook, felt that splintering in my baseball knees, my bat spine, my glove of a skull. Wondered what power he had running through him. Where it come from.

I lay my head on the seat in Leonie's car, rubbing the pouch Pop gave me, and wonder if he ever gave a small sack, full of things to balance, to anyone else. His brother, Stag? Mam? Uncle Given? Or even the boy Richie? And then I hear Pop:

Richie wasn't built for work. He wasn't built for nothing, really, on account he was so young. He ain't know how to work a hoe, didn't have enough years in his arms for muscle, or to know how to break the earth good, or to pull with just enough power to clean the bolls from a plant instead of leaving little half tufts of white, ripping the cotton in two. He wasn't like you; you already filling out, getting longer through the shoulders, longer in the leg. You built like me, like my papa—good stock. But whoever his daddy was must have been skinny, weak-muscled. Maybe short. He was a bad worker. I tried to help him. Tried to break his line when he was hoeing, dig a little deeper in his grooves. Reach over and clean his plants better when we was harvesting. Pull his weeds. And mine. And for a while, a few months, it worked. I was able to save him, kept him from getting beat. I worked myself so hard I was sleep before my body even hit my bunk. Sleep on the fall. I kept my eyes on the ground. Ignored the sky, all that open space pushing down that made fear gather in my chest, a bloated and croaking toad. But then one Sunday when we was doing laundry, scrubbing our clothes on the washboards with soap that was so weak everything smelled a little less like wet-stink but still didn't smell good, Kinnie Wagner rode by with the dogs.

Kinnie was the inmate caretaker for the dogs. He was a legend even then. I knew about Kinnie. All of us did. They sang songs about him in the hill country of Tennessee, down through the Delta, all the way to the coast. He bootlegged and brawled and stole and killed. Had the truest shot I ever saw. Even though he'd already escaped Parchman once, and one of them break-proof prisons in Tennessee, too, they still put him over the dogs. Even though he put more than one lawman in the dirt. Poor White people all through the South loved him for it, loved him for spitting in the eye of the law. For blinding it. For being lawless in the lawless South, which was worse than the frontier, for standing like David in an Old Testament place, where, for a century before Parchman, law had been meted out like this, Jojo: eye for an eye, tooth for tooth, hand for hand, foot for foot. I think even the sergeants respected him. Anyway, Kinnie and some of the men he'd chosen to help him was on their way to drill the dogs, to train to scent. And one of the men that ran with the dogs was dragging. Maybe he was sick. Maybe he had been whipped. I don't know. But the short man fell, and his dogs broke loose, ran away from his dusted-over face, his receding belly, and ran to me. Hopped around me like big barking rabbits. Let they tongue hang. Kinnie, who was a big White man, six foot three, probably damn near three hundred pounds, laughed. Told the Black man on his knees in the clay: Nigger, you more trouble than you worth. And then pointed one of them big sausage fingers at me and said: You look skinny enough. I hung the pants I was wringing on the line on the way over to him. Took as much time as I could, because he was the type of man who expected me to run. To look at his big, healthy whiteness in awe. When I came, the dogs came with me, ears flopping, big black eyes rolling. Happy as pigs in shit. Can you run, boy? Kinnie said. I looked up at him; his horse was big and dark brown, but with a red tinge. Looked like you could see the blood boiling just under his coat, a river of blood bound by skin, knit together with muscle and bone. I'd always wanted a horse like that. I stood close enough to Kinnie so he know I'd come, but far enough away he couldn't kick me. Yes, I said. Kinnie laughed again, but there was a knife underneath, because then he turned them blue eyes on me and said, But do you know your place? Shifted his rifle so the muzzle was facing me. A great black Cyclops eye. I let him think what he would about my place,

*but I said: Yes, sir. And hated myself a little bit for saying it. One
of the dogs licked my hand. They like you, Kinnie said, and I need
myself another dog trusty. I didn't say nothing. Animals had always
come to me. Mama said one time she left me wrapped in a basket
on the chicken stump out in the back when I was a little baby, not
more than a month, and stepped inside to get a sharpening stone
for her knife; when she came out, one of the goats was licking my
face and my hand. Like it knew me. So I just looked at the top of
Kinnie's head, his bushy blond hair. He looked at my neck, and
he said: Come on. And turned his horse and kicked, and took off.*

*Once, we tracked a gunman through ten miles of swamp to
an abandoned cabin, and I saw Kinnie put a bullet through that
running gunman's head at two hundred yards: the gunman's skull
burst. Kinnie had killed him as the sun was going down, so we
camped next to a stream. The clouds rolled in, and the night was
twice black and fogged with mosquitoes. We'd smoked the fire;
all the inmates working with Kinnie and the dogs leaned in to it.
Everyone but me and Kinnie. I mudded myself to help with the
bites. The smoke boiled his face, melted it to nothing, but I still felt
him watching me in the darkness. Knew it when he stopped his
story about how a woman sheriff had caught him in Arkansas,
sent him back to Parchman this last time, and then said: I could
never hurt a woman; they knew that. And then his gaze is on me.
I looked right back. Everybody got a line—something to break
them, he said. I thought about Richie scrawling through the dirt
with his hoe. Everybody, Kinnie said, and spat chew into the fire.*

When I wake up, it's midmorning, and Leonie done pulled
off the highway. The atlas says we should take Highway 49

all the way up, deeper north, into the heart of Mississippi, and then get off and drive a ways to get to the jail, which Leonie has marked on the state map with a black star, but we're not following the map anymore. We pass a grocery store, a butcher. A sagging building with a flat roof and a faded sign: *Lumber Wholesale*. The buildings thin and the trees thicken until we're at a stop sign and there's nothing but trees, and when we roll through the intersection, the road turns to dirt and rocks.

"You sure you know where we going?" Leonie asks Misty.

"Yeah, I'm sure," Misty says. It's stopped raining, and the air is fuzzy with fog. Misty rolls down the window and holds her cell phone out. Aside from the chug and pull of Leonie's car, it's quiet; the trees are still and tall. To the left of the car, the trunks are brown and healthy, the undergrowth sparse. To the right of the car, the forest looks recently burned. The trunks are black halfway up, and the undergrowth is thick and bright green. I wonder at the stillness of it all. We are the only animals rooting through.

"Ain't shit out here," Leonie says.

"If I could get a signal, I could call him and ease your mind, but we too far out." Misty wipes her phone on her shirt and slides it into her pocket. "I been here before with Bishop. I know where I'm going."

"Where we going?" I ask the front of the car. Leonie half turns, so I can see her frown at Misty before she turns to the road.

"Got to stop for a minute. See some friends," Misty throws over her shoulder. "Then we getting back on the road."

We round a bend and there is a gap in the trees, and suddenly we are among a little cluster of houses. Some have siding like Mam and Pop's, some have insulation paper and no siding. One is an RV that looks years off the road, with wisteria draping along the top and crawling down the side. It's like the thing has green, living hair. Chickens run in bunches as a dog, a pit bull with gray-blue fur and a gaping maw, chases them. The chickens scatter. A boy, probably four, is sitting on the ground in front of the porch steps of a house with no siding, and he is stabbing the mud with a stick. He wears a baby's onesie that fits him like a shirt, yellow underwear, and no shoes. He wipes his hand across his face as Leonie comes to a stop and turns off the engine, and it turns his skin from pale milk to black.

"Told you I knew where we was going," Misty says. "Blow the horn."

"What?"

"Blow the horn. Ain't no way I'm getting out of this car with that dog running loose." Leonie blows, and the dog, who has stopped chasing the chickens and trotted around to the car to sniff the tires and pee on them, begins to bark. I know what he says. *Get out.* Inhale. *Get out!* Inhale. *Trespasser, get out!* Kayla wakes up and starts to cry.

"Take her out," Leonie says, so I unbuckle her.

The little White boy waves his stick in the air, and then grabs it with both hands, pointing it like a rifle. His blond hair sticks to his head, curls into his eyes like worms. "Pow pow," he says. He is shooting at us.

Leonie cranks the car.

"We don't need this—"

"Yes, we do. Cut it off. Blow the horn again."

Leonie compromises. She doesn't cut the car off, but she does blow the horn again, one long, loud honk that makes Kayla cry harder and burrow in to my chest. I try to shush her, but she can't hear me over the barking dog, the shooting boy, the silence in that clearing in the pines, a sound as heavy and loud as the others, but not. I want to jump out of the car with Kayla, and I want to outrun that boy and his dog and that fake gun, and I want to walk us all the way home. My insides feel like they want to fight.

A White woman steps out the door of the house with no siding, steps past the dirt-faced child. Their hair is the same blondish-reddish color, with the same curliness. Hers is long, down to her waist, and except for her nose, which seems swollen in her face and burns red, she's prettier than Misty. She's also barefoot. Her toes are pink. She coughs, and it sounds like a scraping in her throat, and walks toward the car. The dog runs up to her, but she ignores it. At least it stops barking. Misty opens the car door and sticks the top half of her body out while holding on to the frame.

"Hey, bitch!" Misty says, like it's a term of endearment. The woman smiles and coughs at the same time. The mist is settling like dew on her hair, turning it white. "Told you we was coming." The boy is still shooting us with his stick gun while the dog licks his face. I want to run back home. Leonie drags her hand through the hair over her right ear, scratching at her scalp. She does this when she is nervous. *You going to make yourself bleed*, Mam told her once, but I don't think Leonie realizes when she does it. She scrapes so hard it sounds like nails pulled over canvas. Misty is hugging the woman, who is staring into the car. When Leonie opens her door and steps out and says hey, I barely hear it over Kayla's crying. She scratches again. The little boy hops up the concrete steps and disappears into the house. When Leonie walks up to the woman and all three of them begin talking to each other, her hands hang weak-jointed at her sides.

The floors are uneven. They are highest in the middle of each room in the naked house, and then slope down to the four shadow-sheathed corners. The inside of the house is dim through the porch, which is crowded with boxes so all that's left is a walkway into the living room, which is also dim and crowded with boxes. There are two sofas here and one recliner, and this is where the shooting boy sits. He is eating a pickle Popsicle. The television sits on top of a box instead of a TV stand, and it's playing some sort of reality show about people who buy islands to build resorts.

"Through here," the woman says to Misty and Leonie, who follow behind. Leonie stops me with a raised arm in the living room.

"Y'all stay here," she says before leaning forward to touch Kayla's nose with her pointer finger and smile. Kayla's face is still wet with tears, but she is sniffing and holding on to my neck and staring at the shooting boy as if there is something she wants to say to him, so I let her down. "I'm serious," Leonie says, and then follows the woman and Misty into the kitchen, which is the brightest room in the house, lit by a chandelier hanging from the ceiling, laden with bulbs. There is a curtain hanging over the doorway, and the woman pulls it halfway shut and coughs and motions at the table for Misty and Leonie to sit. She opens the refrigerator. I sit on the edge of the sofa so I can watch the shooting boy in the armchair and Kayla, who is squatting feet before him with her hands in her lap, and the gap in the curtain where the women sit in the kitchen.

"Hi," Kayla says, drawing the word out so that it's two long syllables, her voice rolling up and down a hill. It's the same thing she says to her baby doll when she picks it up first thing in the morning, the same thing she says to the horse and the pig and the goat, the same thing she says to the chickens, the same thing she says to Leonie when she first sees her. The same thing she says to Pop. She won't talk much to Mam: when I carry her in the room to see Mam's still body, Kayla shrinks into my chest and shoulder, puts on her brave face, and after five minutes of cringing away from Mam and saying *shhhh* with her finger in front of her lips, she says *out*. She never says hello to me. She just sits up or crawls over to me and puts her arms around my neck and smiles.

The boy looks at Kayla like she's his dog, and Kayla hops closer.

"Hi," she says again. There is a worm of snot running down the boy's face. He jumps up to stand in the recliner, and seems to make a decision because he smiles, and his teeth are all capped with silver, the metal stopping them from rotting out of his mouth. He begins jumping in the chair like it's a trampoline, and a few of the boxes stacked to the side of the chair wobble.

"Don't get up there, Kayla." They'll both fall out. I know it. Kayla ignores me and swings one leg up and pulls herself into the chair, where the two begin talking to each other and jumping, having a conversation. I catch words: *chair,* TV, *candy, all gone, move.* I cup my hand around my ear, look at the women in the kitchen, watch the way their mouths move, and try to hear.

"I was sleep. That's why I didn't hear y'all at first. We all been sick back here."

"It's the weather," Misty says. "One day it's freezing, the next it's in the eighties. Damn Mississippi spring."

The woman nods, drinks a plastic cup of something, clears her throat.

"Where Fred?" Misty asks.

"Out back, working."

"Business still good?"

"It's booming, baby," the woman says, then coughs.

Leonie is worrying the table with her hands.

"The warmer it gets, the better it gets."

"You still got me?" Misty says.

The woman nods.

"Y'all want something to drink?" she asks.

"You got a cold drink?" Misty asks. The woman hands her a Sprite. I remember how thirsty I am, but I won't say anything. Leonie would kill me.

"No thanks," Leonie says, and the only reason I know it's what she's said is because I read her lips and the shake of her head. She speaks so low.

"You sure?" Misty asks her.

Leonie shakes her head.

"We need to get back on the road soon."

There are cases of cold drinks stacked up against the wall: Coke and Dr Pepper and Barq's and Fanta. When we drove up, I never would have imagined this much plenty in one house: it is stuffed with it, so much food and so many things, so much bulk—cases of soup, cases of crackers, cases of toilet paper and paper towels, three microwaves still in the box, rice cookers, waffle makers, pots. So much food the boxes of it reach to the ceiling in the living room, so many appliances, they are as tall as the lights in the kitchen. I am hungry and thirsty: my throat a closing hand, my stomach a burning fist. And Leonie at the table, Leonie who doesn't usually care whether we accept food when it's offered, Leonie who normally will take everything given to her with an open hand—now she says no. Now, when the goat and rice I ate is silt in my gut.

The woman crosses her arm over her chest and frowns. She's trying to keep the coughs inside, but they come out in sputters. She shakes her head, and I know what she's thinking because I can see it in the way she's standing and staring at Leonie. *Rude.*

If Pop was here, he wouldn't call this boy no *rascal*. Wouldn't call him a *scalawag*, neither. And he definitely wouldn't call him *boy*. He'd call him *badass*. Because he is. He's tired of playing Kayla's game of chase, so he's stopped running. He crouches in front of the television, turns on one of his four game systems, and begins playing a game. It's Grand Theft Auto, and he doesn't know how to play it. He drives the car over medians, into stores, gets out of the car at stoplights, and runs. Kayla is bored. She walks back over to me and climbs into my lap, grabbing a bunch of my shirt, and begins talking to me seriously about wanting juice and graham crackers, so I can't see the women, can't see the glass of water that Leonie drinks now that she's been bullied into accepting something, can't see Misty and the woman leaning toward each other over the table, whispering to each other. Drawing pictures on the table with their fingers.

The boy is screaming at the television. His video game has frozen.

"No! No!" he yells in a voice that sounds like his nose is stuffed with snot.

The boy's car has sailed off a road that winds around a cliff. The car has jumped the railing but is frozen in the air. The car is red with a white stripe down the middle of it, splitting it in two. The boy punches the buttons on the controls, but the game does nothing.

"Take it out," the woman yells from the table.

"No!"

"Start it over," the woman says, and then bends toward Misty again.

The boy throws the controller at the television. It hits and clatters to the floor. He bends and begins fiddling with the game station, pressing buttons, but nothing changes.

"Don't want to lose my spot!" he yells.

The women ignore him.

Kayla jumps up from my lap and bends to pick up a blue plastic ball from the floor, about the size of two of her fists, and starts playing with it.

"If you take it out, it won't lose your spot. It'll save it," I say.

I know this not because I have a game system but because I played Michael's when he lived with us, so I know how they work. He took it with him when he left. The boy ignores me. He makes a sound halfway between a cry and a growl in his throat, something gurgling and whiny, and when he comes up in front of the shelf of game systems, he doesn't stand or turn around and begin playing with Kayla again. He doesn't grab another ball off the floor, a black one or a green one or a red one, all that I can see, and roll one toward us. He stands up and punches the TV. He hits it with his right hand first, then his left, and then his right, windmilling his arms so that his small fists connect with the plastic so hard it sounds like it's cracking. It is cracking. His fist hits again and there is a firework on the car that bursts and stays, one shot through with white and yellow and red. He hits with his left and it does nothing, but then he hits with his right again and there is another firework burst on the car. It stays.

"What are you doing?" the woman yells from the kitchen. She's half risen from the table. "You better not be messing with them boxes again!"

The boy hits again with his left. Nothing.

"What I say!" the woman yells, and she's all the way standing now. The boy bends to the floor, grabs a T-ball bat, and swings. There's a loud crunch, the sound of glass and plastic cracking, and for one moment, the entire car is one brilliant burst of fireworks, and then the TV winks black, and there is nothing on the screen, but before the screen there are the woman and the boy. She stalks past Kayla, who runs and launches herself into my lap and grabs my shirt with both hands, and corners the boy in front of the TV. He turns with the bat and whacks her on the left leg with it.

"MotherFUCK!" she half coughs and screams, and then she grabs the bat from him. She picks up the boy by one arm and holds the bat with another and yells, "What did you do?" Each word is a swing. Each swing makes the boy run. He shrieks. "What did you do!"

The boy's legs are red wherever she hits him with the bat. He laps the woman like a horse on a merry-go-round, his face like that: open mouth, grimace, rictus. She hits him so many times, his cry goes silent, but that mouth is still open. I know what he is saying: *Pain, please, no more pain, please.* The woman drops the bat and the boy's arm all at once, the bat dropping in a straight line to the floor, the boy sagging into a heap.

"Wait till your daddy come out the shed. He's going to kill you."

Leonie walks across the living room and takes Kayla from me. When she talks, she looks at Misty, who still stands in the doorway of the kitchen, holding back the sheet.

"We really got to get back on the road soon."

"He'll be in soon," the woman pants.

"Y'all got a bathroom?" I ask.

"It's broke," the woman says. She's sweating and wiping her hair back away from her face. "We use the toilet in the shed, but if you got to pee, it's best you just go do it out in the yard."

When I walk out, the boy has crawled back into his recliner, and he has curled himself into a ball and is crying noisy tears. Kayla reaches for me when I open the door, but Leonie holds her in a tight hug and walks back into the kitchen with her, away from the crying boy and the shattered television, as if that is what she needs to protect Kayla from. The woman is already there, drinking a cold drink, shaking her head. "This the second one he done did that to," she says. "It's called birth control," says Misty. The woman coughs.

The front yard is still cloaked in mist, still empty. The dog has disappeared, but my hands still burn when I run to the car, the sweat coming in spikes with the fear of teeth. Nothing chases me to the car, where I open the doors on the driver's side to make a shield and pee by the driver's seat. I half hope Leonie will step in it. I zip and ease the doors shut, wonder where all the people that live in this small circle of houses are. Nothing comes for me when I glance at the house, study the closed front door, or when I creep around the back. There is a shed there, brown with a dark tin roof, papered like the house with weatherproofing liner, but no siding. There is a light coming through slits in one of the windows, which have been blacked out with aluminum foil. Someone is listening to country music inside, and when I put my eye to the slit, I see a shirtless man with a beard. He is tattooed, like Michael, but has shaved his head. There are tables with glass beakers and tubes and five-gallon buckets on the ground and empty cold-drink liter bottles, and I know I've seen this before, know that smell because when Michael built his lean-to in the woods behind Mam and Pop's house, it looked and smelled like this. The reason he and Leonie fought, the reason he left, the reason he's in jail. The man is cooking, moves as easy and sure as a chef, but there is nothing to eat here. My stomach burns. I sneak back around to the front of the house, fingering Pop's bag in my pocket, wondering if that tooth is a raccoon's, if it makes me so quiet and quick that even the dog won't hear me when I circle around to the front of the house and ease inside.

When we leave fifteen minutes later, I'm not nervous and I don't sweat. Misty's trying to act like she's not holding a paper bag tucked into a plastic bag, her arm straight as a yardstick at her side, the bag crinkling and hissing when she walks. Leonie looks everywhere but at Misty. She doesn't hand Kayla off, but instead buckles Kayla in herself. When we pull away from that sad circle of houses with all that plenty inside, Misty is bent down fiddling with Leonie's floor mats, and the bag disappears. I slide a pack of saltines and two bottles of juice I stole out of that house into my own plastic bag. After we leave the half-burnt room of pine trees, and we're back on pavement and the highway, Leonie turns on the radio and lets it play louder than she ever has. I open my stolen bottle and drink the juice down, then pour half the other bottle into Kayla's sippy cup. I hand one cracker to Kayla and slide one into my mouth. We eat like that: one for me and one for her. I let the saltines turn mealy and soggy on my tongue before chewing and swallowing so I don't crunch. I am silent and stealthy in another way. Neither of the women in the front seat pay us any attention. When I eat and drink, I have never tasted anything so good.

Chapter 4

Leonie

The night of Jojo's birthday, Misty said: *If we do this,
the trip's paid for.* And then: *You and Michael could have
enough for a deposit. Y'all could get your own place. You always
say the problem is y'all parents. Yours 'cause you live with them;
his because they're assholes.* Given was even more still when
she said that, like stone. Through Misty's narrow kitchen
window, I could see the tops of the trees turning from a
dark velvet gray to orange, from palest orange to a pink
the color of the inside of my mouth. *How you think I paid
for all my trips up to Bishop? From tips?* She shook her head
and snorted. *You better take advantage.*

I hear them four words over and over again when we get
in the car and I watch Misty put the package in the pocket
under the floorboards. *You better take advantage.* She said
them words as though decisions have no consequences,
when, of course, it's been easier for her. The way she said
it, *take advantage*, made me want to slap her. Her freckles,
her thin pink lips, her blond hair, the stubborn milkiness
of her skin; how easy had it been for her, her whole life,
to make the world a friend to her?

Before Michael went to jail, he installed the envelope in the bottom of my car. He elevated the car on a jack and crawled underneath with his welding tools, and he cut what looked to be a perfect square in the floor of the car, then inserted another piece of metal with a hinge, fixed the hinge, and then welded the bottom of the car back together. *Two doors*, he'd said, and then kissed me twice. *One to hold, and the other to let it go. If I need to.* He'd been home from the oil rig for six months by then, and we'd had to move back in with Mama and Pop. We'd run through the money he saved, plus his severance. He'd worked on the *Deepwater Horizon* as a rig welder. After it blew up, he came home with his severance money and nightmares. At the time, I'd talked him into buying a full-size bed for us to share in our new apartment, *so no matter how we moved*, I said, *we'd sleep close*, so every time he kicked in his sleep, every time he twitched or mumbled and threw up his arms, drawing back from something, I woke. I'd spent the days after the accident with Jojo in the house watching CNN, watching the oil gush into the ocean, and feeling guilty because that's not what I wanted to see, guilty because I didn't give a shit about those fucking pelicans, guilty because I just wanted to see Michael's face, his shoulders, his fingers, guilty because all I cared about was him. He'd called me not long after the story broke on the news, told me he was safe, but his voice was tiny, corroded by static, unreal. *I knew those men—all eleven of them. Lived with them*, he said. When he came home, I was happy. He wasn't. *What we supposed to do?* he asked, taking two bites of his grits before leaving them to jelly on his plate. *We'll figure it out*, I said. When he started getting skinny, I thought it was because of his nightmares. When his cheekbones started standing out on his face like rocks under water, I thought it was because he was stressed out over money. When his spine rose under his skin, a line of knuckles punching up his back, I thought it was because of his grief and the fact he couldn't find another welding job anywhere in Mississippi or Alabama or Florida or Louisiana or the Gulf of Mexico. But later I found out the truth. Later, I learned he'd figured everything out without me.

"You don't have to be so nervous," Misty says.

"I'm not nervous."

"This ain't the first time I done this."

"I know."

"I'm talking about with Bishop."

Misty's sipping on one of the cold drinks she took from her friends' house. The woman's name was Carlotta, and her husband, the one who cooked and gave us the bag, was Fred.

"First time I did this was when I was visiting Sonny, my ex."

"That's how you know them?"

"Yeah. First time I did it, I was scared to death. Like you. But then after that, each time was easier."

I glance in the rearview mirror. Michaela's shoving a blue ball in her mouth and babbling around the ball at her brother, who is trying to coax it away from her, his face very close to hers, his voice low and serious: "No, don't put that in your mouth, Kayla; it's nasty and done been on the floor." Michaela grins and spits the ball in his hand and begins clapping and saying: "Nasty, that's nasty." Jojo looks like he's paying all his attention to Michaela, but I know he's not. There's something about the way he leans, about how he says the same thing to Michaela, again, "That floor was nasty," that makes me realize he's listening to what we're saying, even as he's trying to look like he's not. Me and Misty already talked about it when I picked her up: we're not going to refer to it by name, not going to use any words that hint to what's in the bag, what we're sneaking north with us: meth, crystal, crank. We'd talk around it, avoid it like a bad customer in the bar who's too drunk for more, who smells like sweet alcohol fermenting and diesel, yet keeps grabbing my hand when I walk by, saying something fucked up to me like: *One more, you sweet Black bitch*. And when we have to call it some other name, we're going to call it the most embarrassing thing we can so Jojo will lose all interest.

"If we get pulled over and they find those goddamn tampons, Misty, I'm going to kill you."

I figure that will make Jojo stop listening. Never mind the fact that the statement doesn't make any sense. He's a boy, and periods are one of those things about the human body he most likes to ignore: kidney stones, pimples, boils. Cancer.

"Jojo, I need the atlas."

I'm right. He jerks when I say this before rooting around for the book and handing it over the seat to me, trying to find my eyes in the rearview mirror. When his brown don't find my black, Misty takes it from him. He shrinks back into the backseat, still looking at the floor. Michaela calls him, "Jojo," and he leans toward her again.

"Where are we?" I ask.

"I'm looking," Misty mumbles.

I look for mile markers. We stopped at Carlotta and Fred's just north of Hattiesburg, in north Forrest County.

"Mendenhall. We're in Mendenhall," Misty says. There's a stoplight ahead of us, so I slow. She's not looking at the atlas.

"How you know that?"

Misty points up, and there's a billboard. *Mendenhall*, it reads, *Home of Mississippi's Most Beautiful Courthouse.*

"I want to see it."

The light turns green. I step on the gas.

"I don't."

"Why not? What if it's really pretty?"

In the backseat, Jojo is moving his mouth around like he's chewing something. He looks away from Michaela and up to me, and his eyes dark as mine. I was smaller when I was his age, weedier, more delicate at my joints and bones. He looks like Given, but he never jokes. Sometimes, when Jojo's playing with Michaela or sitting in Mama's room rubbing her hands or helping her turn over in the bed, I look at him and see a hungry girl.

"I bet it has big columns and everything. Probably even bigger than Beauvoir," Misty says.

"No," I say, and leave it at that.

Michael never used to write me anything about the violence in jail, those things that happened in the dead of night in dark corners and locked rooms: the stabbings and the hangings and the overdoses and the beatings. But I told him he had to tell me. In a letter, I said: *If you don't tell me what's going on, I imagine the worst.* So in the next letter, he told me about somebody getting jumped in the showers, beaten purple and black. In the one after, he told me how his cellmate started messing with one of the female guards, how they snuck around and have sex in the jail, hunching like rodents. Bent on procreating. And in the next letter, he told me about the guards beating an eighteen-year-old boy who had been convicted of kidnapping and strangling a five-year-old girl in a trailer park. They heard him screaming and then nothing, and then got word he bled to death like a pig in his cell. *That,* I want to say to Misty, *is your pretty courthouse.* But I don't say anything. I watch the road roll out before me like a big black ribbon and I think about Michael's last letter before he told me he was coming home: *This ain't no place for no man. Black or White. Don't make no difference. This a place for the dead.*

Michaela's sick. She was quiet for the first hour after we left the house, but then she started coughing, and the tail end of the cough caught in her throat and she gagged. For the past thirty minutes, she's been crying and fighting with her seat belt, trying to get out. I hand a palmful of napkins to Jojo, and every other time I look in the rearview mirror, I see him bending over her, frowning, wiping at her drooling mouth. The napkins soak in seconds. We were supposed to drive the rest of the way today and stay with Michael and Bishop's lawyer in the next town over from the jail, but all her crying is making me feel like someone

is squeezing my brain, tighter and tighter. I can't breathe.
Then she coughs and gags again, and I look back and the
front of her is orange and mauve. She's thrown up all her
puffy Cheetos, digested soggy, all her little careful bites of
her ham sandwich. The meat has turned what isn't yellow
pink. Jojo is holding napkins in both hands, frozen. He
looks scared. Michaela cries harder.

"We gotta stop," I say as I pull over on the shoulder of
the road.

"Oh shit," Misty says, and waves her hand in front of
her mouth like she's shooing away gnats. "That smell is
going to make me throw up."

I want to slap her, even though the smell of the stomach acid, harsh and intense in the small car, makes me feel
queasy, too. Want to yell at her: *Bitch, how you work around
all them drunks and can't stand a little throw-up?* But I don't.
Once we're on the side of the road, and I'm swiping globs
of the vomit away with the napkins I snatched from Jojo,
the queasiness turns flips and somersaults in my stomach
like a kid on a trampoline. Jojo doesn't look scared anymore.
He puts both hands in the vomit cascading down Michaela's
front and unbuckles her chest harness. She pauses in her
frantic straining, her little chest pushed out against the belt
again to give a thank-you cry before she starts pulling at the
lap buckle, anxious for him to undo that, too, to free her.
He's frowning. He unbuckles the last buckle and pulls her
out, and before I even have a moment to admonish him,
to say his name sharply, say "Jojo," Michaela is smashed
to his chest and her little arms are around his neck again,
the length of her laid along him, shaking, mewling, him

breathing: "It's all right, Kayla, it's all right, Kayla, Jojo got you, Jojo got you, I got you, shhh."

"You almost done?" Misty asks, tossing it over her shoulder to the backseat like a piece of gummy burger wax paper.

"I'm tired of this shit," I say. I don't know why I say it. Maybe because I'm tired of driving, tired of the road stretching before me endlessly, Michael always at the opposite end of it, no matter how far I go, how far I drive. Maybe because part of me wanted her to leap for me, to smear orange vomit over the front of my shirt as her little tan body sought mine, always sought mine, our hearts separated by the thin cages of our ribs, exhaling and inhaling, our blood in sync. Maybe because I want her to burrow in to me for succor instead of her brother. Maybe because Jojo doesn't even look at me, all his attention on the body in his arms, the little person he's trying to soothe, and my attention is everywhere. Even now, my devotion: inconstant.

I mop up the rest of the slimy residue in her seat, throw the napkins on the asphalt, take a few baby wipes, and swipe them across the seat so that it smells like stomach acid and flowery soap.

"It smells better," Misty says. She's half leaning out the window of the car, her formerly fluttering hand now cupped over her nose like a mask.

The drive to the next gas station seems miles, and the sun breaks through the clouds and beams directly overhead.

When we pull into the parking lot of the station, the

attendant is sitting on the front porch of the wooden building smoking a cigarette. She almost blends in to the wall she leans against, because her skin is as brown as the stained boards. She opens the door for me and follows me in, and the string of silver bells hung across the door jingles.

"Slow day," she says as she slides behind the counter. She's skinny, damn near as thin as Mama, and her buttoned-up work shirt hangs on her like a flat sheet spread to dry on a clothesline.

"Yeah," I say, and wander toward the drink coolers in the back. I palm two bottles of Powerade and set them on the counter. The woman smiles, and I realize she's missing her two front teeth, and a scar meanders in a scratchy line across her head. I wonder if she just has bad teeth, or if whoever gave her that forehead scar knocked them out.

Misty's walking around the parking lot, holding her phone above her head, searching for a signal. All the car doors are open, and Jojo is sitting sideways in the back while Michaela climbs over him, rubbing her face into his neck and whining. He caresses her back, and their hair is molded to their heads. I pour half of a bottle into one of Michaela's juice bottles and hold out my arms.

"Give her here."

"Kayla, go," Jojo says. He isn't looking at me or the damp day or the empty road, but at Kayla, who begins to cry and grabs at his shirt and holds so tightly, her little knuckles turn white. When I pull her into my lap and sit in the front seat, she plants her chin in her chest and sobs, her eyes closed, her fists tucked under her chin.

"Michaela," I say. "Come on, baby. You need to drink

something." Jojo is standing above me, his hands shoved into his pockets as he studies Michaela. She doesn't hear me. She hiccups and wails. "Michaela, baby."

I put the nipple of the sippy cup in her mouth, and she blocks it with her clenched teeth and whips her head to the side. I grip her harder, trying to hold her still, and her little milk muscles give under my fingers, soft as water balloons. We wrestle like this as she stands and sits and bends backward and writhes and says two words, over and over again.

"No. Jojo."

I've had enough.

"Goddamnit, Michaela! Can you get her to drink some of this?" I ask.

Jojo nods, and I'm already handing her over. Without her, my arms feel weightless.

Michaela drinks a quarter cup, and then she slumps over Jojo's shoulder, one arm around his neck, rubbing. I wait fifteen minutes, and just as Misty is buckling herself into the driver's seat so we can get back on the road, Michaela vomits again. It is electric blue, the color of Powerade.

"You might as well take that off," I tell Misty. She rolls her eyes and unbuckles her seat belt before squatting on a parking block in the shade to smoke a cigarette. "We going to be here for a minute."

I don't want Michaela to throw up in the car again, to retch in the backseat while I'm strapped in the front. We'd just have to pull over again so I can clean her up. The heat rises from the asphalt parking lot, along with steam from the rain. Jojo sits sideways, his feet on the ground, Michaela draped over him.

"You want to lay down, Kayla?" he asks. "You might feel better if you lay down."

He slides his hands under her armpits and tries to ease her off of him and onto the seat, but she sticks to him, sure as a burr: her arms and legs thorny and cleaving. He gives up and rubs her back.

"I'm sorry you feel sick," Jojo says, and Michaela begins to cry. He rubs her back and she rubs his, and I stand there, watching my children comfort each other. My hands itch, wanting to do something. I could reach out and touch them both, but I don't. Jojo looks part bewildered, part stoic, part like he might start crying. I need a cigarette. I squat next to Misty on the concrete block and bum a smoke: the menthol shores me up, stacks sandbags up my spine. I can do this. I wait until the nicotine laps at my insides like a placid lake, and then I go back to the car.

"Make her drink more," I tell Jojo.

Thirty minutes later, she vomits that up. I give her fifteen minutes and I tell Jojo again: "Make her drink." Even though Michaela is letting out a steady whine now, bewildered at the cup in her brother's hand, Jojo does what I ask. Twenty minutes later, she vomits again. Michaela is desolate, hanging on Jojo, blinking at me when I stand inside the car door with more electrolytes. "Make her drink," I say again, but Jojo sits there as if he does not hear me, his shoulders hunched up around his ears like he knows I'm out of patience, like he knows that I want to hit him.

"Jojo," I say. He flinches and ignores me. Michaela rubs her snotty nose and leaking mouth in his shoulder. "Jojo, no," she says. The attendant steps out onto the porch, her cigarette already lit.

"Y'all all right?" she asks.

"Y'all got something for vomiting? For kids?"

She shakes her head, and her straightened hair flies free at the temples, waving around like insect antennae.

"Nope. Owner won't stock nothing like that. He say only the basics. But you'd be surprised how many people come through here carsick, needing Pepto-Bismol."

Weeds are flowering in bushes at the edge of the gas station lot; purple and yellow and white blooms nod at the edge of the pines. I palm the back of Michaela's neck where she slumps over on Jojo, who is sitting on the trunk of my car, jiggling his knee and watching me and Misty, frowning.

"Hold on," I say, and walk off the parking lot and along the tree line.

Mama always told me that if I look carefully enough, I can find what I need in the world. Starting when I was seven, Mama would lead me out in the woods around the house for walks, and she'd point out plants before digging them up or stripping their leaves and telling me how they could heal or hurt. The wind moved high in the trees, but nearly everything was silent below, except for me and Mama, who said: *That right there is cow parsnip. You can use the young leaves like celery when you cook, but the roots is more useful. You can make a decoction for cold and flu. And if you make them into a poultice, you can ease and heal bruises, arthritis, and boils.* She dug around the roots of the plant with a small shovel she carried on our walks, and then pulled the whole plant up by its leaves and doubled it up before putting it in the bag she carried across her chest. She searched the ground until she found another plant, and said: *This pigweed. Ain't good for any medicine, really, but you can cook with it, use it like you use spinach. Got a lot of vitamins in it, so it's good for you. Your daddy like it sautéed with his rice, and he say his mama used to make bread with the ground-up seeds. I ain't never tried that, though.* On our way back to the house with the day's haul, she quizzed me. As I grew older, it was easier for me to remember, to answer her quickly as we picked our way around tree roots. *Wormseed,* I would say. *Good for getting rid of worms if you use it like seasoning in food.* But it was hard for me to remember everything. Every day, Mama would point out a plant that had parts that could help women, specifically, seeing as how it was mostly women that searched her out, needing her skills and knowledge. She'd say: *Remember you can use the leaves to make a tea that helps with cramps. And it could bring on a period, too.* I'd look away and roll my eyes to the pines, wishing I were in front of the TV, not out trudging through the woods with my mama talking about periods. But now, as I walk through the clearing and peer into the woods, looking for milkweed, I wish I'd listened more carefully. I wish I could remember more than the fact that it has pinkish-purple flowers. And even though milkweed grows wild on parcels of land like this and flowers in the spring, I don't see its white-beaded, downy leaves anywhere.

When Mama first realized that something was seriously wrong with her body, that it had betrayed her and turned cancerous, she began by treating it herself with herbs. I'd come home on those spring mornings to find her bed empty. She'd be out in the woods, picking and slowly dragging bushels of young pokeweed shoots behind her. Every time, she said: *I'm telling you, it's going to cure it.* I'd take the bundles from her, put my arm around her waist, and help her up the steps and into the house, where I'd set her in a chair in the kitchen. I was always buzzing from the night before, so while I chopped and cleaned and boiled and made pitcher after pitcher of tea for her to drink, the high would trill through my veins like a discordant song. But it didn't cure it. Her body broke down over the years until she took to her bed, permanently, and I forgot so much of what she taught me. I let her ideas drain from me so that the truth could pool instead. Sometimes the world don't give you what you need, no matter how hard you look. Sometimes it withholds.

If the world were a right place, a place for the living, a place where men like Michael didn't end up in jail, I'd be able to find wild strawberries. That's what Mama would look for if she couldn't find milkweed. I could boil the leaves at Michael's lawyer's house, where we're staying before we go pick Michael up in the morning. Put a little sugar in it, a little food coloring like Mama used to do whenever I had an upset stomach as a child, and tell her it's juice.

But the world ain't that place. Ain't no wild strawberries at the side of the road. It ain't boggy enough up here. But this world might be a place that gives a little luck to the small, sometimes shows a little mercy, because after I walk awhile down the side of the road out of sight of the gas station, after I leave Misty gesturing out the window with her arm, yelling, "Fucking come on," I find wild blackberries. Mama always told me they could be used for upset stomach, but only for adults. But if there was nothing else, she said I could make a tea and give it to kids. Not a lot, I remember her saying. From the leaves. Or was it from the vine? Or the roots? The heat beats down so hard I can't remember. I miss the late-spring chill.

This is the kind of world it is. The kind of world that gives you a blackberry plant, a doughy memory, and a child that can't keep nothing down. I kneel by the side of the road, grab the thorny stems as close to the earth as I can get them, and pull, and the vine pricks my hand, tears at the skin, draws blood in tiny points that smear. My palms burn. *This the kind of world*, Mama told me when I got my period when I was twelve, *that makes fools of the living and saints of them once they dead. And devils them throughout.* Even though the words were harsh, I saw hope in her face when she said them. She thought that if she taught me as much herbal healing as she could, if she gave me a map to the world as she knew it, a world plotted orderly by divine order, spirit in everything, I could navigate it. But I resented her when I was young, resented her for the lessons and the misplaced hope. And later, for still believing in good in a world that cursed her with cancer, that twisted her limp as an old dry rag and left her to disintegrate.

I kneel and lean back on my haunches. The day pulses like a flush vein. Wipe my eyes, smear dirt across my face, and make myself blind.

Chapter 5

Jojo

Kayla need to eat. I can tell by the way she keep crying, the way she keep hunching over and then knocking her head back and arching against her seat once we get back on the road. And screaming. I can tell there's something wrong with her stomach. It won't stop hurting her. She need to put something in it, so I take her out and let her sit on my lap, thinking it might make her feel better, but it don't. She scream a little softer, her cries a little less high-pitched and sharp. The pain's knife edge dulls. But she still knocks her head against my chest, and her skull feels thin against my bones, against the stone where my ribs meet, her skull easy to break as a ceramic bowl. Leonie done laid her plants on the armrest between her and Misty, and minute by minute, mile by mile, those blackberry leaves get more and more wilted, the roots get stringier and stringier, sling their dirt loose in clumps. Kayla growls and cries. I don't want Leonie giving her that. I know that's what she think she need to do, but she ain't Mam. She ain't Pop. She ain't never healed nothing or grown nothing in her life, and she don't know.

107

She bought me a betta fish when I was six, after I kept telling her the same story, every day, about the tanks we had in my class at school, the betta fish, red and purple and blue and green, swimming lazily in the tanks, flashing brilliant and then dull. She came home with one on a Sunday, after she'd been out all weekend. I hadn't seen her since Friday, since she told Mam she was going to the store to buy some milk and some sugar and didn't come back. When she came back, her skin was dry and flaking at the corners of her mouth, her hair stuck out in a bushy halo, and she smelled like wet hay. The fish was green, the color of pine needles, and he had stripes down his tail the color of red mud. I called him Bubby Bubbles, since he blew bubbles all day, and when I leaned over his tank, I could hear him crunching on the fish food Leonie had brought home in a sample-size bag. I imagined even then that one day I could lean over his bowl, and instead of crunching, little words would pop out the bubbles that fizzed up to the surface. *Big face. Light.* And *love.* But when the sample size of fish food ran out, and I asked Leonie to buy me more, she said she would, and then forgot, again and again, until one day she said: *Give him some old bread.* I figured he couldn't crunch like he needed on some old bread, so I kept bugging her about it, and Bubby got skinnier and skinnier, his bubbles smaller and smaller, until I walked into the kitchen one day and he was floating on top of the water, his eyes white, a slimy scrim like fat, no voice in his bubbles.

Leonie kill things.

*   *   *

Outside the car, the trees thin and change, the trunks shorten and they get fuller and green, the leaves not sharp dark pine but so full, hazy almost. They stand in thin lines between fields, fields of muddy green, bristling with low plants. The sky darkens. The forests and fields around us turn black. I put my mouth to Kayla's ear and tell her a story.

"You see them trees over there?" She groans. "If you look at the ground under them trees, there's a hole." She moans. "Rabbits live in them holes. One of them is a little rabbit, the littlest rabbit. She got brown fur and little white teeth like gum." She's quiet for a second. "Her name Kayla, like you. You know what she do?" Kayla shrugs and sinks back in to me. "She the best at digging holes. She dig them the deepest and the fastest. One day it was dark and a big storm come and the rabbit family's hole started filling up with water, so Kayla started digging. And digging. And digging. You know what she did?" Kayla's breath hitches, and then she turns to face me and puts her mouth in my shirt and sucks in more air. I rub her back in circles, rub it like I could rub away the cramping, the hurt, whatever's making her sick. "She dug and dug and the tunnel got longer and longer. The water wasn't even coming in where Kayla was digging, but she kept on until she popped up out the ground, and you know what?" Kayla digs her fingernails in to my arm, then raises up a little to look out the window and points at the dark fields, at the thin line of trees with the rabbit hole underneath it. "Getting dark," she says. Then she leans back in to me and slumps. "Uh-huh. Little rabbit saw the gray barn and the fat pig and the red horse and Mam and Pop. She dug all the way to our house, Kayla. And when she saw Mam and Pop she loved them, and she decided to stay. So when we get home, she going to be waiting for us. You want to see her?" I ask. But Kayla is asleep. She twitches and for a blink I imagine I know what she's dreaming, but then I stop. She smells sharp like sweat and throw-up, but her hair smells like coconuts from the oil Mam used to put in it, the one that I use now when I pull her hair into little ponytails: two little cotton balls on the sides of her head. I block out the image of her in the wet earth, the size of a rabbit, digging a hole. I don't want to know that dream.

When we pull off the highway and onto a back road, the sky is dark blue, turning its back to us, pulling a black sheet over its shoulder. The world shrinks to the headlights coming from the car, twin horns leading through the darkness, the car an old animal, limping to another clearing in the woods. Pop always told me you can trust an animal to do exactly what it's born to do: to root in mud or canter through a field or fly. That no matter how domesticated an animal is, Pop say, the wild nature in it will come through. Kayla is her most animal self, a worm-ridden cat in my arms. When we finally pull into a yard and the trees open up, this place is different. It's not like the huddle of houses in Forrest County. There is only one house here, and it is wide. There are windows all along the front, and warm yellow light shines through all of them. Leonie stops the car. Misty gets out and waves at us to follow. I walk to the porch with Kayla asleep in my arms, snoring, breathing out of her mouth, and I see up close the paint is peeling in thin strips with marker-thin lines of brown-gray showing through. The windows look a little cloudy, like the water my fish died in. The wisteria planted on each side of the front steps has rooted thick into the earth, grown as big around as a man's muscley arm, and has twisted and twined up the railings to weave thick as a curtain along the front of the porch. Here, the animal coming out. Misty knocks on the door.

"Come in," a man's voice sings, and there is music behind it.

He's a big man. We find him in the kitchen, boiling noodles for spaghetti. My mouth turns to water. I have never been so hungry.

"Smells good, doesn't it?" he says as he walks toward us. He bounces, seems to walk on his tiptoes. He has a white long-sleeved shirt on, except it's rolled up to his elbows. The shirt is like his porch, the thread coming loose at the neck, something that looks like green paint splattered across the front. His kitchen is green. I ain't never seen a green kitchen. That's when I smell the sauce. It pops in its pot on the stove and streaks his arm as he stirs it. He licks it off. The noodles he put in the water slowly sink, disappear down the edges of the pot as their bottoms turn soft. I frown when he licks his furry arm. His hair is pulled back on his head, and he has it in a little ponytail that sticks out, short as Kayla's. "Figured y'all would be hungry," he says. He's the whitest White man I've ever seen.

"You figured right." Misty hugs the man as she says this, turns her face so that she speaks it into his paint-splattered shirt. "Took us longer to make it here because the little one got sick."

"Ah yes, the little girl!" he said. Leonie looks like she wants to shush him, but she doesn't. "She's—" He pauses.

"Sticky." Now Leonie looks like she wants to punch him. *Her mulish look,* Pop says. "Is the young man sick too?" I already like him better, even though when he looks at me, I see something like sadness in his face, and I don't know why.

"No," Leonie says. She crosses her arms when she says it. "We're not hungry."

"Nonsense," the man says.

"Leonie," Misty says, and looks at Leonie. I know it's the kind of look that says something else without saying it, but I can't read Leonie's eyebrows, her lips, the way she nods her head forward and her long bangs fall in her eyes. Whatever Misty says, Leonie understands and nods back.

"We'll eat." Leonie clears her throat. "I was wondering if I can use your stove. I got something I need to cook."

"Of course, my dear, of course."

Up close, the man smells like he ain't took a bath in a few days, but it's not a musty smell. Smells sweet and wrong at the same time, like sweet liquor that done sat out in the heat and started turning to vinegar.

"Excuse the French, Al, but I'm fucking starving." Misty smiles.

When I sit in the living room, Kayla stays asleep, breathing hot into my shirt with little puffs. The room has high ceilings and bookshelves on every wall. There is no TV. There's a radio in the kitchen, where Misty is sitting at a counter stool, drinking a glass of wine Al has poured for her in a mason jar. The music, all violins and cellos, swells in the room, then recedes, like the water out in the Gulf before a big storm. When Leonie comes in from the car, holding her weeds in one hand, she trips on the rug covering the wooden floor, red and orange and white and frayed, and a bag falls from under her shirt, hits the carpet, and what was inside the crinkled brown paper slides out. It is clear, a whole pack of broken glass, and I've seen this before. I know what this is. The man is laughing at something Misty says, and Leonie will not look at me as she picks it up, scoops it back in the bag, and slumps over the counter before sliding it to Misty, who passes the bag to Al. He picks it up, tosses it into the air, and then makes it disappear like a magician.

Al is Michael's lawyer.

"Boy's around his age," he says, pushing his sleeves up his arm and frowning after pointing at me, "and they thought he was selling weed in school."

Misty swigs her drink.

"And do you know what they did to him?"

She shrugs.

"Brought him into the principal's office with two other boys his age. Friends. Made them drop their pants and strip so they could search them."

Misty shakes her head, her hair swinging around her face.

"That's a damn shame," she says.

"It's illegal, is what it is. It's pro bono, and the school will probably get off with some sort of censure from the courts, but I couldn't not take it," he says, shrugging and drinking. "Long moral arc of the universe and all."

Misty nods like she knows what he's talking about. She's pulled out her ponytail to let her hair hang, and every time she nods or shakes her head, she does it so violently her hair swings, as languid and pretty as Spanish moss, across her back. She's pulled her shirt down at the collar, let it sag, so her shoulder is a gleaming globe in the living room light. Al has all the lamps lit. The more she drinks, the more her hair swings.

"You do what you can." Al smiles, touches her shoulder, and lifts his cup of wine. "How do you like it? It's good, right? I told you it was a good year."

"So what you doing about my man?" Misty leans toward him and raises her eyebrows and smiles.

"Okay, okay," Al says, leaning back away from her to laugh before coming toward her, talking with his hands, telling her about whatever he's doing to help free Bishop.

Leonie is sitting on the sofa next to me, sippy cup in hand. It took her around thirty minutes to cut the black-berry plant, boil the roots and the leaves. She boiled the root in one pot and the leaves in the other, while I hunched over my plate shoving spaghetti into my mouth, hardly chewing. She let it cool. She stood at the counter, squinting and talking to herself with her arms crossed, and then she poured half from one pot and half from the other pot into Kayla's cup. It was gray. I shoved the last of the food in my mouth, went to rinse my plate off and put it into the dishwasher, which smelled sour, and watched while she asked Al if he had any food coloring and sugar. He did. She dumped a few spoons of sugar and drops of food coloring into the cup and shook it until it looked like muddy Kool-

Aid. Now she's sitting next to Kayla, who we left sprawled, asleep, on the couch, and she's trying to nuzzle her awake. Every time she asks Kayla to wake up, kisses her ear and neck, Kayla reaches up and puts her arm around Leonie's neck and pulls like she wants her to lay down, to go to sleep with her. Like she doesn't want to be woken.

It scares me.

"Come on, Michaela," Leonie says, and she tugs Kayla upright. Kayla opens her eyes and slumps like Leonie did in the kitchen when she passed that package across, whining and trying to lie back down. "You thirsty?" Leonie whispers, putting the cup in front of Kayla. "Here. Drink," she says.

"No," Kayla says, and slaps the cup away. It flies out of Leonie's hand and rolls across the floor.

"She don't want it," I say.

"Don't matter what she want," Leonie say, rolling her eyes at me. "She need it."

I want to tell her: *You don't know what you doing.* And then: *You ain't Mam.* But I don't. The worry bubbling up in me like water boiling over the lip of a pot, but the words sticking in my throat. She might hit me. I did a lot of talking when I was younger, when I was eight and nine, in public. And then one day she slapped me across the face, and after that, every time I opened my mouth to talk against her, she did that. Hit me so hard her slaps started feeling like punches. Made me twist to the side, my hand on my face. Made me sit down once in the middle of the aisle in Walmart. So I stopped. But she doesn't know how to make medicine out of plants, and I worry for Kayla. Two years ago, when I was so sick with a stomach bug that I could hardly get up off the sofa and make it to the bathroom, Mam told Leonie to go gather some plant in the woods and make a tea out of the roots. She did it. And because Mam told her to do it, I trusted her, and I drank it, even though it tasted like rubber. Leonie must have picked the wrong plant, or prepared it wrong, because whatever she gave me made me even sicker. She poured the gritty, bitter mess by the back steps, and a few days afterward, when I had worked whatever she gave me and the bug out of my system, I found a stray cat dead, carbuncular and rotting, by the steps. It had drunk whatever she'd poured into a pool on the ground.

Leonie's picked up the cup, holding it to Kayla's lips.

"You thirsty, right," she says, and it's an answer, not a question. Kayla coughs and grabs at the cup. My underarms spike and sweat, and I want to grab that sippy cup and throw it like she did, bat it across the room and snatch her out of the loose circle of Leonie's arm. But I don't. And then she's sucking at the spout and turning up her cup and drinking, and I feel like I lost a game I didn't know I was playing.

"She just need to sleep it off," Misty says then. "Probably carsick, that's all."

Kayla is thirsty. She's drunk half of it, and she's pulling hard on the spout, her lips puckered like it's a bottle. When she's done, she lets the cup clatter to the floor, and then she crawls across the sofa and into my lap, grabbing my hand and saying, "Down," which means up. She wants me to tell her a story. I lean in.

"I have a better vintage in the kitchen," Al says, looking at Leonie. "Maybe we could sample it this evening."

"Sounds good to me," Misty says.

"I don't know," Leonie says. She's looking at Kayla in my lap, Kayla who is beginning to fuss because I haven't begun the story yet. She's beginning to squirm and cry again like she did in the car before she threw up. "She ain't feeling good."

"I'm telling you, it's probably carsickness. Let her sleep it off," Misty says. "She'll be fine." And then she looks at Leonie like she's saying two things at once, one with her mouth and the other with her eyes. "You been driving all day. Might be nice to unwind and take a break."

I can't read her yet. Leonie reaches out and smooths Kayla's hair down, but it springs back up. Kayla curves away from her.

"You probably right," Leonie says.

"You know how many times I threw up with my head out the window when I was a kid? I lost count. She'll be fine," Misty says.

It looks like Misty's said the right thing this time, because Leonie sits back then. There is a wall between us.

"Michael got motion sickness bad. He can't even ride in the backseat without feeling like throwing up." It makes sense to Leonie then. "Must have got it from him."

"See?" Misty nods. Al nods. They all nod and rise and head off to the kitchen. I take Kayla into the bedroom Al pointed us to earlier, with two twin beds. I take off Kayla's shirt, which smells like acid, and wet and soap a rag from the bathroom next to the bedroom, and then wipe her off. She's hot. Even her little feet. So hot. I take off everything but her drawers and lay down with her in one of the twin beds, and she puts her little arm over my shoulder and pulls me to her, like she does every morning we wake up together. "Doe-doe," she says.

I lay there until the music goes quiet in the kitchen and I hear them moving out to the back porch. No glasses clink, no wine. I figure they're opening up that pack Leonie brought. I lay there until I can't no more, and then I carry Kayla into the bathroom and stick my finger down her throat and make her throw up. She fights me, hitting at my arms, crying against my hand, sobbing but not making no words, but I do it three times, make her vomit over my hand, hot as her little body, three times, all of it red and smelling sweet, until I'm crying and she's shrieking. I turn off the light and go back into the room and wipe her with my shirt and lay in the bed with her, scared that Leonie's going to walk in and find all that red throw-up in the bathroom, find out I made Kayla throw up Leonie's potion. But nobody comes. Kayla sniffs and dozes off, hiccupping in her sleep, and then I clean all of it up with soap and water until the bathroom is as white as it was before. All the while, my heart beating so hard I can hear it in my ears, because I knew what Kayla was saying. I knew.

I love you, Jojo. Why you make me, Jojo? Jojo! Brother! Brother. I heard her.

I try to sleep, but for hours, I can't. All I can do is lay there and listen to Kayla breathe. Outside, somewhere far away off in the dark reach of the woods, a dog barks. It's a hacking sound, full of anger and sharp teeth. At the heart of it all: fear. When I was younger, I wanted a puppy. I asked Pop for one, and he said ever since his time in Parchman, he couldn't keep a dog. He said he tried when he got let out, but every one of the dogs he got, mutts and hounds, died within the first year of him getting it. When he was in Parchman, Pop said, once he started working with the hounds the prison used to track escapees, all he could smell, when he was eating or waking or falling asleep, was dog shit. All he could hear was the dogs, yipping and howling and baying, raring to tear. Pop said he tried to get Richie on with dogs so he could get him out the fields, but it didn't work. I close my eyes and imagine Pop sitting on the high-backed chair in the corner of the room. Pop, with his straight back and his hands like tree roots, telling me more stories, speaking me to sleep.

Was one of them days when the sun bear down on you so hard feel like it's twisting you inside out, and all you do is burn. One of them heavy days. Down here, it's different; we got that wind coming off the water all the time, and that eases. But up there, they ain't got that, just the fields stretching on, the trees too short with not enough leaves, no good shade nowhere, and everything bending low under the weight of that sun: men, women, mules, everything low under God. Was a day like that the boy broke his hoe.

I don't think he meant to do it. He wasn't nothing but a scrawny thing, littler than you, I already told you that, so he must have hit a rock or leant on it the wrong way, and that's what did it. Kinnie had me running the dogs around the fields, working on they sense of smell. I was circling Richie's field when I saw him walking with the two pieces in his hand, just dragging the handle in the dirt, little trail following him to the wood line. The driver, the man who set the pace for the day's work, something like an overseer, saw Richie. He sat up on his mule and watched the boy's back, and he looked more and more mad, like a snake drawing down and bunching up before he strike. I edged around the field until I could get close enough to Richie to hiss at him.

"Pick the handle up, boy. Driver watching you," I said.

"He going to beat me anyway," Richie said, but he picked the handle up.

"Who say?"

"He say."

The boy was jittery around the eyes, even though he walked like he wasn't scared. Them marks I saw on him when he came in Parchman told me he knew what it was to be beat, whether it was his mama taking a belt buckle to him or some man. But I knew the boy wasn't ready for the whip. I knew he wasn't ready for Black Annie.

I was right. Sun went down, and after supper, sergeant tied him to some posts set at the edge of the camp. So hot the sun still felt like it was up, and the boy laid there spread-eagle on the ground in the dirt with his hands and legs tied to them posts. When that whip cracked in the air and came down on his back, he sounded like a puppy. Yelped so loud. And that's what he kept doing, over and over. Just yelping for every one of them lashes, arching up off the ground, turning his head like he wanted to look at the sky. Yelling like a drowning dog. When they untied him, his back was full of blood, them seven gashes laid open like filleted fish, and sergeant told me to doctor on him. So I cleaned him up as he lay there throwing up with his face in the dirt. I ain't tell him to stop. Sergeant gave him a day to heal, but when *they sent him back out in the field, them lashes on his back wasn't anywhere near healed, and they oozed and bled through his shirt.*

I can almost hear Pop in the dim room, which feels wet and close from all the hot water I ran to cover the sound of Kayla throwing up and to clean up after. He would shift and lean on his elbow, and his voice would rise out of the black like smoke. I wipe Kayla's hair away from her head, and she sweats. Whenever Pop talked about Richie getting whipped, he told me about Kinnie, his boss in charge of the hunting hounds, who escaped the day after they flayed Richie's back.

Kinnie Wagner pulled his last escape that day. It was 1948. Walked right out the front gates of Parchman with a machine gun he'd stole out of munitions. Warden was pissed.

"I'll look a fool," he said, "being the warden who let the damn man escape a third time. You want your job, you better catch him. Let the dogs," he told the sergeant.

Sergeant looked at me and I got the best of the pack: Axe and Red and Shank and Moon, all dogs Kinnie'd named, and I let them loose and started tracking. But the dogs wouldn't track the man that fed them, the man that first touched them, the man that raised them. Kept walking slow and sad in circles through that country, slinking through those thin trees under that heavy sky, and I followed them, catching Kinnie's tracks clear, but slowed down by the animals so I had to go back at the end of the day, tell the sergeant the dogs wouldn't track they master.

Him and two other sergeants and a gang of trusty shooters came out with me the next day, and it was the same. The hounds smelled that son of a bitch and thought he was they daddy. Couldn't savage him because when they slept, they dreamed of him, of his big red hands and his gray mouth. The stink that came off of him from all his sweating as dear to them as the scent from they mama's ears.

I can tell Leonie ain't slept. She never came in the room last night, and this morning, the music is still playing in the kitchen on Al's stereo, and all three of them look wrinkled: their clothes, their hair, their faces. Leonie's looking at the empty chair across from her, so she misses when I walk in the room, Kayla in my arms, her head on my shoulder. Normally, she'd be asking for a *dog* (she likes hot dogs for breakfast), or pointing outside and pulling my hand and saying *Pop*. But I woke to her touching my cheek right underneath my eye, looking very serious, not smiling. Her little hand like a stick burned with fire and now throwing off heat, red and black. As I walk into the kitchen, Kayla breathes little huffs into my neck. I rub her back, and Leonie finally notices us.

"They got oatmeal on the stove," Leonie says. All three of them are drinking coffee, black and strong. "Did she throw up again?"

"No," I say. Leonie looks toward that empty chair again. "She hot, though."

Leonie nods, but she don't look at me. She look at the chair. Raise her eyebrows like somebody said something surprising, but Al and Misty are leaning in to each other, murmuring things, whispering. Leonie ain't part of that conversation. I walk over to the pot and see the oatmeal crusted to the sides, burnt crispy on the edges, and jelly in the middle with cold.

"Let's go get your man," says Misty, and they all stand. "But they haven't eaten," Al says. "They have to be hungry." "I'm not," I say, and my mouth tastes like old gum chewed almost to paste. I figure I'll eat some of the food I stole in the backseat on the way to the jail, ease the grinding suck of my stomach. Sneak some to Kayla if she'll let me. She burns in my arms, her neck against my neck, her little chin digging in to my collarbone. Her legs dangle, lifeless as a carcass's from a hook.

"Let's go get your father," Leonie says.

The jail is all low, concrete buildings and barbed-wire fences crisscrossing through fields. The road stretches onward, out into the distance, and for a while, this road points us toward the men housed here. There's no other sign, nothing in those fields: no cows, no pigs, no chickens. There are crops coming in, baby plants, but they look small and stunted, as if they'll never grow. But a great flock of birds wheels through the sky, swooping and fluttering, moving graceful as a jellyfish. I watch them as Kayla mewls in my ear, as we pass another sign, old and wooden, that says *Welcome to Parchman, Ms.* And then: *Coke is it!* But by the time we get out of the car in the parking lot, the birds have turned north, fluttered over the horizon. I hear the tail end of their chatter, of all those voices calling at once, and I wish I could feel their excitement, feel the joy of the rising, the swinging into the blue, the great flight, the return home, but all I feel is a solid ball of something in my gut, heavy as the head of a hammer.

When we get to the jail proper, Leonie and Misty sign our names into a book, and then we're led into a room with cinder-block walls painted yellow. Misty follows a guard through a door set at the opposite end of the room, where we sit at a table ringed by low benches, like we could be taking a picnic while we wait on Michael, but there is no food, no blanket, and there is white pockmarked ceiling above us: no sky. Leonie rubs her arms, even though it's warm in here, warmer even than outside. It feels like there's no air-conditioning. She leans forward and rubs at her eyes, smooths her hair back from her face so for a second I see Pop, his flat forehead, his nose, his cheeks. That hammer in me twists, and then Leonie frowns, and her hair flops back over her forehead, and she's just Leonie, and Kayla whimpers again, and I want to go home.

"Juice," Kayla says. I look at Leonie, asking the question without saying nothing: raised eyebrows, wide eyes, frown. Leonie shakes her head.

"She got to wait."

She reaches out to Kayla, brushes her fingers along the back of her neck, but Kayla says no and burrows in to my chest, her skull hard, her nose smushed into my shirt, trying to get away from Leonie's hand. I'm looking at Leonie's frown so hard that I don't even see Michael when he appears at the door, two guards at his shoulders, who stop at the door and let him pass as it opens and clangs shut, and then all at once, he's standing in front of us. Michael's here.

"Baby," he says. I know he ain't talking to me or Kayla, but only Leonie, because it's her who drops her arm and turns, her who rises and walks stiff-kneed to him, her that he hugs, his arms wrapped around her like a tangled sheet, tighter and tighter, until they seem one thing standing there, one person instead of two. He's bigger than I remember around the neck and shoulders and arms, wider than he was when the police took him away. They're both shaking, speaking so low to each other I can't hear them, whispering and shivering like a tree, juddering in the wind.

It takes less time than I thought it would to check Michael out. Maybe he done all his paperwork beforehand. Misty is still in another room, talking to Bishop, but Michael says: "I can't stay in here another minute. Let's go." Before I know it, we're walking back out into the weak spring light. Leonie and Michael have their arms around each other's waist. When we get back to the parking lot, they stop and begin kissing, wet, openmouthed, their tongues sliding onto faces. He looks so different than he did when he left, but he's still the same Michael underneath, in the neck, in his hands, kneading Leonie's back the way Mam used to knead biscuits. Kayla points out to the fields, fields covered in a fog, and says, "Jojo." I walk across the parking lot, closer to the fields with her.

"What you see, Kayla?" I ask.

"All the birds," she says, and coughs.

I look out at the fields but I don't see birds. I squint and for a second I see men bent at the waist, row after row of them, picking at the ground, looking like a great murder of crows landed and chattering and picking for bugs in the ground. One, shorter than the rest, stands and looks straight at me.

"See the bird?" Kayla asks, and then she lays her head

on my shoulder. I blink and the men are gone and it is just fog rolling, wisping over the fields that stretch out endlessly, and then I hear Pop, telling me the last bit of the story he is willing to share about this place.

After the sergeant beat Richie, I told him: "You got to keep that back clean." Got clean rags and put them on him, and then changed them with supplies I stole from the dogs' stash. I bound them around Richie's chest with long strips. His skin was hot and runny.

"It's too much dirt," Richie said. His teeth was chattering, so his words came out in stutters. "It's everywhere. In the fields. Not just my back, Riv. It's in my mouth so I can't taste nothing and in my ears so I can't hardly hear and in my nose, all in my nose and throat, so I can't hardly breathe."

He breathed hard then, and ran out the shack where our group of trusty shooters bunked, and threw up in the dirt, and then I remembered again how young he was, how his big teeth was still breaking through his gums in some places.

"I dream about it. Dream I'm eating it with a big long silver spoon. Dream that when I swallow, it go down the wrong hole, to my lungs. Out there in the fields all day, my head hurt. I can't stop shaking."

I touched his narrow back, pushed one of the cuts to see if pus would come out, trying to see if it was infected, if that's why he was sick with fever and chills, but it oozed a little clear and that's it.

"Something ain't right," I said to myself, but the boy was kneeling over his sick in the dirt, listening to the trusty shooters calling to each other on they patrol, shaking his head like I'd asked him a question, right to left, right to left. And then he said:

"I'm going home."

*   *   *

"See the birds?" Kayla asks.

"Yeah, Kayla, I see," I tell her.

"All the birds go bye," Kayla says, and then she leans forward and rubs my face with both hands, and for a second I think she's going to tell me something amazing, some secret, something come from God Himself. "My tummy," she says, "Jojo, tummy hurts."

I rub her back.

"I ain't had a chance to give y'all a good hello," comes a voice, and I turn around and it's Michael. He's looking toward Kayla.

"Hello," he says.

Kayla tenses up, grips me with her little legs, grabs both of my ears, and pulls.

"No," she says.

"I'm your papa, Michaela," Michael says.

Kayla puts her face in my neck and starts to shake, and I feel it like little tremors through my gut. Michael lets his hands drop. I shrug, look past Michael's face, clean-shaved and pale, purple under his eyes, sunburn high on his forehead. He got Kayla's eyes. Leonie's behind him, letting go of his hand to grab him around the waist. He reaches behind him to her, and rubs.

"She got to get used to you," I say.

"I know," he says.

*   *   *

When we get back to the car, Leonie pulls out her little cooler and then hands out sandwiches that the lawyer must have made before me and Kayla woke up, sandwiches on brown bread thick with nuts with slabs of smelly cheese and turkey slices thin as Kleenex layered in between. I eat mine so fast I have trouble breathing, and I start to hiccup around the food, big bites, lodged in my throat. Leonie frowns at me, but it's Michael who speaks.

"Take your time, son."

He says it so easy. *Son.* He got his arm on the back of the driver's seat, his hand wrapped around the back of Leonie's neck, rubbing it, squeezing it soft. It's something like the way Mam would hold me by the neck when we went to the grocery store when I was little and both of us could walk, up and down the grocery aisles. If I'd get too excited, like when we got to the checkout and saw all the candy, she'd squeeze. Not too hard. Just enough to remind me that we was in the store, around a whole bunch of White people, and that I needed to mind my manners. And then: she was behind me, with me, loving me. Here.

If I wasn't hiccupping, I would cut my eyes at Michael, but the hiccupping is so bad I can't breathe. I think of Richie and wonder if this is how he felt in them dusty rows, how they must have stretched to the end of the earth before him, how this place must have gone on forever. But even as I'm gulping to swallow past the food, to breathe easier, and another hiccup shakes through me, I know it must have been worse for the boy.

A rain begins, so light it's like a gentle spray from a water bottle, and it turns the air white, and everything looks hazy.

I want another sandwich, but Michael is sitting where Misty sat, and he's eating his sandwich slow, tearing off his bites before putting them in his mouth. It's one of the things I heard Pop say about Michael when he moved in with us: *Mike eat like he too good for the food*, he told Mam. She shook her head and cracked another pecan, picking out the meat. We were sitting next to each other on the porch swing. I'm still so hungry I can imagine the taste of those pecans, how the dust around the nut taste bitter, but the pecan is wet and sweet. Mam knew, but she ignored my thieving and let me eat. There's only one sandwich from the lawyer left in the bag, and Misty still hasn't eaten hers yet, so I swallow.

"We got some water?" I ask.

Leonie passes me a bottle of water the lawyer must have given her. The plastic is thick and has mountains painted on the front. The water is warm, not cold, but I'm so thirsty and my throat is so clogged I don't even care. The hiccups stop.

"Your sister finish hers?" Leonie asks.

Kayla's fallen asleep in her car seat, which I had to move to the middle. Misty's back, and she's sitting with me now that Michael's here. Kayla has half of a sandwich in her hand, her fingers curled around it tight. Her head tilted back and hot. Her nose is sweating, and her curls are getting stringy. I pull the sandwich from her grip and it comes, so I eat the rest of it, even though it's a little soggy where she was gumming it.

"Most of it," I say.

"She look much better." Leonie is lying. She don't look much better. Maybe a little, but not much. "I knew the blackberry would work."

"Something wrong with her? She sick?" Michael asks. His hand done stop moving, and he turns around to look at us. I stop chewing. In the gray foggy light, and in the close car, his eyes look bright green, green as the trees pushing out new spring leaves. Leonie looks disappointed he's stopped touching her and leans across the seat toward him.

"Just some kind of stomach virus, I think. Or she was carsick. I gave her one of Mama's remedies. She better."

"You sure, baby?" Michael looks closely at Kayla, and I swallow the last of her sandwich. "She still looks a little yellow to me."

Leonie gives a little half laugh and waves at Kayla.

"Of course she's yellow. She's our baby." And then Leonie laughs, and even though it's a laugh, it doesn't sound like one. There's no happiness in it, just dry air and hard red clay where grass won't grow. She turns around and ignores all of us and looks out the front windshield, gummy with bug splatter, so she doesn't even see when Kayla startles, her eyes open wide, and throw-up, brown and yellow and chunky, comes shooting out her mouth and all over the back of the front seat, all over her little legs and her red-and-white Smurfs shirt and me because I'm pulling her up out of her seat and into my lap.

"It's going to be all right, Kayla, it's going to be all right," I say.

"I thought you gave her something for that," Misty says.

"Baby, I told you she didn't look good," Michael says.

"Goddamnit sonofabitch," Leonie says, and a dark skinny boy with a patchy afro and a long neck is standing on my side of the car, looking at Kayla and then looking at me. Kayla cries and whines.

"The bird, the bird," she says.

The boy leans into the window and blurs at the edges. He says: "I'm going home."

Chapter 6

Richie

The boy is River's. I know it. I smelled him as soon as he entered the fields, as soon as the little red dented car swerved into the parking lot. The grass trilling and moaning all around, when I followed the scent to him, the dark, curly-haired boy in the backseat. Even if he didn't carry the scent of leaves disintegrating to mud at the bottom of a river, the aroma of the bowl of the bayou, heavy with water and sediment and the skeletons of small dead creatures, crab, fish, snakes, and shrimp, I would still know he is River's by the look of him. The sharp nose. The eyes dark as swamp bottom. The way his bones run straight and true as River's: indomitable as cypress. He is River's child.

When he returns to the car and I announce myself, I know he is Riv's again. I know it by the way he holds the little sick golden girl: as if he thinks he could curl around her, make his skeleton and flesh into a building to protect her from the adults, from the great reach of the sky, the vast expanse of the grass-ridden earth, shallow with graves. He protects as River protects. I want to tell him this: *Boy, you can't*. But I don't.

Instead, I fold myself and sit on the floor of the car.

*   *   *

In the beginning, I woke in a stand of young pine trees on a cloudy, half-lit day. I could not remember how I came to be crouching in the pine needles, soft and sharp as boar's hair under my legs. There was no warmth or cold there. Walking was like swimming through tepid gray water. I paced in circles. I don't know why I stayed in that place, why every time I got to the edge of the young stand, to the place where the pines reached taller, rounded and darkened, draped with a web of green thorny vines, I turned and walked back. In that day that never ended, I watched the tops of the trees toss, and I tried to remember how I got there. Who I was before this place, before this quiet haunt. But I couldn't. So when I saw a white snake, thick and long as my arm, slither out of the shadows beneath the trees, I knelt before It.

You are here, It said.

The needles dug into my knees.

Do you want to leave? It asked.

I shrugged.

I can take you away, It said. *But you have to want it.*

Where? I asked. The sound of my voice surprised me.

Up and away, It said. *And around.*

Why?

There are things you need to see, It said.

It raised its white head in the air and swayed, and slowly, like paint dissolving in water, its scales turned black, row by row, until it was the color of the space between the stars. Little fingers sprouted from its sides to grow to wings, two perfect black scaly wings. Two clawed feet pierced its bottom to dig into the earth, and its tail shrunk to a fan. It was a bird, but not a bird. No feathers. All black scales. A scaly bird. A horned vulture.

It bounced up to alight on the top of the youngest pine tree, where it bristled and cawed, the sound raw in that silent place.

Come, It said. *Rise.*

I stood. One of its scales dislodged and floated to the earth, wispy as a feather.

Pick it up. Hold it, It said. *And you can fly.*

I clenched the scale. It was the size of a penny. It burned my palm, and I rose up on my tiptoes and suddenly I wasn't on the ground anymore. I flew. I followed the scaly bird. Up and up and out. Into the whitewater torrent of the sky.

Flying was floating on that tumbling river. The bird at my shoulder now, a raucous smudge on the horizon then, sometimes atop my head like a crown. I spread my arms and legs and felt a laugh bubbling up in me, but it died in my throat. Because I remembered. I remembered before. I remembered being spread-eagle in the dirt, surrounded by hunched, milling men, and a teenage boy at my shoulder who stood tall under the long shadows. River. River, who stood as the men flayed my back, as I sobbed and vomited and turned the earth to mud. I could feel him there, knew that he would carry me after they let me loose from the earth. My bones felt pin-thin, my lungs useless. The way he carried me to my cot, the way he bent over me, made something soft and fluttery as a jellyfish pulse in my chest. That was my heart. Him my big brother. Him, my father.

I dropped from my flight, the memory pulling me to earth. The bird screamed, upset. I landed in a field of endless rows of cotton, saw men bent and scuttling along like hermit crabs, bending and picking. Saw other men walking in circles around them with guns. Saw buildings clustered at the edges of that field, other fields, unto the ends of the earth. The bird swooped down on the men's heads. They disappeared. This is where I was worked. This is where I was whipped. This is where River protected me. The bird dropped to the ground, dug its beak into the black earth, and I remembered my name: Richie. I remembered the place: Parchman prison. And I remembered the man's name: River Red. And then I fell, dove into the dirt, and it parted like a wave. I burrowed in tight. Needing to be held by the dark hand of the earth. To be blind to the men above. To memory. It came anyway. I was no more and then I was again. The scale hot in my hand. I slept and woke and rose and picked my way through the prison fields, lurked in the barracks, hovered over the men's faces. Tried to find River. He wasn't there. Men left, men returned and left again. New men came. I burrowed and slept and woke in the milky light, my time measured by the passing of all those Black faces and the turning of the earth, until the scaly bird returned and led me to the car, to the boy the same age as me sitting in the back of the car. Jojo.

I want to tell the boy that I know the man who sired him. That I knew him before this boy. That I knew him when he was called River Red. The gunmen called him River because that was the name his mama and daddy give him, and the men say he rolled with everything like a river, over the fell trees and stumps, through storms and sun. But the men added the Red because that was his color: him the color of red clay on the riverbank.

There's so much Jojo doesn't know. There are so many stories I could tell him. The story of me and Parchman, as River told it, is a moth-eaten shirt, nibbled to threads: the shape is right, but the details have been erased. I could patch those holes. Make that shirt hang new, except for the tails. The end. But I could tell the boy what I know about River and the dogs.

When the warden and sergeant told River he was going to be in charge of the dogs after Kinnie escaped, he took the news easy, like he didn't care if he did it or if he didn't. When they named River to keep the dogs, I heard the men talking, especially some of the old-timers: said all the dog keepers were always older and White, long as they been there, long as they remembered. Even though some of those White men had been like Kinnie, had escaped and then been sent back to Parchman after they'd been caught fleeing or had killed or raped or maimed, the sergeant still chose them to train the dogs. If they had any talent for it, they were given the job. Even if they were flight risks, even if they had done terrible things both in and out of Parchman, the leashes were theirs. Even though they were terrible, dangerous White men, the old-timers still took more offense when they knew Riv would be their hunter. They didn't like Riv taking care of the dogs. *It's different*, they said, *for the Black man to be a trusty, with a gun.* Said: *That's unnatural, too, but that's Parchman.* But it was something about a colored man running the dogs; that was wrong. There had always been bad blood between dogs and Black people: they were bred adversaries—slaves running from the slobbering hounds, and then the convict man dodging them.

But River had a way with animals. The sergeant saw that. It didn't matter to him that Riv couldn't make the hounds hunt Kinnie. The sergeant knew there wasn't another White inmate who could wrangle those dogs, so Riv was his best bet for training them, for keeping them keen. The dogs loved Riv. They turned floppy and silly when he came around. I saw it, because Riv asked them to transfer me out the fields and over to him so I could assist him. He saw how sick I was after I got whipped. He thought if I were left to my despair, my slow-knitting back, I would do something stupid. *You smart,* he said. *Little and fast.* He told the sergeant that I was wasted in the fields.

But I didn't have River's way with the dogs. I think some part of me hated and feared them. And they knew it. The dogs didn't soften to silly puppies with me. Their tails stiffened, their backs straightened, and they stilled. When they saw Riv in the dark morning, they bounced and yapped, but when they saw me, they ossified to stone. River held out his hands to the dogs like he was a reverend and they were his church. They were quiet with listening, but he didn't say anything. Something about the way they froze together in the blue dawn was worshipful. But when I held out my hand to them, like Riv told me, and waited for them to acclimate to my scent, to listen to me, they snapped and gurgled. Riv said: *Have patience, Richie; it's going to happen.*

I doubted. Even though the dogs hated me, and I still got up when the sun was a dim shine at the edge of the sky and spent all day hauling water and food and running after those mutts, I was still happier than I had been before, still lighter, almost, maybe okay. I know River hasn't told Jojo that, because I never told River that when I ran, it felt like the air was sweeping me along. I thought the wind might pick me up and hurl me through the air, buoy me up out of the shitty dog pens, the scarred fields, away from the gunmen and the trusty shooters and the sergeant up into the sky. That it would carry me away. When I was lying on my cot at night while River cleaned my wounds, those moments blinked around me like fireflies in the dark. I caught them in my hands and held them to me, a golden handful of light, before swallowing them.

I would tell Jojo this: *That was no place for hope.*

It only got worse when Hogjaw returned to Parchman. They called him Hogjaw because he was big and pale as a three-hundred-pound pig. His jaw was a hard square. His mouth a long thin line. He had the jaw of a hog that would gore. He was a killer. Everybody knew. He had escaped Parchman once, but then he committed another violent crime, shooting or stabbing someone, and he was sent back. That's what a White man had to do to return to Parchman, even if he was free because he had escaped: a White man had to murder. Hogjaw did a lot of murdering, but when he came back, the warden put him over the dogs, over Riv. The warden said: "It ain't natural for a colored man to master dogs. A colored man doesn't know how to master, because it ain't in him to master." He said: "The only thing a nigger knows how to do is slave."

I wasn't light anymore. When I ran to fetch, I didn't feel like I was racing the wind. There were no more firefly moments to blink at me in the dark. Hogjaw smelled bad. Sour like slop. The way he looked at me—there was something wrong about it. I didn't know he was doing it until one day we were out running drills with the dogs, and Hogjaw said, *Come with me, boy.* He wanted me to follow him to the woods so we could run the dogs up trees. Hogjaw told River to run a message to the sergeant and leave us to the drills. Hogjaw put his hand on my back, gently. He grabbed my shoulders all the time, hands hard as trotters; he usually squeezed so tight I felt my back curving to bend, to kneel. River gave Hogjaw a hard look, and stood in front of me that day, and said, *Sergeant need him.* He looked at me, tilted his head toward the compound, and said, *Go, boy. Now.* I turned and ran as fast as I could. My feet running to darkness. The next morning Riv woke me up and told me I wasn't his dog runner anymore, and I was going back out in the field.

I want to tell the boy in the car this. Want to tell him how his pop tried to save me again and again, but he couldn't. Jojo cuddles the golden girl to his chest and whispers to her as she plays with his ear, and as he murmurs, his voice like the waves of a calm bay lapping against a boat, I realize there is another scent in his blood. This is where he differs from River. This scent blooms stronger than the dark rich mud of the bottom; it is the salt of the sea, burning with brine. It pulses in the current of his veins. This is part of the reason he can see me while the others, excepting the little girl, can't. I am subject to that pulse, helpless as a fisherman in a boat with no engine, no oars, while the tide bears him onward.

But I don't tell the boy any of that. I settle in the crumpled bits of paper and plastic that litter the bottom of the car. I crouch like the scaly bird. I hold the burning scale in my closed hand, and I wait.

Chapter 7

Leonie

We got to leave the windows down because of the smell. I done used all the napkins I had shoved in the glove compartment to clean up the mess, but Michaela still look like she been smeared with paint, and she done rubbed it all over Jojo, and he won't let her go so he can clean the throw-up off him, too. "I'm all right," he said. "I'm all right." But I can tell by the way he keep saying it that it ain't all true. The part of me that can think around Michael knows what Jojo is saying ain't true. That he ain't all right, because he's so worried about Michaela. Jojo keeps looking over at Misty, who is half leaning out the window, complaining about the smell ("You ain't never going to be able to get that out," she said), and I expect him to look mad in the rearview like he did earlier when Misty complained. Instead, there's something else there, something else in his wide-open eyes and his lips that done shrunk to nothing.

* * *

Michael knocks on the door. All of us are huddled on the porch, smelling like vomit and salt and musk, when Al opens it.

"Hello. I'm surprised they processed you so quickly!" Al says.

He has another cooking spoon in his hand, a hand towel tossed over his shoulder like a scarf. I feel sorry for his house-keeper, if he has one, because I'm pretty sure he never washes any of his pots, just stacks one on the other on his counter. Whenever he's not at his office, he must be cooking.

"Michaela's still sick." Misty shoulders her way past all of us and through the front door.

"Well, that just won't do," Al says, and he steps back so the rest of us can file past him. Jojo is last; Michaela won't let him go, and he won't put her down.

"Clean towels are in the hall closet," Al says. "Y'all should wash up. I'll borrow Misty and we'll go to the store for medicine." Misty nods, looks relieved at being able to ride in a vehicle not splashed with vomit. "Bread and ginger ale are in the pantry," Al says. "I don't know why I didn't think of that yesterday." Al studies the carpet, then looks up and passes the towel over his face. "Oh yes, I remember." He smiles at me and Michael. "I was dazzled by my company and their gifts, no?"

Michael holds out his hand. It is callused from the farm work he did in Parchman: looking after dairy cows and chickens, tending to some vegetable patches. He told me the warden thought it would be a good idea to get the inmates to working the land again, that he thought it was a shame all that good Delta soil was going to waste with all them able-bodied men there, with all them idle hands. But it had put a bug in Michael. He liked it, he told me in his letters. When he finally got home, he wanted us to put in a garden, wherever we ended up at. Even if it was a cluster of pots on a concrete slab. *Can't nothing bother me when I got my hands in the dirt,* he said. *Like I'm talking to God with my fingers.* Al's hand looks soft, big, and when he shakes Michael's hand, his flesh is an envelope, swallowing.

"Thank you," Michael says. "For everything you done for my family and me."

Al shrugs, looks down at their hands, turns redder than he already is.

"It's my job," Al says, "for which I am well compensated. Thank *you.*"

After Misty and Al leave, I strip Michaela and make Jojo take off his shirt, and then I throw it all in Al's washing machine, a fancy upright that takes me five minutes of jabbing buttons and turning dials to figure out how to work. Michaela shrieks the entire time she's in the bathtub, her eyes rolling to Jojo, and I'm rougher than I should be with her, soaping her little lean belly, her legs, her back. Picking chunks out of her hair. Pushing that rag against her face to wipe the slime and crust and tears from it, pushing harder than I should, because I'm so pissed. Mama carried an orange bracelet always, woven orange yarn with little orange beads on it, and she knotted it and put it in the pocket of her skirt every day, and when me or Given done something stupid, something like Given getting drunk for the first time and showing up with a sick mouth throwing up all over her herbs on the porch, or like when I pulled up some plant she was growing in the garden, mistaking it for a weed, she'd grab that little piece of orange and start praying: *Saint Teresa*, I'd hear. *Our Lady of Candelaria*, she'd mutter. And then: *Oya*. And I don't know the French, just words here and there, but sometimes she'd say it in English, and I was there often enough to understand: *For Oya of the winds, of lightning, of storms. Overturn our minds. Clean the world with your storms, destroy it and make it new with the winds of your skirts.* And when I asked her what she meant, she said: *Ain't no good in using anger just to lash. You pray for it to blow up a storm that's going to flush out the truth.*

"Saint Teresa," I mutter. "Oya," I say, and rinse Michaela, dumping a cup of water over her head. She wails. I wrap a towel around her that soaks at the bottom, turns heavy with water, before picking her up and lifting her out of the tub. She kicks. I want to hit her. *Don't make me feel this for nothing*, I think. *Give me some truth.* But ain't no truth coming when I dry her off, ignore the lotion for her flailing, and shoulder past Jojo, who been cleaning off his chest at the sink and mirror and, I know, watching, like a blue jay mother, ready to dart in and peck if I do her wrong. Ready to take the hits for himself if I do lose my temper and start swatting at her bottom, still clammy with water and fever. He's at that age where skinny boys either stretch and get skinnier and leaner and harder, or where skinny boys get fat and spend their early teen years trying to learn how to move bodies made bulky by hormones. Jojo is a mix of both: fat collects all along his belly, but avoids his

chest and arms and face. With a shirt on, he still looks as
lean as he did when he was younger. I can tell by the way
he washes himself he's ashamed of it, that he don't know
like I do that in a few years that stomach's going to melt
away, layer by layer, as he gets taller and more muscular,
and he'll emerge, his body an even-limbed machine like
Michael's. Tall like Pop.

"Make sure you get in them rolls," I say. Jojo flinches
like I've hit him. Shies closer to the mirror. It feels good
to be mean, to speak past the baby I can't hit and let that
anger touch another. The one I'm never good enough for.
Never Mama for. Just Leonie, a name wrapped around the
same disappointed syllables I've heard from Mama, from
Pop, even from Given, my whole fucking life. I dump Michaela, the wailing bundle, on the bed and begin toweling
her off and she's still kicking and screaming and moaning
and now saying "Jojo," and I just want to give her one slap,
or maybe two, enough to sting her good, but I don't know
if I'll be able to stop, Saint Teresa, I won't be able to stop,
help me. I leave her trembling and walk to the door and
yell at the bathroom, at Jojo, who stands with his hands
tucked in his armpits, his arms like football pads across his
chest, and watches us.

"Get her dressed. Put her to sleep for a nap. Don't leave
this room."

I slam the door.

When I run out of the hallway and see Michael standing
in the milky light, my anger turns so quickly to love I stop,

silenced. All I can do is watch him walk the four corners of the room, and then shrug.

"He ain't got no TV," Michael says. "He got this big old nice house, but no TV."

I laugh and it's like the badass little boy who ruined the TV down the road is in the room with us: the delighted trembling he must have felt at his wickedness rushes like water through me.

"He got something better than that," I say.

The fireplace is big, the molding blackened at the edges and the paint long since sloughed off like a snake's skin. There are three ceramic bowls capped with tops on the mantel, vases at least five shades of blue. *Like the ocean,* Al said the night before. *Not like your ocean—I mean seriously, they shouldn't even call that a gulf since it's the color of ditch water. I mean real water. I mean Jamaica and Saint Lucia and Indonesia and Cyprus.* He smiled away the insult and pointed at the two larger urns at the corners of the mantel. *Mater and Pater,* he said. And then he slid the small center urn across the sooty wooden plane and cradled it in his arms. *And my Baby: my Beloved.* When Al pulled out the pack, and said *She's here to party,* Misty yelped, excited. I pull out the pack and Michael looks as if he wants to turn and run—and then like I am holding his favorite food, macaroni and cheese, and he wants to eat. Instead, he grabs my hand and pulls me toward him, surrounds me, breathes heavy into the hair at my temple, making it flutter. Five minutes later, we are high.

* * *

It's the drug but then it's not the drug. He is all eyes and hands and teeth and tongue. His forehead against mine: his head down. He is praying, too low for me to hear, and then I feel it. "Leonie, Loni, Oni, Oh," he says, his voice there and then nothing, his fingers there and then nothing and then there again, and my skin itches and tingles and burns and sears. So long since I had this. My chest is hollow and then full; now a ditch dusty dry, now rushing with water after a sudden, heavy spring rain. A flood. There are no words. All around me, then through me, a man praying, and silent, praying and silent, a man who is more than man, a man with a shining shock of hair and clear eyes, a man who is all fire, fire in his mouth, flames his hands, smoldering coals the V of his hips. Fire and water. Drowned clean. Born up. Blessed. Like that, yes. Like that. Yes.

I pee in Al's cold white half bathroom, listen for the kids, hear nothing. Walk back into the living room, the windows sparking dust to gold in the air. There is something wrong. Michael smiles at me, rubs his neck where I sucked on him, says, "I think you left a mark." And Given-not-Given, black-shirted, sits slumped at the other end of the sofa. He waves his arm for me to come sit between them. The buzz loops through me and drops. I sit, and Michael takes my face in his warm, real hands, and his lips meet mine, and I am opening all over again. Losing language, losing words. Losing myself in that feeling, that feeling of being wanted and needed and touched and cradled, all the while marveling that the one doing it is the one that wants, that needs, that touches, that sees. This is a miracle, I think, so I close my eyes and ignore Given-not-Given, who is sitting there with a sad look on his face, mouth in a soft frown, and think of Michael, real Michael, and wonder if we had another baby, if it would look more like him than Michaela. If we had another baby, we could get it right.

I expect him to be gone when I pull my mouth from Michael's, but Given-not-Given's not on the sofa anymore, he's standing by the mantel, looking just as solid as the Michael I'm straddling, but still as those urns. Michael groans and wipes a hand over his face, his neck and chest red, the freckles on him welted as ant bites.

"Sugar baby, what you do to me?" he says.

I don't know what to say because Given-not-Given is watching me closely, waiting for my reply, so I say nothing and shake my head and root into Michael's neck with my face, inhaling the smell of him. So alive: so here. Hoping that when I sit up, Given-not-Given will be gone back to wherever he stays when he's not haunting me, back to whatever weird corner of my brain calls him up when I'm high: the hollow figment. But Given's still there, and he's standing outside of the hallway to the kids' room, sitting on the floor with his back to the wall. He rubs his face with his hands.

"I love you," I tell Michael, and he cups me to him and kisses me again. Given-not-Given frowns and shakes his head. As if I have given the wrong answer. I look at Michael beneath me, and I ignore the phantom, don't even look toward the kids' room, so that for the rest of the hour and a half that Misty and Al are gone, Given-not-Given is a light smudge at the corner of my eye, sitting outside the kids' room, guarding them. But Michael is rubbing my back and scalp, and that is all that matters.

They sleep as one: Michaela wraps herself around Jojo, her head on his armpit, her arm over his chest, her leg over his stomach. Jojo pulls her in to him: his forearm curled under her head and around her neck, his other arm a bar across them both to lay flat against her back. His hand hard in protection, stiff as siding. But their faces make me feel two ways at once: their faces turned toward each other, sleep-smoothed to an infant's fatness, so soft and open that I want to leave them asleep so they can feel what they will. I think Given must have held me like that once, that once we breathed mouth to mouth and inhaled the same air. But another part of me wants to shake Jojo and Michaela awake, to lean down and yell so they startle and sit up so I don't have to see the way they turn to each other like plants following the sun across the sky. They are each other's light.

"Wake up," I say, and Jojo sits straight up, still hugging Michaela to him. Given-not-Given sat outside their door until Misty and Al came back: it's strange to see echoes of him in the way Jojo's shoulders curl inward over Michaela, in his wide-open eyes that scan the room and stop on the one dresser, in how still he suddenly is. "It's time to go," I say.

"Home?" he says.

Michael has to sit on the trunk to close it. With three people in the back, we ain't got room for the bags we rode up here with, so even though Jojo whined about it, I made them put everything in the back, including the sandwiches Al's sending us down the road with. Jojo's still pouting, and I'm two minutes away from turning and leaning over the backseat and slapping the expression off his face: the thread line, the moue of his lips, the low eyebrows, all wiped smooth. He sings nursery rhymes to Michaela through the pout: the baby claps her hands and works her fingers like little spiders and looks bored and fascinated in flashes. Every fifth word, she touches Jojo's nose. Misty's asleep after complaining for a good hour that the car still smells like throw-up, and Michael's driving, so I watch the kids when I ain't watching Michael, when I ain't noting the way his skin eats up the light from the growing day.

When Al handed Michael the sandwiches, Al was sweating all over, damp with salt and smelling like raw onions. He'd packed the sandwiches in a small hard plastic bag, a portable cooler with a Chimay logo printed on the side. "We don't want to take your bag," Michael said. "I insist," Al said, his breath shuttering in and out of him fast, his eyes everywhere: the woods, the yard, the house sinking in gentle decline. Al was high again. "For services rendered," he said, and smiled at me then. His teeth were bad, each one ringed with black like a dirty bathtub, his gums red. *He never brushes*, I thought. The men shook hands, and Michael curled a loose fist over whatever Al gave him. Michael slid it into his pocket.

"Come here," Michael says. His blood thuds thickly under my ear, the skin of his arm like tepid water. The road winds through fields and wood, all the way south to the

Gulf, and the light that cuts through the windows flutters all around. Where the road meets the Gulf, it skirts the beach for miles. I wish it ran straight over the water, like the pictures of the bridge I've seen that links the Florida Keys to the coast, wish it was an endless concrete plank that ran out over the stormy blue water of the world to circle the globe, so I could lie like this forever, feeling the fine hair on his arm, my kids silenced, not even there, his fingers on my arm drawing circles and lines that I decipher, him writing his name on me, claiming me. The world is a tangle of jewels and gold spinning and throwing off sparks. I'm already home.

I've never had enough of this. After Michael and I got together in high school, I got pregnant with Jojo in just under a year: I was seventeen. Ever since then we had Jojo and Michaela around us, making those spaces bigger between us. I remember it in flashes, mostly when I'm high, that feeling of it just being me and Michael, together: the way I swam up and surfaced out my grief when I was with him, how everything seemed so much more alive with him. We parked out in a field under the stars, in his pickup truck. We'd sneak and swim in his parents' aboveground pool, sinking under the water in the blurry blue and kissing. On the beach near a seafood festival, with the lights from the carnival rides flickering in the distance, bad zydeco music sounding over the loudspeakers, he'd twirl me and make me dance with him until we tripped and fell in the sand.

"It ain't healthy," Mama said after I brought Michael home the first time, and we sat on the sofa and watched TV. Pop walked through the house and looked past us.

After Michael left, Mama began cooking. I sat at the kitchen table and polished my nails, a soft pastel pink, the color of cotton candy, because I thought it looked good on my hand. I hoped the color would make Michael take my fingers in his mouth and say: *I gotta get me some of this sweet.*

"All you hear, all you see, is him," Mama said.

"I see plenty else," I said. I wanted to defend myself, but I knew I was lying, because when I woke up in the morning, I thought of Michael's laugh, of the way he flipped his cigarettes before he lit them, of the way his mouth tasted when he kissed me. And then I remembered Given. And the guilt I felt when I realized it.

"Every time you say something, you look at him like a little puppy dog. Like you waiting for him to pet you."

"Mama, I know I ain't a puppy."

"You exactly that."

I blew on the fingers of my right hand and waved them in front of my face, breathed in the hot smells of the kitchen: beans bubbling on the stove, corn bread cooling, the smell of the nail polish, which made my stomach turn, but in a way that I liked. I'd huffed before I got pregnant with Jojo, on my knees in a shed in one of Michael's friends' yards, one of the many friends that Michael had whose parents were never home. The world had tilted and spun, and my brain had seemed to break out of my skull and float off. Michael had grabbed my shoulders, anchored me, pulled me back into myself.

"So you don't like him?" I asked.

Mama breathed out hard and sat across from me at the

wooden table. She grabbed my unpolished hand and turned
it palm up and tapped it as she spoke.

"I . . . it ain't his fault what he was born to. Where."
Mama took a deep breath. "Into that family." She took
another hitching breath, and the way her face folded and
smoothed, I knew she was thinking of Given. "He just a
boy, a boy like any other his age. Smelling his piss for the
first time and thinking with his nether-head." *Like your
brother*, she didn't say. But I knew the sentence was in her.

"I ain't doing nothing crazy."

"If you ain't already having sex with him, you will be
soon. Protect yourself." She was right, but I didn't listen.
Ten months later, I was pregnant. After Michael got the
test and I took it, I brought it to Mama and told her. I told
her on a Saturday because Pop worked on Saturdays, and
I didn't want him to be there. It was an awful day. It was
early spring, and the rain had been booming all night and
all morning: sometimes the thunder was so close, it made
my throat judder, closed my windpipe, made it hard for
me to breathe. I'd always been scared of lightning, always
thought it would hit me one day, burn through the air
and touch me with a great blue arc, like a spear streaming
straight for me, and me helpless when the sharp head sank
in. I'd grown up paranoid, thought the lightning followed
me when I was in my car, when it rattled my windows.
Mama was hanging plants to dry in the living room on
string that Pop had hung on a zigzag back and forth across
the room, so the plants listed in the electric air, and Mama
half laughing and muttering, the soft backs of her arms
flashing white and then not: a kitten showing its belly.

"Here he come. Been singing for weeks."

"Mama?"

She stepped down from the pine step stool Pop had built her. He'd carved her name into the top of it; the letters looked like wisps of smoke. *Philomène.* It had been her Mother's Day present years before, when I was so little the only help I could give was to scratch a little star, four lines crossed at the middle, on the side of her name, and Given had carved a rose that looked like a muddy puddle, now worn smooth by Mama's feet.

"I was wondering how long it was going to take you to build up the nerve to tell me," she said, the stool tucked under her arm like she would put it away, but instead of walking to the kitchen, she sat on the sofa and let the step stool hang over her legs across her lap.

"Ma'am?" I asked. Thunder boomed. I felt hot around the neck and armpits, like someone had splashed hot grease across my face and chest. I sat down.

"You're pregnant," Mama said. "I saw two weeks ago."

She reached across the wood in her lap and touched me then, not with the pitiless hand of the lightning, but with her dry, warm hands, soft under the skin she'd worked hard, just a second of a touch on my shoulder, like she had found a piece of lint there and was brushing it off. I surprised myself and curled in to it, leaning forward, put my head on the wood while her hand rubbed circles on my back. I was crying.

"I'm sorry," I said. The wood hard against my mouth. Unyielding. Wetting with my tears. Mama leaned over me.

"No room for sorries now, baby." She grabbed me by

the shoulders, pulled me up to look at my face. "What you want to do?"

"What you mean?" The closest abortion clinic was in New Orleans. One of the more well-off girls in my school whose daddy was a lawyer had taken her after she'd gotten pregnant, so I knew it was there, and it was expensive. I thought we had no money for that. I was right. Mama gestured at the hanging plants, the listing jungle above our heads bristling in the cool electric air.

"I could give you something." She let the end of the sentence trail off, disappear. She looked at me like I was a smudged book she was having trouble reading and cleared her throat. "It was one of the first things I learned how to do, in my training. It's the one tea I never have enough of." She touched my knee then; she'd found another piece of lint. She leaned back again, and her culottes stretched tight across her knees. Years later, that's where she'd first start feeling the pain from the cancer: in her knees. Then it moved up to her hips, her waist, her spine, to her skull. It was a snake slithering along her bones. Sometimes I think back to that day, to her sitting on the sofa, giving me those little touches, little touches that didn't want to turn me one way or the other, even though she wanted Jojo, I think, because her grief for Given was hungry for life. Sometimes I wonder if the cancer was sitting there with us in that moment, too, if it was another egg, a yellow egg knit of sorrow, bearing the shape of bullet holes, wiggling in the marrow of her bones. That day, she was wearing a blouse she'd sewn herself from a print full of pale yellow flowers. Roses, looked like. "You want this baby, Leonie?"

A whip-crack of lightning lit the house, and I jumped as the thunder boomed.

I choked and coughed; Mama patted my back. The humidity made her hair alive around her face, tendrils of it standing up and curling away from her buttery scalp. The lightning cracked again, this time like it was right on top of us, feet away from arcing through the house, and her skin was white as stone and her hair waving, and I thought about the Medusa I'd seen in an old movie when I was younger, monstrous and green-scaled, and I thought: *That's not it at all. She was beautiful as Mama. That's how she froze those men, with the shock of seeing something so perfect and fierce in the world.*

"Yeah, Mama," I said. It still twists something in me to think of that: the fact that I hesitated, that I looked at my mama's face in that light and felt myself wrestle with wanting to be a mother, with wanting to bear a baby into the world, to carry it throughout life. The way we were sitting on that sofa, knees tight, backs curved, heads low, made me think of mirrors and of how I'd wanted to be a different kind of woman, how I'd wanted to move somewhere far away, go west to California, probably, with Michael. He talked about moving west and working as a welder all the time. A baby would make that harder. Mama looked at me and she wasn't stone no more: her eyes were crumpled and her mouth crooked, and that told me she knew exactly what I was thinking, and I worried that she could read minds, too, that she would see me shying away from who she was. But then I thought of Michael, of how happy he would be, of how I would have a piece of him with me always, and that unease melted like lard in a cast-iron pot. "I do."

"I wish you would have finished school first," Mama said. Another piece of lint, this time on my hair at the crown of my head. "But this is now, and we do what we do." She smiled then: a thin line, no teeth, and I leaned forward and put my head in her lap again, and she ran her hands up and down my spine, over my shoulder blades, pressed in on the base of my neck. All the while shushing like a stream, like she'd taken all the water pouring on the outside world into her, and she was sending it out in a trickle to soothe me. *Je suis la fille de l'océan, la fille des ondes, la fille de l'écume,* Mama muttered, and I knew. I knew she was calling on Our Lady of Regla. On the Star of the Sea. That she was invoking Yemayá, the goddess of the ocean and salt water, with her shushing and her words, and that she was holding me like the goddess, her arms all the life-giving waters of the world.

I'm asleep and I don't know it until Michael is shaking me awake, his fingers digging into my shoulder. My mouth is so dry, my lips are sealed shut.

"The police," Michael says. The road behind us is empty, but the tension in his hand and the way his eyes widen and roll make me know this is serious. Even though I can't see them and don't hear any sirens, they are there.

"You don't have a license," I say.

"We have to switch," he says. "Grab the wheel."

I grab it and push my feet into the floorboards and raise my rear off the seat so he can put a leg over in the passenger seat and begin sliding over. He takes his foot off the gas, and the car begins to slow. I put my left foot over near the pedal, and I am sitting in his lap in the middle of the car for one awful, hilarious moment.

"Shit shit shit." He laughs. It's what he does when he's frightened. When I went into labor, my water breaking in the snack aisle of a convenience store in St. Germaine, he scooped me up in his arms and carried me to his truck, laughing while cussing. He told me that once, when he was a boy, a cow kicked one of his friends in the middle of the night when they were out cow-tipping with flashlights: his friend, a redhead with pencil arms and a mouthful of rotten teeth from years of not brushing and chewing dip, braced himself as he fell, and his arm snapped like a tree limb. The elbow bent wrong, a piece of bone sticking out of his upper arm, pearly as a jagged oyster shell. Michael said his own laughter scared even him, then: high and breathless as a young girl's. Michael lifts me off his lap, slides into the passenger seat, and I am behind the wheel when I see the lights behind me coming up fast on this two-lane highway, flashing blue, siren stuttering.

"You got it?" I ask.

"What?"

"The shit. You know, the stuff from Al."

"Fuck!" Michael fumbles in his pockets.

"What?" Misty wakes up in the backseat, twisting to look back. I begin slowing down. "Oh, shit," she says when she sees the lights.

I look in the rearview and Jojo is looking straight at me. He's all Pop: upside-down mouth, hawk nose, steady eyes, the set of his shoulders as Michaela wakes up crying.

"I don't have time," Michael says. He's fumbling for the

carpet, about to shove the plastic baggie out of the little
door in the floor of the car, but there's too much in the way
with a balled-up shirt I bought for him in a convenience
store when we stopped to get gas, with plastic bags of potato
chips and Dr Pepper and candy we bought with the money
Al gave us. "And it got a fucking hole in it." The bottom
of the plastic baggie is scored and jagged, the white and
yellow crystal dry and crumbly at the corners.

I snatch the small white baggie. I shove it in my mouth.
I work up some spit, and I swallow.

The officer is young, young as me, young as Michael. He's
skinny and his hat seems too big for him, and when he leans
into the car, I can see where his gel has dried and started
flaking up along his hairline. He speaks, and his breath
smells like cinnamon mints.

"Did you know you were swerving, ma'am?" he asks.

"No, sir, Officer." The baggie is thick as a wad of cotton
balls in my throat. I can hardly breathe.

"Is something wrong?"

"No, sir." Michael speaks for me. "We been on the road
for a few hours. She tired is all."

"Sir." The officer shakes his head. "Can you step out of
the car, ma'am, with your license and insurance?" I catch
another whiff of him: sweat and spice.

"Yes," I say. The glove compartment is a mess of napkins
and ketchup packets and baby wipes. As the officer walks
away to talk with a static-garbled voice on his walkie-talkie,
Michael leans in, puts a hand on the small ribs of my back.

"You all right?"

"It's dry." I cough, and pull out the insurance paper. I snatch up my whole wallet and get out the car and wait for the officer to return, everybody but Michaela frozen in the backseat. Michaela flails and wails. It's midafternoon, and the trees list back and forth at the side of the road. The newly hatched spring bugs hiss and tick. At the bottom of the shoulder, there is a ditch filled with standing water and a multitude of tadpoles, all wriggling and swimming.

"Why isn't the baby in her car seat?"

"She been sick," I say. "My son had to take her out."

"Who are the man and the other woman in the car?"

My husband, I want to say, as if that would validate us. Even: *My fiancé*. But it's hard enough to choke out the truth, and I know with this ball in my throat, I will surely choke on a lie.

"My boyfriend. And my friend I work with."

"Where y'all going?" the officer asks. He doesn't have his ticket book in his hand, and I feel the fear, which has been roiling in my belly, rise in my throat and burn hot like acid, push against the baggie on its slow descent down to my stomach.

"Home," I say. "To the coast."

"Where y'all coming from?"

"Parchman."

I know it's a mistake soon as I say it. I should have said something else, anything else: Greenwood or Itta Bena or Natchez, but Parchman is all that comes.

The handcuffs are on me before the *n* is silent.

"Sit down."

I sit. The ball in my throat is wet cotton, growing denser and denser as it descends. The officer walks back to the car, makes Michael get out, puts him in handcuffs, and marches him back to sit next to me.

"Baby?" Michael says. I shake my head no, the air another kind of cotton, humid with spring rain, all of it making me feel as if I am suffocating. Jojo climbs out of the car, Michaela hanging on to him, squeezing him with her legs: she has her arms wrapped tightly around his neck. Misty climbs out the backseat, her hands palms forward and her mouth moving, but I can't hear anything she's saying. The officer looks between the two and makes his decision and walks toward Jojo, his third pair of handcuffs out. Michaela wails. The officer gestures for Misty to take Michaela, and Michaela buries her face in Jojo's neck and kicks when Misty pulls her from Jojo. She's never liked Misty: I brought her with me to Misty's one day after a run to the convenience store by the interstate for cigarettes, and when Misty leaned into the car to say hello to Michaela, Michaela turned her face, ignored Misty, and asked a question: "Jojo?"

"Just breathe," Michael says.

It's easy to forget how young Jojo is until I see him standing next to the police officer. It's easy to look at him, his weedy height, the thick spread of his belly, and think he's grown. But he's just a baby. And when he starts reaching in his pocket and the officer draws his gun on him, points it at his face, Jojo ain't nothing but a fat-kneed, bowlegged toddler. I should scream, but I can't.

"Shit," Michael breathes.

Jojo raises his arms to a cross. The officer barks at him,

the sound raw and carrying in the air, and Jojo shakes his head without pausing and staggers when the officer kicks his legs apart, the gun a little lower now, but still pointing to the middle of his back. I blink and I see the bullet cleaving the soft butter of him. I shake. When I open my eyes again, Jojo's still whole. Now on his knees, the gun pointing at his head. Michaela thrashes against Misty.

"Sonofabitch!" Misty screams, and drops Michaela, who runs to Jojo, throws herself on his back, and wraps herself, arms and legs, around him. Her little bones: crayons and marbles. A shield. I'm on my knees.

"No," Michael says. "Don't, Leonie. Baby, don't."

I snap. Imagine my teeth on the officer's neck. I could rip his throat. I don't need hands. I could kick his skull soft. Jojo slumps forward into the grass, and the cop is shaking his head, reaching under Michaela, who kicks at him, to cuff Jojo with one hand. He motions to Misty, who runs forward and grips Michaela under her armpits, wrestles her like an alligator.

"Jojo!" Michaela screams. "Have Jojo!"

The officer stands in front of me again.

"I need your permission to search the car, ma'am."

"Take me out of these cuffs." If he would come close enough, I could head-butt him blind.

"Is that a yes, ma'am?"

I swallow, breathe. Air shallow as a muddy puddle.

"Yes."

Jojo only has eyes for Michaela. He twists his neck to look at her, speaks to her, his voice another murmuring, like the trees as they sway in the wind. The clouds, like great gray waves, are sliding across the sky. The air already feels wet. Michaela is beating Misty around the neck, and I am sure Misty is cussing, her words indecipherable, but her syllables split the air as cleanly as railroad spikes riven into wood.

"He put up the gun, baby?" Michael asks.

I nod and groan.

The officer is picking his way through the trunk, which is all junk. I see that now, handcuffed, suffocating. Plastic bags filled with faded, misshapen clothes. Al's bag of sandwiches. A tire iron. Jumper cables. An old cooler littered with empty potato chip bags and cold drink bottles, mold eating at the seams. The baggie down my throat, disappeared to my stomach; my breath coming in a great whoosh, and I can breathe but the high from the meth comes fast. It squeezes me, a great hand, and shakes. It is a different kind of suffocation. I shudder, close my eyes, open them, and Phantom Given is sitting next to Jojo on the ground, reaching out as if he could touch him. Given-not-Given drops his hand. Half of Jojo's face is in the dirt, but I can still see his frowning mouth, quivering at the corners: it is the face he made when he was a baby, when he was fighting the urge to cry.

"Have Jojo!" Michaela shrieks. The officer straightens from the car and walks over to Misty, who hoists Michaela up in the air to wrangle her. Phantom Given rises, walks to the officer, Michaela, and Misty.

"You all right, babe?" Michael asks.

I shake my head no. Given-not-Given reaches out again, this time to Michaela, and it looks as if she sees him, as if he can actually touch her, because she goes rigid all at once, and then a golden toss of vomit erupts from Michaela's mouth and coats the officer's uniformed chest. Misty drops Michaela and bends and gags. Phantom Given claps silently, and the officer freezes.

"Fuck!" he says.

Michaela crawls to Jojo, and the officer yanks at Jojo's pocket, pulls out a small bag Jojo had, and looks within it before shoving it back in Jojo's face like it's a rotten banana peel. He stalks back to stand in front of us again, and he is opening our cuffs, and he shines. The bile glistens, the blue flashes.

"Go home," he says. There is no cinnamon and cologne anymore. Just stomach acid.

"Thank you, Officer," Michael says. He grabs my arm and walks me toward the car, and I cannot hide the shudder of pleasure as the meth licks and his fingers grip and the officer undoes Jojo's cuffs.

"Boy had a damn rock in his pocket," the officer says. "Go home, and keep that child in the seat as much as you can."

Phantom Given frowns at me as I slide into the passenger seat. My body lolls. I can't blink. My eyes snap open, again and again. Given-not-Given shakes his head as the real Michael slams the passenger door.

"Fuck fuck fuck fuck fuck," Misty breathes in the backseat. Jojo straps Michaela's legs in her seat and hugs her and the whole contraption: the plastic back, the padding. Michaela sobs and grabs handfuls of his hair. I expect him to tell her it's okay, but he doesn't. He just rubs his face against her, his eyes closed. My spine is a rope, tugged north, then south. Michael puts the car in gear.

"You need milk," Michael says. Phantom Given wipes his hand across his mouth, and it is then I realize that streams of spit are coming from my mouth, thick as mucus. Given-not-Given turns away from the car and disappears: I understand. Phantom Given is the heart of a clock, and his leaving makes the rest of it tick tock tick tock, makes the road unfurl, the trees whip, the rain stream, the wipers swish. I bend in half, my mouth in my elbow and knees, and moan. Wish it was Mama's lap. My jaw clacks and grinds. I swallow. I breathe. All delicious and damned.

Chapter 8

Jojo

I can't look at him straight. Not with him sitting on the floor of the car, squeezed between Kayla's car seat and the front, facing me. He don't say nothing, just got his arms over his knees, his mouth on his wrists. One hand balled into a fist. I ain't never seen knees like his: big dusty beat-up tennis balls. Even though he's skinny, arms and legs racket-thin, he should be too big to fit in the space he done folded himself into. He's sharp at the edges, but there's too much of him, so all I can think when I look at him is *Something's wrong.* The phrase keeps flying around in my head like a bat, fluttering and flapping and slapping at the corners of an attic. I don't know I've fallen asleep until I wake up to the car stopping, to the lights flashing, to the policeman in the window telling Leonie to step out of the car and the boy on the floor sinking farther down, covering his ears with his hands.

"They going to chain you," he says.

When the officer comes around to the back door and says, "Step out of the car, young man," the boy curls up smaller into himself, like a roly-poly, and he grimaces.

"I told you," he says.

It's my first time being questioned by the police. Kayla is screaming and reaching for me, and Misty is complaining, her shirt sliding farther down her shoulder, showing the tops of her breasts. I don't have eyes for that. All I have eyes for is Kayla, fighting. The man telling me sit, like I'm a dog. "Sit." So I do, but then I feel guilty for not fighting, for not doing what Kayla is, but then I think about Richie and then I feel Pop's bag in my shorts, and I reach for it. Figure if I could feel the tooth, the feather, the note, maybe I could feel those things running through me. Maybe I wouldn't cry. Maybe my heart wouldn't feel like it was a bird, ricocheted off a car midflight, stunned and reeling. But then the cop has his gun out, pointing at me. Kicking me. Yelling at me to get down in the grass. Cuffing me. Asking me, "What you got in your pocket, boy?" as he reaches for Pop's bag. But Kayla moves so fast, small and fierce, to jump on my back. I should soothe Kayla, should tell her to run back to Misty, to get down and let me go, but I can't speak. The bird crawling up into my throat, wings spasming. *What if he shoot her?* I think. *What if he shoot both of us?* And then I notice Richie looking out of the car window, even though the cuffs are grinding into my wrists. He distracts me from the warm close day, from Misty pulling Kayla away, but only for a second because I can't help but return to this: Kayla's brown arms and that gun, black as rot, as pregnant with dread.

The image of the gun stays with me. Even after Kayla throws up, after the police officer checks my pants and lets me out of them biting handcuffs, even after we are all in the car and riding down the road with Leonie bent over sick in the front seat, that black gun is there. It is a tingle at the back of my skull, an itching on my shoulder. Kayla snuggles in to me, quickly asleep, and everything is hot and wet in the car: Misty's sweating about the hairline, wet beads appear on Kayla's snoring nose, and I can feel water running down my ribs, my back. I rub the indents in my wrists where the handcuffs squeezed and see the gun, and the boy starts talking.

"You call him Pop," Richie says. I think it should be a question, but he says it like it's a statement. I look up at Misty, who's biting her fingers and looking out the window, and I nod.

"Your grandpa," the boy says, his eyes looking up to his forehead, the roof of the car, like he's reading the words he says in the sky. Michael ain't paying attention to anything going on in the backseat, either; he's driving and rubbing Leonie's back. She's doubled over, moaning. I nod again.

"My name?" he says.

Richie, I mouth.

He looks like he wants to smile but he doesn't.

"He told you about me?"

I nod.

"He tell you how he knew me? That we was in Parchman together?"

I huff and nod again.

"They don't send them there as young as you no more."

My wrists won't stop hurting.

"Sometimes I think it done changed. And then I sleep and wake up, and it ain't changed none."

It's like the cuffs cut all the way down to the bone.

"It's like a snake that sheds its skin. The outside look different when the scales change, but the inside always the same."

Like my marrow could carry a bruise.

"You look like Riv," Richie says. He puts his chin on his forearms and breathes hard, like he just finished running a long way. I move Kayla onto my lap, and she is making me so hot. I have to look away from the wrong of the boy folded onto the floor of the car, so I stare out the window at the tall trees flashing past and think about the gun. Even though it reminded me of so much cold, I think it would have been hot to touch. So hot it would have burned my fingerprints off.

It's after one of them long stretches, after at least two hours seeing nothing but trees, we finally run up on a gas station, and Michael pulls off the road. The boy's been sitting quiet, I been singing to Kayla, and Misty been playing with her cell phone, so we all look up when we pull into the parking lot. The sun burns with a steady midafternoon bore. Leonie's still bent over in the front seat, but she ain't moaning no more. She quiet as the boy, but she ain't still like him. She got her arms crossed over her chest and she rubbing her stomach and her sides and her back like she's miming kissing, her fingers digging into the thin shallows between her ribs. And every five seconds or so, her head smacks back like someone hit her in the face with a basketball, like I got hit when I was seven in a game down at the park. My cousin Rhett threw the ball to me and yelled *catch* too late.

I wasn't paying attention to him or the game: I was looking to the bleachers, where Leonie was sitting with Michael, thigh to thigh in the cold winter air, puffed up in jackets, huddled together like nesting hens. I turned around to the ball slamming into my nose and mouth, so hard I saw white and left spit on the ball. They all laughed, and I thought it was funny and horrible at the same time.

Michael's digging through Leonie's purse, and he pulls out ten one-dollar bills and waves them.

"I need you to get two things. Milk and charcoal."

"Kayla's asleep."

"Your mama's sick. She need this for her stomach."

I remember the gray water, the black stew from the leaves she boiled for Kayla.

"She gave Kayla something she made. So she wouldn't be sick no more. She ain't got no more of that?"

I wonder if whatever medicine she cooked would help Leonie now. If it would make her so sick that whatever poison is inside her would come out.

"She gave it all to Kayla," Misty says.

"What you need charcoal for?"

"Jojo, you always talk this much when somebody asks you to do something?"

He could hit me right now. Leonie did most of the hitting, but I know Michael could hit, too. Never with a closed fist, though. Always with his palm open, but his hand felt like a small shovel every time he hit me on the thin plate of my shoulder, the knobby middle of my chest, my arm where the muscle ain't enough to take the pain out of the blow.

"Kayla's asleep," I say again, meaning it to be firm, but

it comes out soft as a mumble, and it don't sound like what I want it to sound like. Michael don't hear *We don't need you*. He hear *I'm weak*.

"Put her in her seat."

"She going to wake up," I say. She's a heavy sleeper. Plus she don't feel good, which means she'll probably stay sleep. But I don't want to put her down. I don't want to leave her in her seat with Richie sitting at her feet, her toes by his head, her little feet dangling by his mouth. What if she sees him?

"Goddamnit, I'll go get it," Misty says, and opens the car door.

"No," Michael says. "Jojo, get your goddamn ass up out this car and go inside and get what I told you. Right now."

"He going to hit you. In the face," Richie says, but he doesn't look up, doesn't raise his head. Just says it and keeps his head down. "I ain't going to touch her."

"Kayla," I say.

Michael throws the money at me and sharpens his hand to a blade. The other one he got on Leonie's shoulder, keeping her still.

"She too young to help me," Richie says. "I need you."

"I'll go," I say.

Michael doesn't turn back around. He watches me lay Kayla in her seat, watches me try to fix her head so it doesn't flop forward, so her little chin doesn't dig into her chest, watches me glance at Richie on the floor, who waves his fingers but doesn't raise his head.

"I ain't going nowhere," Richie says.

The inside of the store is so cool and the outside air so

hot and wet that the windows are fogged up. I can't see
Leonie's car from inside, only the smeared gray on the
glass. The man at the counter got a big brown bushy beard,
every hair going every which way on his face, but the rest
of him is thin and yellow, even his hair, which he's combed
over his head to hide the baldness underneath. It works,
too, because his scalp is yellow as the rest of him, so it's
hard for me to tell where his skin ends and the hair sprouts.

"That's all?" he says when I put the quart of milk and the
small briquettes of charcoal on the counter. He stretches
out his words so they seem to loop between us, and I have
to translate to understand what he says through the ac-
cent. I lean forward. He moves back just a step: small as a
slivered fingernail. A twitch. I remember I'm brown, and
I move back, too.

"Yeah," I say, and slide the money over the counter.

When I bring the bag to the car, Michael is disappointed.

"Go back inside," he says, "and get a hammer or a screw-
driver or something. Go look where they got all the home
stuff and the car stuff at. They got to have something. How
you expect me to break the charcoal up?"

"Guess that wasn't all?" the man asks when I slide the
tire-pressure gauge across the counter.

"Nope," I say. He smiles at me, and each tooth is gray.
His gums red. His mouth the only thing about him that's
vivid, a red surprise coming out of his beard. I take a Tootsie
Pop out the display bin.

"How much is it?"

"Seventy-five cents," the man says. His eyes say different:
I would give it to you if I could, but I can't. Got cameras in here.

"I got it," I say, "and I don't need no receipt."

The change is cold in my pocket when I stop at Michael's side of the car and hand him the gauge.

"You got my change?"

I was hoping he'd forget, that at the next place we stopped, I could sneak inside with Kayla, buy a beef jerky and a drink for myself. My insides feel like a balloon again, full with nothing but air. I pick the change out around the bag Pop gave me, and when I slide into the back of the car, Michael's handing me a dirty saucer Leonie had slid under the driver's seat, and a brick of charcoal, and the gauge.

"Fucking charcoal was expensive," he says. "Crush it."

"Candy," Kayla says, and reaches for me.

"Michaela, leave your brother alone," Michael says. He's rubbing Leonie's hair, bending over to whisper in her ear, and I catch little bits of it. "Just breathe, baby, breathe," he says.

"Shhh," I tell Kayla, put my knees to the door, and hunch down over the plate and the charcoal. I hit the charcoal light because I don't want the gauge to break the plate. Kayla whines and the whine rises. I think she's going to start screaming *candy, candy*, but I look back at Kayla and she has her two middle fingers in her mouth, and I know then by the way she's studying me, her little eyes round as marbles, calm in her seat, rubbing her seat belt clasp with her other hand, that she has it. Like me. That she can understand like I can, but even better, because she know how to do it now. Because she can look at me and know what I'm thinking, know *I got it, Kayla, got you a sucker but you got to wait for me to finish doing this and you can get it, I promise, because you been a good girl*, and she smiles around her wet fingers, her little teeth perfect and even as uncooked rice, and I know she hears me.

"Mike, you sure about this?" Misty asks.

"It's what they give you in the hospital," Michael says.

"I ain't never heard of nobody using the kind you cook with."

"Well," Michael says.

"What if it make her worse?"

"You know what she did?"

"Yes," Misty says, almost swallows the words, her voice quiet.

"Well, then you know she need something."

"I know."

"This what I got," Michael says, something about his voice set, like concrete firming, like he answered a question: final.

"It's done," I say.

"The whole piece?"

I raise the saucer up so he can see it, see the tiny pile of black-gray powder, smelling strong of sulfur. Some kind of bad earth. Like the bayou when the water's low, when the water runs out after the moon or it ain't rained and the muddy bottom, where the crawfish burrow, turns black and gummy under the blue sky and stinks. Michael takes the powder. He peels the plastic off the milk top, pops it, and drinks two big gulps. I am so hungry I can smell it on his breath, smell it in the car when he takes the charcoal and dumps it into the milk, puts the top on, and shakes. The milk shades gray. He flicks the top off again, and there is a new smell in the car, the kind of smell that makes the back of my throat get thick, the kind of smell that makes me want to swallow, so I do.

"Jesus Christ, that stinks!" Misty says. She pulls her shirt over the bottom half of her face like a veil.

"It ain't supposed to smell good, Misty," Michael says. He hoists Leonie up and her head falls back. I expect her eyes to be closed but they aren't: they are wide open, and her lashes are fluttering fast as a hummingbird's wings. A white open shock. "Come on, baby. You got to drink this."

Leonie twists and turns like she has no bones, her body winding as a worm's.

"Candy?" Kayla asks.

Michael's nostrils flare and his lips are spread like he wants to smile, but there is no curve here. His teeth gleam yellow and wet as a dog's. He won't know. All his attention is on Leonie, on her winding neck and her hands trying to bat him away.

I unwrap the sucker. It is red and glossy and I hide it in the curve of my hand as I pass it to Kayla. If Michael ask where she got it, I'm going to say I found it on the floor of the car.

"What's that?" Richie asks.

"Come help me, Misty," Michael says. The milk drips down his forearm. Leonie is fighting him. "Hold her nose!"

"Shit!" Misty says, and she's out the backseat and in the front seat and they are both wrestling Leonie back and Michael's pouring what he can down Leonie's throat, and she's swallowing and breathing and choking and there's gray milk everywhere.

"Hold me!" Kayla says, and she's climbing into my lap.

Her hair is soft on my face, and I can smell the sucker on her breath, sugary and tart, and she turns her head and it's like having a faceful of cotton candy, rough and sweet.

"It's a sucker," I whisper. Richie nods and stretches his hands over his head.

"That's your mama?" he ask.

"No," I say, and I don't explain, even when Michael pull her from the car and they both on they knees in the grass on the side of the station, and she's vomiting so hard her back curves like an angry cat's.

I am singing nursery rhymes with Kayla while Leonie throws up because I want Kayla to pay attention to me. Don't want her to see Leonie hunched over and sick, don't want her to see Michael with that pinched look on his face like he's going to cry, don't want her to see Misty running from the station to where they are on the grass with cups of water and her voice high-pitched and her face red. But I sing the nursery songs all wrong; Leonie sang them to me so long ago I remember them only in snatches, light shining on a moment here or there when I was on her lap, both of us singing in the kitchen, steamy with onions and bell pepper and garlic and celery, the smell so delicious I wanted to eat the air. Mam would laugh at my pronunciation, the way I called cows *tows*, the way I called cats *tats*. I must have been Kayla's age, but I could smell Leonie, too, smell her breath, the red cinnamon gum she chewed as she sang past my ear. Even when I grew older and she stopped giving me kisses, every time somebody chewed that gum, I

thought of Leonie, of her soft, dry lips on my cheek. Kayla
doesn't care, even if the songs are patched together from my
memory, pieces of a puzzle that almost fit: Old MacDonald
has a llama, and there's a cow on the bus, mooing as the
wheels go around and around, and the itsy bitsy spider is
crawling with a pout. I make up pantomimes for all of it,
but Kayla's favorite is a spider crawling upward, because
I cross my thumbs and my fingers splay and segment and
move, and there is a spider in the car, inches from Kayla's
face, crawling upward against the rain. Foolishly. When the
boy begins speaking, I sing in a whisper, and Kayla sings
in a whisper because she thinks it's fun, and I listen. Then
Kayla stops singing and she listens, too, but she waves her
arms in the air and whines when I stop, so I sing.

"Is Riv old?" Richie asks.

I nod and warble.

"He was skinnier than you. Taller. Always had a way
about him. He stood out. Not just because he was young.
But because he was Riv."

The sun is creeping across the sky. The sun beams past
the boy's face to land on Kayla, to make her eyes shine.

"Got a lot of men in there ain't so friendly. Then and
now. It's full of wrong men. The kind of men that feel better
if they do something bad to you. Like it eases something
in them."

Where the sun should hit the boy's face and make it
glow, it only seems to make it turn a deeper brown.

"They beat you in there. Some people look at boys our
age and see somebody they can violate. See somebody who
got soft pink insides. Riv tried to keep that from me. But

he couldn't keep it all, and I was too small. I couldn't bear it. Kept thinking about my brothers and sisters, wondering if they was eating. Wanted to know what it would feel like to wake up and not feel like a thicket of thorns was up inside of me."

This is a brown that skims black.

"I couldn't live with it. So I decided to run. Did Riv tell you that?"

I nod.

"I guess I didn't make it." Richie laughs, and it's a dragging, limping chuckle. Then he turns serious, his face night in the bright sunlight. "But I don't know how. I need to know how." He looks up at the roof of the car. "Riv will know."

I don't want to hear no more of the story. I shake my head. I don't want him talking to Pop, asking him about that time. Pop has never told me the story of what happened to Richie when he ran. Every time I ask about it, he changes the subject or asks me to help him with something in the yard. And I understand the sentiment when he looks away or walks off, expecting me to follow. I know what Pop's saying: *I don't want to talk about this. It wounds me.*

"What's wrong?" Richie asks. He looks confused.

"Shut up," I say softly. And then I nod at Kayla, who wiggles her fingers in the air and says, "Spider, spider."

"I got to see him again," he says. "I got to know."

Michael done picked Leonie up like a baby, one arm under the crook of her knees, the other under her shoulders. Her head flops back. He's talking into her throat, carrying her to the car. She's shaking her head. Misty's wiping her

forehead with paper towels. Richie raises up a little, like
he has a body, has skin and bones and muscle, needs to
stretch before he settles back down into his too-small spot
on the floor.

"It's how I get home."

It's afternoon. The clouds are gone, the sky a great wash
of blue, soft white light everywhere, turning Kayla gold,
turning me red. Everything else eating light while Richie
shrugs it off. The trees clatter.

"You ain't even from Bois." I say it like it's a fact, when
I know it's a question.

Richie leans forward, leans so close that if he had breath,
it would be hitting me in the face, stinking up my nose. I
done seen pictures of toothbrushes from the '40s. Big as
hair brushes, bristles look metal. I wonder if they even had
them up there, in Parchman, or if they gnawed a twig to a
brushy softness and rubbed their teeth with that, the way
Pop said he had to do when he was growing up.

"There's things you think you know that you don't."

"Like what?" I spit it out fast because Misty's opening
the front door, and Michael's laying Leonie in the front seat,
and I know the rest of my words have to be quiet.

"Home ain't always about a place. The house I grew up
in is gone. Ain't nothing but a field and some woods, but
even if the house was still there, it ain't about that." Richie
rubs his knuckles together. "I don't know."

I raise my right eyebrow at him. Mam can do it, and I
can do it. Pop and Leonie can't.

"Home is about the earth. Whether the earth open up
to you. Whether it pull you so close the space between you

and it melt and y'all one and it beats like your heart. Same time. Where my family lived . . . it's a wall. It's a hard floor, wood. Then concrete. No opening. No heartbeat. No air."

"So what?" I whisper.

Michael starts the car and pulls out of the narrow gravel parking lot beside the gas station. Wind kneads my scalp.

"This my way to find that."

"Find what?"

"A song. The place is the song and I'm going to be part of the song."

"That don't make no sense."

Misty glances over at me. I look out the window.

"It will," Richie says. "It's why you can hear animals, see things that ain't there. It's a piece of you. It's everything inside of you and outside of you."

"What else?" I lower my hand and mouth.

"What?"

"What else I don't know?"

Richie laughs. It's an old man's laugh: a wheeze and a croak.

"Too much."

"The biggest ones," my lips form.

"Home."

I roll my eyes.

"Love."

I point at Kayla. Richie shrugs.

"There's more," he says. He wiggles like the floor is too hard, like he doesn't like talking about love. The way he looks at me then, like the secretary at the school did when I was seven and I had an accident and peed myself and Leonie never showed up with clean clothes, so I sat on a hard orange plastic chair in the office and shivered for an hour until they got in touch with Mam, and she came and walked me out of the AC into the hot day. Like he's sorry for me, for what I got to learn.

"And time," he says. "You don't know shit about time."

Chapter 9

Richie

I know Jojo is innocent because I can read it in the un-
marked swell of him: his smooth face, ripe with baby
fat; his round, full stomach; his hands and feet soft as his
younger sister's. He looks even younger when he falls
asleep. His baby sister has flung herself across him, and
both of them slumber like young feral cats: open mouths,
splayed arms and legs, exposed throats. When I was thirteen, I knew much more than him. I knew that metal shack-
les could grow into the skin. I knew that leather could split
flesh like butter. I knew that hunger could hurt, could scoop
me hollow as a gourd, and that seeing my siblings starving
could hollow out a different part of me, too. Could make
my heart ricochet through my chest desperately. I watch
Jojo and Kayla's sprawled sleep and wonder if I ever slept
like that when I was young. I wonder if Riv ever looked
at me and saw a wild, naïve thing in the cot next to him.
I wonder if he felt pity. Or if there was more love. Jojo
snores to a snort and stops, and I feel something in my
chest, where my heart would be if I were still alive, soften
toward him.

*   *   *

I didn't understand time, either, when I was young. How could I know that after I died, Parchman would pull me from the sky? How could I imagine Parchman would pull me to it and refuse to let go? And how could I conceive that Parchman was past, present, and future all at once? That the history and sentiment that carved the place out of the wilderness would show me that time is a vast ocean, and that everything is happening at once?

I was trapped, as trapped as I'd been in the room of pines where I woke up. Trapped as I was before the white snake, the black vulture, came for me. Parchman had imprisoned me again. I wandered the new prison, night after night. It was a place bound by cinder blocks and cement. I watched the men fuck and fight in the dark, so twisted up in each other I couldn't tell where one man ended and another began. I spent so many turns of the earth at the new Parchman. I watched for the dark bird, but he was absent. I despaired, burrowed into the dirt, slept, and rose to witness the newborn Parchman: I watched chained men clear the land and lay the first logs for the first barracks for gunmen and trusty shooters. I thought I was in a bad dream. I thought that if I burrowed and slept and woke again, I would be back in the new Parchman, but instead, when I slept and woke, I was in the Delta before the prison, and Native men were ranging over that rich earth, hunting and taking breaks to play stickball and smoke. Bewildered, I burrowed and slept and woke to the new Parchman again, to men who wore their hair long and braided to their scalps, who sat for hours in small windowless rooms, staring at big black boxes that streamed dreams. Their faces in the blue light were stiff as corpses. I burrowed and slept and woke many times before I realized this was the nature of time.

It was a small mercy that I never surfaced in the old Parchman, the one where Riv and I lived. I only visited that Parchman in memory, memories that rose like bubbles of decay to the surface of a swamp. Riv had a woman in Parchman; she shines golden in the dark blanket of memory that surrounds me when I sleep. She was a prostitute who serviced the Black men in the prison, and she looked like she could have been my mama, skinny as me, as dark, eyes inky like the trees when night falls. She wore a lot of yellow. I asked Riv once why he liked her and he told me that was something I would know when I was older. I asked him if he loved her, and he shook his head and I wondered if there was somebody he loved down on the Gulf, some saltwater girl.

It was that yellow-wearing woman, that Sunshine Woman, all the other men called her, who told me and Riv about the lynching. It was her last day at Parchman, but neither of us knew it, and she sat with her arms across her chest and one hand covering her mouth, watching the trusty shooters. We sat in a corner of the yard, in the shade of a shed, and she told us about the latest hanged man. *Was a Black man*, she said, *from outside of Natchez*. He went into town one day with his lady, and he didn't get off the sidewalk when a White woman walked by. *Stepped too close to her*, Sunshine Woman said, *and brushed up against her real close-like. Felt her softness through her clothes*, Sunshine Woman said. *The White woman spat, cursed the Black man and woman, and the Black woman say she sorry. That her man ain't mean to do it.* Sunshine Woman thought the truth of it was he didn't want his woman to have to step down into the street, as it was rutted with puddles because there had been bad rains and flooding. Maybe the Black man was prideful, thought he could be courteous to his woman, keep her walking and clean. *She was wearing her best dress,* Sunshine Woman said. The White woman went home and told her husband that the Black man molested her and his woman disrespected her. The Black man and woman were on their way home when the mob caught up with them. *That's them,* the White woman said, *that's them right there.* Sunshine Woman said it was over a hundred of them. The people from the community saw all the lights out there, the torches and lanterns that lit up the night to dawn.

And that's when Sunshine Woman started to whisper. She said their people went out in the woods and found them the next day. Said the mob beat them so bad they eyes disappeared in they swollen heads. There was wax paper and sausage wrappings and bare corncobs all over the ground. The man was missing his fingers, his toes, and his genitals. The woman was missing her teeth. Both of them were hanged, and the ground all around the roots of the tree was smoking because the mob had set the couple afire, too. *A person ain't safe,* Sunshine Woman said, *and that's why this the last you seeing of me around here, Riv. I'm heading north to Chicago with my auntie and uncle,* she said, *and you be a fool if you don't come north when you get out.*

Riv looked like he had swallowed something nasty, some

bug or a rock in his meal, and he said: *Naw, Sunshine Woman, I got to go back south.* Riv glanced at me and said: *Maybe you shouldn't have told both us that story. Maybe you should have waited.*

He grown enough to be in here, Riv, Sunshine Woman said. *That mean he grown enough to know.*

Riv had pulled his arm from her then and stepped out into the sun.

Just 'cause he in here don't mean he can bear that. He shouldn't have to, Riv said.

Sunshine Woman seemed disappointed in Riv, angry, but she hooked her hand through his arm even though it look like it hurt her to do so, and she said: *I'm sorry, Riv. Sorry, boy.* She pulled him away, and they left me standing in the lee of the building. I looked up at the rusted tin of the walls and realized I could have told Sunshine Woman that she hadn't told me something I didn't already know. I wondered if that would have made Riv less angry with her. Once, when I was playing in the woods with my brothers and sisters, we found what had once been a man, hanging from a tree. He was a short man, short as me, but rubbery with rot and stinking and his mouth was open like he was grinning. That grin was the devil. My little brothers and sisters ran home screaming, and when I walked into the house, my mama slapped my face for being the oldest and leading us where we shouldn't go. But when I thought about the way Riv admonished Sunshine Woman, how he stepped away from her to protect me, I began to understand love. I began to understand that what Riv and Sunshine Woman did wasn't an expression of love, but Riv's standing in the sun for me was. I sagged and sat on the ground with the weight of it. I wanted to call to Sunshine Woman and tell her I would do it: I would go north when I was free. Riv looked back at me and his eyes were glassy and dark; it was as if he could hear my thoughts, as if he knew what I wanted to say. As I watched Sunshine Woman pull Riv away from me, I felt a stinging in my toes, in my soles, in my legs, up my butt, and through my back, where it burst to fire in my bones, licking all through my ribs, a loose powerful feeling, like a voice freed from a throat, a screaming note all through me, and it was then I knew I was going to run.

I began to understand home when Riv and I slept next to each other and Riv told me stories in the dark. Once, River told me about the ocean. He said: *We got so much water where I'm from. It come down from the north in rivers. Pool in bayous. Rush out to the ocean, and that stretch to the ends of the earth that you can see. It changes colors,* he said, *like a little lizard. Sometimes stormy blue. Sometimes cool gray. In the early mornings, silver. You could look at that and know there's a God,* he said to me as the other gunmen coughed and tossed. *Maybe one day, when you and me get out of here, you could come down and see it,* Riv said.

Kayla has her palm curled around Jojo's neck, and he throws an arm over her back, and I wonder if they dream the same dreams. I wonder if they dream of home: of jungle-tangled trees, bearing the weight of the sky. Of streams leading to rivers leading to the sea. I wonder if the reason I couldn't leave Parchman before Jojo came was because it was a sort of home to me: terrible and formative as the iron leash that chains dogs, that drives them to bark hysterically and run in circles and burrow to the roots of the grass, to savage smaller animals, to kill the living things they can reach.

Today when Jojo came to Parchman, I woke to the whispering of the white snake, which had dug a nest down into the earth with me so he could speak to me in my ear. So he could curl about my head in the dark and whisper, *If you would rise, I can take you across the waters of this world to another. This place binds you. This place blinds you. Keep the scale, even if you cannot fly. Go south, to River, to the face of the waters. He will show you. Go south.* He curled around my neck and startled me to climb up and out of the dirt, to rise to the smell of Riv's blood, thick as the fragrance of spider lilies in flower. When I saw Jojo and Kayla in the parking lot, the snake transformed to a bird on my shoulder before flying away on a wave of wind, speeding south on a lonely migration. As Kayla whines in her sleep and Jojo rubs her back to quiet her, a shadow alights and crosses over them. Up in the sky, the scaly bird drifts, shining a dark light.

I will follow, I say. I hope he can hear me. I say: *I'm coming home.*

Chapter 10

Leonie

When we first began dating, Michael and I spent a month of nights parking on the boat jetty out on the bayou, kissing, his face against mine, smooth skin, as the wind came in the open windows, briny and sweet. A month of riding everywhere but near his house in the Kill and getting dropped off at my house an hour before dawn. I jumped off the cliff at the river one of those nights. I ran before I leapt to clear the rocky bank; I dropped into the feathery dark heart of the water and went all the way to the bottom, where the sand was more muddy than grainy and downed trees decomposed, slimy and soft at the core. I didn't swim up; the fall had stunned my arms and legs, the thunderous slap of the water numbed them. I let the water carry me. It was a slow rise: up, up, up toward milky light. I remember it clearly because I never did it again, scared by that paralyzing ascent. This is what it feels like to wake with my head in Michael's lap, his fingers still on my scalp, the car rumbling, light slanting sharp through the window. This is what it feels like to rise from a dark deep place. I lift up a little and put my forehead on Michael's thigh and groan.

"Hey." I can hear the smile in his voice; the word sounds higher, thinner. I'm too close to his crotch.

"Hey," I say, and raise up farther. By the time I'm sitting up straight, it feels wrong. Like every bone in my spine, each locking piece, been knocked over and built back up crooked.

"How you feel?"

"What?"

Michael pushes my hair back off my forehead and I close my eyes at the touch. My throat is burning. Michael looks in the rearview and then pulls me over so my head is on his shoulder, his lips at my ear.

"The cops pulled us over, remember? You swallowed that shit from Al because wasn't no time to dump it. The fucking floor was covered in shit. You should clean your car, Leonie." He sounds like Mama when he says it.

"I know, Michael. What else?"

"I got you milk and charcoal from a gas station. You threw up."

I swallow, and the root of my tongue aches.

"My mouth hurts."

"You threw up a lot."

The world outside the car is a green, shaky blur, the color of Michael's eyes, of the trees bursting to life in the spring. The memory that eased me up out the dark, the memory of jumping from that cliff, is a buzzing green, but there is none of that inside of me. Just some water oak limbs, dry and mossy, burned to ash, smoldering. I feel wrong.

"How long to the house?"

"'Bout an hour."

Even the pine trees, with their constant muted green, seem brighter. Through them, I see the sun will set soon.

"Wake me up."

I lie down in the ashes and sleep.

When I wake, Michael's rolled all the windows down. I've been dreaming for hours, it feels like, dreaming of being marooned on a deflating raft in the middle of the endless reach of the Gulf of Mexico, far out where the fish are bigger than men. I'm not alone in the raft because Jojo and Michaela and Michael are with me and we are elbow to elbow. But the raft must have a hole in it, because it deflates. We are all sinking, and there are manta rays gliding beneath us and sharks jostling us. I am trying to keep everyone above water, even as I struggle to stay afloat. I sink below the waves and push Jojo upward so he can stay above the waves and breathe, but then Michaela sinks and I push her up, and Michael sinks so I shove him to the air as I sink and struggle, but they won't stay up: they want to sink like stones. I thrust them up toward the surface, to the fractured sky so they can live, but they keep slipping from my hands. It is so real that I can feel their sodden clothes against my palms. I am failing them. We are all drowning.

"Feel better?" Michael asks.

The sky has turned pink, and everybody looks ragged, even Misty, who has fallen asleep with her face smashed against the window, her hair falling over her forehead and down the line of her nose and cheek: a yellow head scarf.

"I guess," I say.

And I do, except for the dream. It stays with me, a bruise in the memory that hurts when I touch it. I turn around to check on Michaela. Her shirt, cold and wet, clings to her small, hot body.

"We could drop the kids off. Go get something to eat before we go home."

"Home?"

"To your mama and daddy's," Michael says.

I knew that's where we were going, knew there was nowhere else for us to go. Not to the Kill, not to his parents, who've never even seen Michaela in the flesh. We could not go where we aren't welcome. But I guess I had an apartment in my head. Once we're on our feet we'll get to it, but I had so envisioned it that when I thought about us going home, I only saw that place. I imagined us settling in one of the bigger towns on the Gulf Coast, in one of those three-story complexes with metal-and-concrete stairs leading from one level to another. We would have big whitewashed, carpeted rooms, space, anonymity, and quiet.

"Yeah," I say.

"So you want to?"

Michaela kicks the back of my seat. Her hair is matted to her head, and she's chewing on a sucker stick, the cardboard melting and coming away in papery bits to stick on the side of her mouth. I smile at her, wait for her to smile at me, but she doesn't. She kicks again and bares her teeth around the stick, but it is no smile.

"Michaela, stop kicking Mama's seat."

"Ony," she says, and sucks on the stick and waves both

hands in the air. Jojo looks away from the window, down
to her kicking feet, and frowns. "Ony!" she screams.

"She's saying your name," Michael says.

"Mama," I tell Michaela.

"Ony," Michaela says, and for a moment I'm in my
drowning dream again, and I feel her hot, wet back buoyed
up by my palms, slipping, slipping.

"Yeah," I tell Michael. "Drop them off."

Michael turns from one narrow, tree-shrouded road to
another, water dripping from the leaves to dot the windshield, and I know we're in Bois by the map of the limbs.
Two people walk in the distance, and as we cruise through
the green tunnel, I see a man, short and muscled, who leads
a black dog by a chain. And next to him, a skinny little
woman with a sable, coily cloud of hair that moves like a
kaleidoscope of butterflies. It's not until we're right up on
them that I see who it is. Skeetah and Eschelle, a brother
and sister from the neighborhood. The siblings walk in sync,
both of them bouncing. Esch says something, and Skeetah
laughs. We pass as dusk darkens the road.

Michaela kicks my seat again, and I turn around and slap
her leg so hard my palm stings. Jealousy twins with anger.
That girl: so lucky. She has all her brothers.

The house looks like it sunk. Drooping at the crown. Jojo
seems taller than he was when we left as he jiggles the
doorknob, as he disappears through the dark door. But soon
he's walking back out to the car, and it's so dark now that
I can't see his face. Even when he leans into the window

of the car and Michael turns on the overhead light, there is still a black film over his face.

"They not here," he says.

"Mama and Pop?" I ask.

"No."

"Did they leave a note?"

Jojo shakes his head.

"Get in the car," Michael says.

"What?" I ask. I'm so tired that it feels like someone has placed a wet towel over my brain, the weight of it suffocating thought.

"We can wait here." Jojo stands.

"Get in the car," Michael says.

Jojo's lips thin, and he climbs into the back of the car. Michaela has her face hidden in his neck again, one finger twirling a lock of Jojo's hair. Michael reverses into the empty street.

"Where we going?" Jojo says.

"To visit your grandparents."

My heart is a squirrel caught in a snare. The fine hair on my arms stands up and quivers. I see Michael's daddy, fat and sweating, his rifle balanced loosely on his lawn mower, the sound of the motor grinding and whining because he's pushing it as fast as it can go over the lawn, trying to get to my car, to me. I see my hands, black and thin-boned, on the steering wheel. I see Given's hands, fine as mine, but hard with callused coins from the rub of the bowstring.

"Why now?" I ask.

"I'm home," Michael says. "You know they never drove up to Parchman."

"Because they didn't care," I say, even as I know it's not true.

"They do. They just don't know how to show it."

"Because of me. And the kids," I say.

This is an old argument between us. Michael tries something new.

"Plus, Jojo's thirteen. It's time."

"He's thirteen and they ain't gave a shit to see him or Michaela," I say.

Michael ignores me and heads north. The air is cooler up in the Kill, since there are even fewer houses and more dark land sleeping under the deepening sky.

"Maybe they'll surprise us, Leonie," Michael says.

My mouth tastes like vomit.

"Sugar baby."

"No."

Michael pulls to the side of the road. The crickets turn riot.

"Please," Michael says. He rubs the nape of my neck. I want to scramble out the window of the car and run, to disappear.

"No."

"They made me, baby. And we made the kids. They going to look at Jojo and Michaela and see that," Michael says. I feel my shoulders beginning to creep down, to relax, to settle.

"What you told them?" I ask.

Michael looks at the bugs skipping across the windshield like they are dragonflies and it is hard water.

"I told them it was time," Michael says. "That if they

love me, they got to love them, too, because they a piece of me." He looks at me then, his green eyes look brown in the fading light, his hair dark: a stranger sitting in the driver's seat. "Like you," he says.

I bat his hand off my neck, rub where he touched like it's a mosquito bite.

"Fine," I say, and Michael heads north into the Kill.

"Kayla's hungry," Jojo says.

"Chip!" Michaela says. Outside, the world is dark, the fields and trees ink black. I roll up my window, which has been cracked. I woke Misty up when we pulled into her gravel driveway and she grabbed her bag from her feet and struggled out of the car with a sarcastic "Well, it's been fun, folks." She'll hate me for a day or two, but once she washes her clothes and gets the smell of vomit out of her nose, she'll call. I knew it by the way she leaned into my window after she slammed her door shut, glared at Michael, and said: "Good luck." When I stretch over the backseat to roll up the window Misty slept against, Jojo's looking at the floor like he's lost something.

"They got leftovers down there?"

"No," he says.

"We're going to your grandparents' house," Michael says.

"Chip," Michaela says.

"You'll eat soon, Michaela," I say. "Pass her here, Jojo."

Jojo unbuckles her from the seat, and he pushes her forward. Her hair's knotted in the back, curls worn fuzzy from the rub of her car seat. I smooth the hair up, trying to tame it into a puff on the top of her head, but she shakes and cries for a potato chip again. I dig in my purse. There's nothing in the bottom but change and one peppermint I took from the bar. I unwrap it and give it to Michaela, and she sucks and quiets. The car smells like mint and her hair, sweet as sugar. Michael slows to cross the railroad tracks, and just as he does, a tusked wild hog, big as two men and covered in black fur, darts from the woods and sprints across the road, as light on his hooves as a child. Michael swerves a little, and I clutch Michaela but I can't hold her and she flies forward, hitting her head on the dashboard. Michael swerves off the road and stops. Michaela bounces and slides down on my feet, and she is quiet.

"Michaela," I say. I grab her under her armpits and drag her up, see a purple knot weeping red on her forehead. She's alive, because her eyes are open and she's hitching to cry, her breath stuttering in her throat. She wails.

"Kayla!" Jojo says.

"Jojo!" Michaela puts her forearms into my collarbones, pushing away from me, wanting Jojo again. The headlights vanish into the darkness along with the monstrous pig and suddenly I feel boneless, loose as a jellyfish, and I don't have the strength to fight her.

"Shhhh," I say, but even as my mouth is trying to comfort her, I hand her over the backseat, and she's in Jojo's arms. He's patting her back as her arms settle around his neck. Michael and I turn to each other and I frown. We face forward, looking at the mist obscuring the windshield.

"Jojo, buckle her in." I say this without turning to look

at him, because I don't want to see his face, afraid I might
see the hard planes of Pop in his expression: judgment. Or
worse, the soft quiver of Mama's pity.

"You sure?" Michael's shaken: I can tell by the way he
grips the steering wheel and then lets go, grips and lets go,
as if he's testing his reflexes, gauging the nimbleness of his
fingers. One bug crackles and hits the windshield, drunk
in the lights. And then another.

"You want to go," I say.

"Yeah."

"Then let's go."

There is no radio, no talk. Just the growl and pull of the
car, the gravel ground under the tires, gatherings of frogs
singing in hisses and croaks from ponds in woods and some
perfect circles dug into yards. Michael's parents' house is
different at night, and it's been so many years since I've been
there in the dark that it is a hazy memory, even as I look at
it: long, straight gravel driveway, yellow in the moonlight,
leading to the house through the fields; the gravel shimmers,
an after-light left by a sparkler through night air. There are
two lit windows, one at each end of the house. Michael cuts
the lights so the car creeps and crunches down the driveway,
the roll of the rocks under the tires sounding little pops. We
park next to Big Joseph's pickup truck and a blue car with a
short hood, boxy body and back. A rosary hangs from the
rearview mirror. I ease the car door open, and I suddenly
need to pee, desperately. I don't want to be here. Michael
holds out his hand, and I want to climb back in the car, slam
the door, drive off with the kids, who are still sitting in the
backseat. A dog barks in the distance.

"Come on," Michael says.

"Let's go," I tell Jojo. He gets out of the car and stands in the dark. He is as tall as me, maybe a little taller, and I can see him tall as Pop in two or three years. He hoists Michaela up and holds her in front of his chest: her back, his shield. Michaela is touching her forehead, which shows a dark constellation of blood, and asking Jojo questions.

"Mam?" she asks. "Pop? Mam? Pop?"

"No," Jojo says. "These new people."

But he doesn't say who they are, and I want to answer her question, want to be her mother, want to say: *Your other grandma or grandpa, your other family, your other Mam and Pop.* But I don't know what to say, how to explain, so I say nothing and let Michael answer her questions. But he offers nothing, either: he walks up the deck steps to the front porch and the door, pulls the screen door open, and knocks: two sure knocks, hard as a horse's hooves on asphalt. I follow, and Jojo's dragging feet purr through the gravel in the dark. Michael walks down the steps, a white ghost in the dark; grabs my hand; and pulls me up to stand next to him at the door.

Michael knocks again, and I hear movement in the house. Jojo hears like an animal and takes a step back toward the car.

"Come on, Jojo," Michael says.

The door opens and there is light so bright I look down at my feet, Michael's hand hard as metal in mine, gripping so tight I am sure my fingers are purple and white, but I see him, see Big Joseph, wearing overalls and a too-tight T-shirt, his peppered beard, his fleshy arms, all of it too much in the yellow spill. I step back. Michael pulls.

"Daddy," he says.

"Son," Big Joseph says. It is only the second time I've heard him speak in person, and his voice surprises me with how high it is, so different from the rest of him, which seems so rooted, so close to the earth, so low. The first time was in the courtroom, but he didn't mean anything to me then, beyond being the uncle of the boy who shot my brother.

"We here," Michael says. He lifts our clenched hands. Big Joseph lists, an old oak in a bad wind, but does not move, does not step back, does not say: *Come in.* In the dark behind us, Michaela cries.

"Eat," she says. "I eat, Jojo!"

There are footsteps. Not as heavy as Big Joseph's, but a steady, solid thumping, and even though I know it's his mother, know it's Maggie, I still flinch when I hear her smoker's voice: deep and gravelly. She yanks open the door and she looks like a rabbit: her robe like a cream fur, her house slippers like white paws. I've seen her twice outside of this house, know that her body underneath is rabbit, too: the thin arms and legs, the round ball of her stomach.

"Cheese, Jojo!" Michaela screams.

"You heard the child, Joseph," she says. A spasm makes her face twitch, and then it is still. Her hair is a red cap, her eyes unfathomably dark. "Time for supper."

"We already ate," Big Joseph wheezes.

Michaela mewls.

"And she ain't," Maggie says.

"You know they ain't welcome in this house."

"Joseph," Maggie says, and she frowns at him and pushes his shoulder.

Big Joseph makes a sound in his throat and sways again, but then I realize Maggie is the wind. Big Joseph looks at me like he wants that gun across his lap, but he steps out of the doorway. They've talked about this: I can tell by the way Maggie said his name, the way a woman says the name of a man that she has long lived with, long loved. The way she says his name is enough. I know they have spoken about me, about Jojo, about Michaela. Maggie pushes open the screen door. She doesn't say *come in* or *welcome*, just stands there, turned sideways. When I walk past her, she smells like lotion and soap and smoke, but not cigarette smoke: like fallen burnt oak leaves. She has Michael's face. I startle when I walk past because it's so strange to see his face on a woman: narrow jaw, strong nose, but the eyes are all wrong, hard as green marbles. In the house, we stand in a cluster, shying away from the furniture: a herd of nervous animals. Big Joseph and Maggie stand side by side, touching but not. She's taller than the pictures, and he's shorter.

"You going to introduce us?" Maggie's looking at Michael when she says it and he nods his head, just barely: a wink of a nod.

"Yes, ma'am. This—"

"Jojo," Jojo says. He hoists Michaela. "Kayla." She looks at Maggie with her beautiful green eyes, and then I realize those are Maggie's eyes, too, and I squeeze Michael's hand, and my children seem strangers. Michaela a golden, clinging toddler, the tilt of her head and those clear eyes direct and merciless as an adult's. And Jojo, tall as Michael, almost tall as Big Joseph, shoulders back, the line of his back a metal fence post. I have never seen him look so much like Pop as he does right now.

"Nice to meet you," Maggie says, but she does not smile when she says it.

Jojo doesn't even nod. Just looks at her and shifts Michaela to his other hip. Big Joseph shakes his head.

"I'm your grandmother," she says.

There is a large wall clock in the kitchen, and the minute hand ticking its way around the face sounds loud in the uncomfortable silence, so loud I begin counting the seconds. My fingers squeeze tighter and tighter around Michael's as his turn lax as he looks from his mother to his father, frowning. Jojo shrugs, and Michaela sticks her middle two fingers in her mouth and sucks hard. The house smells like lemon cleaner and fried potatoes.

Big Joseph falls into an armchair and wrenches it to the television.

"Figured they'd be rude," he says.

"Daddy," Michael says.

"Won't even say hello to your mother."

"They're shy," Michael says.

"It's all right," Maggie says. She bites the words short.

I must be sweating it out. A fire in my chest licks along my breasts. There's rock in my stomach, at the base of the fire. I squeeze my legs. I don't know whether I want to throw up or pee.

"Say hello," I croak.

Jojo looks at me: mutinous. The corner of his mouth,

frowning; his eyes almost closed. He bounces Michaela and steps backward toward the door. I don't know why I said it. Michaela looks at me as if she has not heard; if nobody knew better, they'd think she was deaf.

"Raised by her, what you'd expect, Maggie?"

"Joseph," Maggie says.

I would throw up everything. All of it out: food and bile and stomach and intestines and esophagus, organs all, bones and muscle, until all that was left was skin. And then maybe that could turn inside out, and I wouldn't be nothing no more. Not this skin, not this body. Maybe Michael could step on my heart, stop its beating. Then burn everything to cinders.

"Hell, they half of her. Part of that boy Riv, too. All bad blood. Fuck the skin." His voice is so high by the end of it that I can hardly hear him over the television, over an enthusiastic car salesman whose prices are miraculously dropping. Maggie's mouth is a seam. Her hands worrying one another, and suddenly I hate her because she can walk and my mama can't. And then I hate Joseph because he's called my daddy a boy. I wonder what he knows of my daddy, how he could look at Pop and see every line of Pop's face, every step Pop takes, every word out of Pop's mouth, and see anything but a man. Pop's at least twenty years older than Big Joseph; he was a grown man when Big Joseph was pissing his diapers. So how can Big Joseph see Pop, see how stonelike he is, like Pop's taken all the hardship of the world into him and let it calcify him inch by inch till he's like one of them petrified trees, and see anything but a man? Pop would whip his ass. And I can see Big Joseph in my mind's eye, standing over Given, breathing down on him like he's so much roadkill, how he would ignore the perfection of him: the long bow-drawing arm, the high forehead over the dead eyes.

"Goddamnit, Daddy!" Michael says.

Quick as he fell into the chair, Big Joseph is up, walking toward us but facing Michael.

"I told you they don't belong here. Told you never to sleep with no nigger bitch!"

Michael head-butts Big Joseph. The crack of their skulls ricochets through the air, and Big Joseph's nose is gushing blood, and then him and Michael are on the floor, but Michael isn't punching him. They're pushing against each other, each trying to pin the other down, rolling like children. Breathing hard. Sweating. Maybe crying. Michael saying over and over: "Goddamnit, Daddy, goddamnit, Daddy," and Big Joseph saying nothing but wheezing so hard it sounds like sobbing.

"Enough!" Maggie screams. "That's enough!" And then she's running away and I can't believe she's going to leave them fighting in the kitchen, but then she's running back with a broom and beating Michael over the shoulders with it because he's on top of Big Joseph now, yelling, "Get up. Get up." And I still feel sick, and cold, and too small for all this, and part of me wants to go grab Jojo's hand and pull them out this house and leave them fighting. And another part of me wants to open my mouth and laugh, because it's all so ridiculous, all of it, and I look over at my son and I think for sure he's smiling, for sure he can see how stupid all of it is, but he ain't looking at them tussling. He's looking at me, and I see a flash of something I ain't never seen before. He's looking at me like I'm a water moccasin and I just bit him, just sank my teeth into the bone of his ankle, bit it to swelling. Like he would step on my head, crush my skull, stomp me into red mud until I wasn't nothing but bone and skin and mud oozing in my slits. Like he ain't no child of mine. Michaela's climbing her brother, getting higher and higher on him until she's almost sitting on his shoulder, so I do it. I stalk over and I grab Jojo's hand even though I half expect him to yank it away, and I pull him toward the door.

"Nice meeting y'all," I say, and it sounds high-pitched and ridiculous coming out of my mouth, with the men still tussling and Maggie still whacking. Big Joseph's on top now, choking Michael, and even though I want to go back and help Michael, I don't. I open the door and pull Jojo and Michaela. I take one look back and see Michael punch his daddy in the throat. Then we're out the door, and the sky in the Kill is wide and open and cold, awash in stars, and we down the porch steps, standing by the car, shivering, listening to the banging in the house. A crash, and a light goes out.

"Get in," I say, and Jojo climbs in the backseat with Michaela.

"Shit," Michaela lisps, and it sounds like *thit*.

"Don't say that," I say. We sit in the car in the dark with the first of the crickets and katydids that come alive in the warmer months and listen to them trill, protesting the frigid air, the unfeeling stars, and we wait.

* * *

It's minutes. Or it's hours. Could be days, too, and maybe we slept through the sunrise and sunset, and woke to the night, again and again, and them still rolling and breaking things inside. Daddy and son. Until Michael and his mama come out the door, Michael kicking right through the screen, Maggie rushing out behind him to grab his shoulders. To turn him to her. To yell at him, then talk to him, then murmur. Michael leans down toward his mother in breaths until he's hunched over her, his head on her shoulder, her rubbing his back like a baby. Her robe turning black where he brushes against it: blood dabbed from his touch. Michael sobbing then. The bugs quiet.

"We should've left," Jojo whispers.

"Shut up," I say.

"Kayla's still hungry," Jojo says.

I should leave. I should leave Michael to his family. Take my daughter home and feed her, fill her stomach, quiet her whimpering. But I don't. I can't. Maggie pulls the door open, disappears inside, and I expect Michael to walk toward the car but he doesn't. He just leans over and crosses his arms and puts them on the porch railing and hunches over, waiting. His mother opens the door again and almost hits him, and then she's passing him a paper grocery bag and hugging him to her and talking to him again, and with each word, she thumps his back with the flat of her hand. And he's a baby again, and it looks like she's trying to burp him. I look down at my lap. Out the driver's side window. Off into the far line of the woods. There's the sound of a door slamming shut, and then a creak, and Michael's opening the car and sliding into the passenger seat. The bugs loud and then dim again. The bag crackles.

"Are you okay?" I ask. I know it's stupid, but still, this is what I say.

"Let's go," Michael says.

The car chokes and cranks to life. I drive slowly down the driveway, swerving around muddy potholes, the bugs scatting our way. When I turn onto the street, the house is all dark. All the windows dim: the siding and beams and glass of the front of it smooth and still as a blank face.

Pop is home when I turn in to the gravel drive. He's sitting on the porch, still as the swing and the potted plants at both sides of the door; he's cut the light off so he is a darkness in the darkness, and the only reason I know it's him is by the way he flicks his lighter to life and then releases it, lets it flutter, and then he flicks again. He smoked when I was younger. Packed and rolled the cigarettes himself. But after he caught me around the back of the shed lighting one of his spent cigarettes with only a fingernail's worth of tobacco in it, he slapped it and the match out of my hand, and I never saw nor smelled the scent of one on him again. The way he looked at me when the cigarette hit the ground. Eyes wide, disappointed: pained. It was the first time I remember Pop looking at me like that. I was eleven and my breasts were budding and my friends at school were already smoking weed and worse, so I wanted to try at least a cigarette, but recalling his face, the way he looked guilty and angry at the same time, made me wish I'd never picked up that bud of rolled tobacco, never stole that match, never lit it, never hid back there for Pop to catch me.

So now whenever Pop is thinking about something but doesn't want to let anyone know he's thinking about something, worrying it over, he does this. *Light, gutter, light, gutter.* Where I was the one hesitant in the Kill, now it's Michael that stands at my elbow, slumped, curled in on himself: like I got a cur dog on a short, frayed leash. He tries to grab Michaela out of the car, but by the time he gets around to her side, Jojo is out and Michaela is patting his face, saying "Eat-eat," with every little tap, and they are already walking toward Pop in the darkness. Michael and I grab bags, so by the time we get up the porch steps, Michaela is disentangling herself from Pop's arms, and Jojo is carrying her into the house. Here, Pop is a dusky smudge, the tattoos on his arms lit up in a flash with the lighter, and then out again. When I was younger, I would sneak and stand next to him when he took a nap on the couch, smell his breath, the way it smelled of tobacco and mint and musk, and I would trace over his tattoos with my pointer finger, without touching him, just follow the illustrations around: a ship; a woman who looked like Mama, clothed in clouds and carrying arrows and a pine branch in her hand; and two cranes: one for me and one for Given. Given's is alight, poised in flight, feet skimming the marsh grass, while mine is beak down in the mud. When I was five, Pop pointed at mine and told me: *This the one I got for you: they a sign of luck when you see them, mean everything is in balance, that it's raining good and there's fish and there's things squirming under the marsh mud, that the bayou grass going to be green soon. They a sign of life.* The light gutters, and they are erased in the dark. Pop speaks and I see his teeth.

"Your mama been asking about you."

"Sir," Michael says. I feel the words as much as I hear them, hot puff of air that caresses my shoulder.

"Michael," Pop says. He clears his throat. "I expect it's good to be home."

"Yes, sir."

"Your mama—" Pop's voice breaks off.

"We getting a place," Michael interrupts. "Soon."

Pop lights and his face flashes. He is frowning, and then the flame dies.

The night is country dark.

"It'll keep until tomorrow." Pop rises. "Leonie, go on and see your mother."

Mama is laying in the bed with her face turned to the wall, and her chest is still, the bones from the spoon of her clavicle close and hard under the skin: a rusted cooking grate over a busted barbecue pit. Her arms are all bone, the skin and thin muscle overlaying them sliding to bunch at odd places: too far away from the elbow, too near the center of her throat. She swallows, and I feel relief wash through me, and I realize I was watching to see if she was breathing, to see if she was moving, to see if she was still here. It's like a quick rain over hot, dry earth.

"Mama?"

Her head moves an inch, and then one more, and then she's looking at me, her eyes too alive in her face. The pain glistens in her black irises, moves like smoke over the whites. The only thing bright while the rest of her dulls.

"Water?" she asks. It's a scratchy whisper, hardly there in the din of the night insects trilling through the open window.

I lift the cup and straw Pop left next to the bed for her to drink. I should have been here.

"Michael's home," I say.

She tongues the straw out of her mouth and swallows. Lays her head back. Her hands curled on the thin white blanket like an invalid's.

"It's time."

"What?" I say.

Mama clears her throat, but her whisper is no louder: too-long pant hems dragging over dirt.

"It's time."

"For what, Mama?"

"For me to go."

"What you mean?"

I set the cup down on the edge of the nightstand.

"This pain." She blinks as if to grimace, but doesn't. "If I lay in this bed for much longer, it's going to burn the heart out of me."

"Mama?"

"I done did everything I could. Brewed all the herbs and medicines. Opened myself to the *mystère*. For Saint Jude, for Marie Laveau, for Loko. But they can't enter. The body won't let them," she says.

Her knuckles bear all the scars: slipped knives, broken dishes, pounds of laundry. I wonder if I pull her hand to my

nose and sniff, if I can smell all the offerings she done placed
on her altar over the years, done used to heal: strings of
peppers, potatoes, yams, cattail, spider lily, Spanish needle,
sweet bedstraw, and wild okra. All the green of the earth
in her hands. But when I sniff, her palms sandpaper-dry,
I smell threshed hay bleached by the winter sun. Dead.
She squeezes, and it is pitiful. When I was a little girl, she
kneaded my scalp when she washed my hair, scraped it
with her fingernails as I sat in the tub with my knees in my
chin. I want to cry. I don't know what she's saying to me.

"I got one left," she says.

"What you mean?"

"The last *mystère*. Maman Brigitte. Let her come into
me. Possess me. She the mother of the dead. The judge.
If she come, maybe she take me with her."

"There ain't another? What about one that heals?" I ask.

"I didn't teach you enough. You won't be able to ap-
pease them."

"I could try." I let the words trail from my mouth and
hang in the air like lax fishing line, dangling a hook nothing
wants to bite. The night bugs call one to another, courting
and threatening and singing, and I can't understand any
of it. Mama looks at me, and for one blink, hope shines,
remote and brilliant as a full moon.

"No," she says. "You don't know. You ain't never met
the *mystère*. They look at you, they see a baby."

I take my hand from hers, and she lays still, her eyes
too wet, too large. Eyelids fluttering. She don't ever blink.

"You can gather for me. I need rocks. From the cemetery.
Enough to stack them in a pile. And cotton."

I want to walk out the room. Walk out the front door. Walk straight to the bayou, to the water, step on it, shimmering glass under my soles, and walk until I disappear over the horizon.

"Cornmeal. And rum."

"That's it? You just going to go? Soon as you seek this spirit? Just like that?"

My voice breaks: my face is wet.

"Why can't Pop do it?" I ask.

"You my baby." She breathes heavy, and the grate cracks and sinks to rusted stillness. "Like I drew the veil back so you could walk in this life, you'll help me draw it back so I can walk in the next."

"Mama, no—"

"Help me prepare." She sighs wetly then, and I reach out to wipe her face, the skin under the tears warm and wet and alive with salt and water and blood. "I don't want to be empty breath. Bitter at the marrow of my bones. I don't want that, Leonie."

"Mama."

The cup falls off the table, spreads a puddle of water around my shoes. The katydids clack in applause or disapproval, I don't know.

"Baby, please," Mama says.

Her eyes wild and wide. She moans, and what could be the pain moves through her, making her legs shuffle under the covers, then lay still: rough wind through bare winter branches. The morphine is not enough.

"Let me leave with something of myself. Please."

I nod, and then her scalp is under my hands, hot to the

touch, and I'm kneading and scratching like she did me, and her mouth is opening and closing in half pleasure, half pain. Opening and closing with what would be sobs, but she chokes them quiet. Relief again, but this time like a flood over dry plains, rushing from where I touch her head down her gaunt face, her sinewy neck, her flattened, etched chest, the dip of her stomach, the empty pot of her hips, the long, swollen black lines of her legs, to her flat feet. I wait, but nothing about her body changes. I expect her to lie slack, but it doesn't happen. I only know she's fallen asleep by her eyelids, the smooth marbles of them, relaxed. I leave her and pull the door behind me. Michael's in the shower. Pop is still out on the porch, flashing in the darkness. Someone has turned a lamp on in the living room, and Given's pictures, year after year of half smiles and angled legs like he's a moment away from jumping up and running, look down on me. A multitude of Givens. And I want him back so bad then, because I want to ask him: *What should I do?*

Michaela's on the second sofa in the living room. Michaela breathes openmouthed, huffing crumbs, and a half-eaten cracker falls from her hand to the floor. I don't even pick it up. In my room, my full bed seems as small and narrow as Mama's, and like her, I turn to the wall. I can feel her on the other side. She sears me. I couldn't see before, but now I feel it: her chest packed tight with wood and charcoal, drenched in lighter fluid, empty no longer—the pain the great blaze, immolating all.

Chapter 11

Jojo

I pulled Kayla out and ran to the porch, to Pop and his lighter, bright as a lighthouse beacon as it flashed in the dark. I skipped the steps and leapt up to the porch, coming to a fast stop in front of Pop like the rabbits that creep around the house when the sun sets: eating, stilling, then running only to freeze again. Saying to me: *So delicious, so delicious, but still, still, yes, I see you.* Calling to one another: *Run run run halt.*

"Son," Pop says, and grabs the back of my neck, his hand large and warm. My wrists feel raw. My mouth comes open and I breathe in. It sounds like a web of phlegm is in my throat. My eyes are burning and I shut my jaw and clench my teeth and try and try and try not to cry. I breathe again and it sounds like a sob. But I will not cry, even though I want to duck down with Kayla, want Pop to fold me in his arms and hug me to him, want to smash my nose in his shoulder so hard I can't breathe. But I don't. I feel his hand on me and rise on my toes so he presses harder. I can feel the heat of his fingers. He lets his hand run down my back to rest at the top of my spine, and I even imagine I can feel the whorl of his fingertips, the blood push back under his skin.

"Pop," I say.

Pop shakes his head, gives my back a little rub.

"Go put your sister to sleep. We'll talk about it tomorrow."

Me and Kayla eat crackers and pimento cheese and some smothered chicken legs Pop got in a skillet on the stove, wash it down with water. I think about putting Kayla in the tub but then I hear the shower, and when I hear Mam's and Leonie's voices in the room and see Pop's lighter flash on the porch, I know it's Michael. Kayla lays her head on my shoulder, grabs my hair, rolls my curls around her finger like a noodle.

"Mam? Pop?"

Her breathing gets slow and then she's slobbering on my throat and I know she's asleep, but I don't put her down because I'm looking at Richie, who's looking at Pop, who's looking out to the black yard, the far road. The boy's face shows in fire, and I ain't never seen that look before. Ain't never seen somebody look at someone else like Richie looks at Pop: all the hope on his face, plain in the circle of his mouth, his wide-open eyes, the wrinkle of his forehead. He step closer and closer to Pop, and he's a cat then, fresh-born, milk-hungry, creeping toward someone he'd die without. I lay Kayla down on the sofa and step out onto the porch. Richie follows.

"Riv," he says.

Pop flicks his light, lets it die, and flicks it again.

"Riv," Richie says again.

Pop pulls phlegm up his throat, spits off the porch. Looks down at his hands.

"It was quiet here without y'all," Pop says. "Too quiet." The lighter flame shows his quick smile, and then it's gone. "I'm glad y'all back."

"I didn't want to go," I say.

"I know," Pop says.

I rub my wrists and look at Pop's profile flare and fade in the light.

"Did you find it?" Pop asks.

Richie takes a step forward, and the look changes. Just a flicker. He glances between me and Pop and he frowns.

"The bag?" I say.

"Yeah," Pop says.

I nod.

"Did it work? It's a gris-gris bag."

I shrug.

"I think so. We made it. Got stopped by the police, though. And Kayla was sick the whole time."

Pop flicks the lighter, and the flame blazes for one half of a second, the fire bright and cold and orange, and then sparks out. Pop shakes the lighter by his ear and lights it again.

"Why can't he see me?" Richie asks.

"It was the only way I could send a little of me with y'all. With Mam"—Pop clears his throat—"sick. And that being a place I can't go back to. Parchman."

Richie is inches away from Pop. I can't even nod.

"See your face every day. Like the sun," Richie says.

Pop pockets the lighter.

"You left me," Richie says.

I slide closer to Pop. Richie reaches out a hand to touch Pop's face and sweeps his fingers across his eyebrows. Pop sighs.

"You better watch out, boy. He used to look at me like that," Richie says. His teeth are white in the black: tiny and sharp as a kitten's. "And then he left me."

I have to talk against the pockets of silence he creates whenever he speaks: the bugs shush for him with every word.

"Do she feel any better, Pop?"

Pop searches in his pocket for something and then stops. "Sometimes I forget. I forget I don't smoke," he says. He shakes his head in the darkness: I can hear the slide of his hair against the wall of the house he sits against. "She got worse, son," Pop says.

"You was the only daddy I ever knew." Richie's voice was soft as a mewl. "I need to know why you left me."

Richie is quiet. So is Pop. I slide down the wall and sit next to Pop on the porch. I want to lay my head on his shoulder, but I'm too old for that. It's enough to feel his shoulder rub mine when Pop passes a hand over his face, when he begins to flip the lighter over and under his knuckles, like he does sometimes with knives. The trees murmur around us, nearly invisible in the black. When I hear Leonie come walking out Mam's room, breathing as hard and deep as if she been running, pulling in her breaths like it hurt, I look up at the glittery sky and search for the constellations Pop taught me.

"The Unicorn," I say as I identify it. *Monoceros.* "The

Rabbit." *Lepus.* "The Great Snake." *Hydra.* "The Bull."
Taurus. I learned the proper names from a school library
book. I know Leonie must be looking out at the porch,
wondering what me and Pop are doing in the dark. "The
Twins," I say. *Gemini.* Leonie's room door opens and shuts,
and I see Michael babying Leonie when she was sick. I see
the way Leonie didn't do nothing when that cop put those
handcuffs on me. Richie looks at me like he knows what I'm
remembering, and then he sits across from us, curls over his
knees, wraps his arms around his back, makes a sound like
crying, and rubs what he can reach of his shoulder blades.

"My wounds were here. Right here. From Black Annie.
And you healed them. But you left and now you won't
see me."

I lay my head on Pop's shoulder anyway. I don't care. Pop
breathes deeply and clears his throat like he wants to say
something, but he doesn't. But he doesn't shrug me away.

"You forgot about the Lion," Pop says. The trees sigh.

When we go inside to lay down, Richie still sits, no
longer rubbing. Instead, he rocks back and forth, faintly,
and the look on his face is broken. Pop shuts the door. I
curl around Kayla on the sofa and try to lie still, to forget
the broken boy on the porch long enough to drift to sleep.
My spine, my ribs, my back: a wall.

"Jojo," she says, and pats my cheeks, my nose. Pulls open
my eyelids. I jump and wake and fall off the sofa, and Kayla
laughs, bright and yellow and shiny as a puppy that just got
the knack of running without tripping over her own legs.

Happy, like that. My mouth tastes like I've been sucking on chalk and licking oyster shells, and my eyes feel grainy. Kayla claps her hands and says, "Eat-eat," and it's then I realize that I smell bacon, and I realize I ain't smelled it ever since Mam got too sick to cook. I sling Kayla on my back and she clings. I think it's Leonie, and I feel something in me soften for a minute, rethink all the bad I thought about her the night before, and something inside me say: *But she do. She do.* And then I step into the narrow kitchen, and it ain't her; it's Michael. He got a shirt on that look like it's been washed and dried a size too small, the letters on it faded: it's one of mine. An old one Mam bought me to wear one Easter. He look all wrong at the counter, the way he reflect too much of the morning light.

"Y'all hungry?" he asks.

"Naw," I say.

"Yes," Kayla lisps.

Michael frowns at us.

"Sit down," he says.

I sit, and Kayla climbs up on my shoulder, straddles my neck, and beats my head like a drum.

Michael takes the pan off the gas, sets it to the side. He lets the fork he was turning the bacon with drip at his side, drip oil on the floor, as he turns to face us.

He crosses his arms, and the oil drips again. The bacon is still sizzling, and I wish he would take it out and drain it so me and Kayla can eat it hot.

"You remember that time we went fishing?"

I shrug, but the memory comes anyway, like someone pouring a bottle of water over my head. *Just the boys*, he'd

told Leonie, and she looked at him like he'd jabbed her in
her softest parts. And I thought he'd renege then, say *I'm
just joking*, but he didn't. It was late, but we went out to
the pier anyway and cast lines. He called me *son* with his
fingers, with the way he tied the sinkers and speared the
bait. Laughed at me when I wouldn't spear the worm, when
I wouldn't touch them. Michael waves his fork at me, and
he knows I'm lying. He knows I remember.

"We going to have more of that now."

He told me a story that night. As the fishermen gigged
for flounder with their lights and their nets, he said: *What
you know about your uncle Given?* And I told Michael that
Mam had showed me his pictures, talked about him, told
me he wasn't here no more, that he was in another world,
but hadn't told me what that meant. I told Michael that
because it was true, and because I wanted him to tell me
what she meant. I was eight then.

"That's what me coming home means."

Michael pokes the bacon. That night on the dock, he
didn't tell me how or why Uncle Given left. Instead, he told
me about working out on the rig. How he liked working
through the night so when the sun was rising, the ocean
and the sky were one thing, and it felt like he was in a perfect egg. How the sharks were birds, like hawks, hunting
the water. How they were drawn to the reef that grew up
around the rig, how they struck under the pillars, white
in the darkness, like a knife under dark skin. How blood
followed them, too. How the dolphins would come after
the sharks left, and how they would leap from the water
if they knew anyone was watching, chattering. How he

cried one day after the spill, when he heard about how all of them was dying off.

"For you and your sister," Michael says, and lifts the piece of bacon he's been poking at. It's already maroon and stiff, but he drops it back in the grease anyway.

I actually cried, Michael told the water. He seemed ashamed to say that, but he went on anyway. How the dolphins were dying off, how whole pods of them washed up on the beaches in Florida, in Louisiana, in Alabama and Mississippi: oil-burnt, sick with lesions, hollowed out from the insides. And then Michael said something I'll never forget: *Some scientists for BP said this didn't have nothing to do with the oil, that sometimes this is what happens to animals: they die for unexpected reasons. Sometimes a lot of them. Sometimes all at once.* And then Michael looked at me and said: *And when that scientist said that, I thought about humans. Because humans is animals.* And the way he looked at me that night told me he wasn't just thinking about any humans; he was thinking about me. I wonder if Michael thought that yesterday, when he saw that gun, saw that cop push me down so I bowed to the dirt.

Michael lifts out the bacon and drops it on the paper towel. That night on the pier, it was as if the pull of the moon on the water, the surge of the tide, drew the words from Michael. He said: *My family ain't always did right. Was one of my dumbass cousins that killed your uncle Given.* I didn't think Michael was telling me the whole story. Whenever Leonie or Mam or Pop talked about how Given died, they said: *He got shot.* But Michael said something different. *Some people think it was a hunting accident.* He wound up his line and got ready to cast again. *One day I'll tell you the whole story*, he said. Now the faint smell of charred bacon wafts through the air, and Michael pulls out another piece, this one curled black and hard.

Kayla claps and pulls at my hair in bunches, the same way she does grass.

"I just want you and Michaela to know that I'm here. I'm here to stay. And I missed y'all."

Michael pulls out the bacon and puts it on the plate. It's all black and burnt at the edges. Char and smoke fill the room. He runs to the back door and opens and closes it, trying to wave out the smoke. The grease hisses to silence. I don't know what he wants me to say.

"We call her Kayla," I say. I pull Kayla up over my head and set her in my lap. "No no no no," Kayla says, and starts kicking. My scalp burns. I bounce her on my knees, but that just pisses her off, and she straightens like an ironing board and slides off my legs onto the floor. Her whine escalates until it's like a police siren. Michael shakes his head.

"That's enough, young lady. Get up off the goddamn floor," he says. His door waving ain't doing much.

Kayla shrieks.

I kneel next to her, bend over, put my mouth next to her ear, and speak loud enough for her to hear me.

"I know you mad. I know you mad. I know you mad, Kayla. But I'm going to take you outside later, okay? Just sit up and eat, okay? I know you mad. Come here. Come here." I say this to her because sometimes I hear words between her howls, hear her thinking: *Why don't he listen why don't he listen I feel!* I put my hands under her armpits, and she squirms and wails. Michael lets the door slam, walks toward us, and then stops.

"If you don't get up off that floor right now, I'm going to whip you, you hear? You hear me, Kayla?" Michael says. He's turning red around his eyes and his throat as he waves his arms in the air, and the smoke just follows him like a blanket he's wrapped around himself. This makes him redder. I don't want him to hit her with the fork.

"Come on, Kayla. Come on," I say.

"Goddamnit," Michael says. "Michaela!"

And then he's hunching over both of us, and his arm whips out, whips in, and he's dropped the fork and he's smacking Kayla hard on the thigh, once and twice, his face as pale and tight as a knot. "What did I say?" He punctuates each word with a slap. Kayla's mouth is open, but she's not wailing: all of her seized up silent, eyes wide from the pain. I know this cry. I swing her up and away from Michael's hand, spin her around and to me. Her back under my rubbing hand, hot. My shushes don't mean nothing. I know what's coming. She lets go of the breath in one long thunderous wail.

"You ain't have to do that," I tell Michael. He's backing away, shaking his spanking hand like it's gone numb.

"I told her," he says.

"You ain't," I say.

"Y'all don't listen," Michael says.

Kayla writhes and shrieks, her whole body coiling. I turn my back on Michael, run out the back door. Kayla rubs her face into my shoulder and screams.

"I'm sorry, Kayla," I say, like I'm the one hit her. Like

she can hear over her crying. I walk around the backyard with her, saying it over and over, until the sun sits higher in the sky, bearing down on us, turning the muddy puddles to vapor. Burning the land dry, and burning me and Kayla: her to peanut butter, me to rust.

I apologize until she quiets to hiccups, until I know she can hear me. And I'm waiting, waiting for her small arms to fold around my neck, her head to drop to my shoulder, and I'm so intent on waiting for it that I don't even see the boy staring at us from the shadow of a tall, many-armed pine tree until Kayla's pinching my arms, saying, "No no, Jojo." In the bright light of the day the shadow swallows him: cool dark bayou water, the color of mud—tepid and blinding. He moves and he is of a piece with the darkness.

"He's slopping the pigs. Your pop."

I blow air hard out my nose, hope it will mean nothing to him. That he will not read it as wanting to talk, that he will not read it as not wanting to talk.

"He don't see me. How come he don't see me?"

I shrug. Kayla says: "Eat-eat, Jojo." All's quiet in the house, and for a stupid second I wonder why Leonie and Michael ain't arguing about him hitting Kayla. And then I remember. They don't care.

"You got to ask him about me," Richie says. He steps out of the shadow and he is a swimmer surfacing for air, glistening in the light. And in the light, he is just a skinny boy, too narrow in the bones, the fat that should be on him starved off. Somebody that I can feel sorry for until his eyes widen, and I squeeze Kayla so hard she cries out. The face he pulls is pinched with hunger and longing.

I shake my head.

"It's the only way I can go." Richie stops, looks up in the sky. "Even if he don't know me no more, don't care about me. I need the story to go." His afro is so long it sprouts from his head like Spanish moss. "The snake-bird says."

"What?" I say, and regret it.

"It's different here," he says. "So much liquid in the air. Salt. And a mud smell. I can tell," he says, "the other waters is near."

I don't know what he's talking about. Kayla says: "Inside, Jojo, inside."

Richie looks at me like he's seeing me the way I seen him. Like Pop looks at a hog at slaughtering time, measuring the meat. He nods.

"You get him to tell you the story. When I'm there," he says.

"No," I say.

"No?" he says.

"No."

Kayla is making little mewling sounds, pulling at my ears. "I want eat, Jojo," she says. "It's enough we brought you back. Brought you here. What if Pop don't want to tell that story? What if it's something he don't want to say?"

"Don't matter what he want. It matter what I need."

I jiggle Kayla. Turn in a circle, my feet sinking in the muddied grass. A cow lows nearby, and I hear: *Cool and becoming of green things, it is. All the new grass.* I stop my spin when I see his fierce eyes again.

"If I get the story, you going to leave, right? You going to go away?" My voice edging up to a question, high as a girl's. I clear my throat. Kayla pulls my hair.

"I told you I'm going home," Richie says. He takes a step before me but parts no grass, squelches no mud, and his face is furrowed: a piece of paper crumpled over on itself, a smudged ball hiding words.

"You ain't answer."

"Yes," he says.

He's not specific enough. If he had skin and bones, I'd throw something at him. Pick up the corner of a cinder block at my feet and hurl it. Make him say it. But he's not, and I don't want to give him cause to change, to stay lurking around the house, around the animals, stealing all the light, reflecting it back wrong: a warped mirror. Casper, the black shaggy neighborhood mutt, lopes around the corner of the house, freezes in a stop, and barks. *You smell wrong*, I hear. *Snake coming through water. The quick bite! Blood!* Richie walks backward into the shadows, his hands palms out.

"Fine," I say.

I let Casper's bark turn me around. Know the dog is keeping him pinned to the tree, so I can jog up the steps and into the house, even as I feel Richie's eyes tightening up my shoulders: a line pulled taut between us, razor-sharp.

The bacon is sitting on a plate lined with paper towels. I put Kayla on the table and pick the meat apart, peeling away what's still a little gummy, still a little brown. I hand the meat to her, bit by bit, to eat. She eats so much I'm left with the charred pieces. I can't even eat them, so I spit it all out and make us peanut butter and jelly sandwiches. Michael and Leonie are in her room, their door closed, conversation a muffled purr. Mam's room is still dark, her blinds closed. I walk in and open them and put the box fan in the window, turn it to a low hum. The air moves. Kayla marches around Mam's bed, singing one of her nonsense songs. Mam stirs, her eyes open to slits. I get her water from the faucet and a straw, hold it up to her so she can drink. She holds the water in her mouth longer than she should, puffing out her cheeks in a balloon, works her way up to swallowing, and when it's down, her face breaks like drinking that water hurt.

"Mam?" I say, pulling a chair up to her bed, propping my chin on my folded fists, waiting for her to put a hand on my head like she always does. Her mouth quivers to a frown, and she doesn't. I sit up, ask a question, and hope that it covers the pain behind my rib cage, which moves like a puppy turning in circles to settle and sleep. "How you feeling?"

"Not good, baby." She speaks in a whisper. I can hardly hear her over Kayla's gibberish song.

"The medicine ain't working?"

"Guess I'm getting used to it," she huffs. The pain pulling all the lines of her face down.

"Michael's back," I say.

She raises her eyebrows. I realize it's a nod.

"I know."

"He hit Kayla this morning."

Mam looks straight at me then, not at the ceiling or off into the air, and I know she done shrugged off her pain as well as she can and she's listening to me, hearing me the same way I hear Kayla when she's upset.

"I'm sorry," she says.

I sit up straight-backed as Pop and frown.

"No," she says. "You old enough to hear this."

"Mam?"

"Shush. I don't know if it's something I did. Or if it's something that's in Leonie. But she ain't got the mothering instinct. I knew when you was little and we was out shopping, and she bought herself something to eat and ate it right in front of you, and you was sitting there crying hungry. I knew then."

Mam's fingers is long and thin. Little more than bone. Cool to the touch, but I can still feel warmth like a small flame in the middle of her palm.

"I never wanted you to be hungry, Jojo. It's why I tried. I would do it if she wouldn't. But now—"

"It's all right, Mam—"

"Hush, boy."

Her fingernails used to be pink and clear. Now they seashells, salt-pitted and yellow.

"She ain't never going to feed you."

Her hands used to be muscled plump from all the work she did in the gardens, in the kitchen. She reaches out and I duck my head up under it so her palm on my scalp and my face in her sheets and I breathe it all in even though it hurts, and it smells like metal and sunburned grass and offal.

"I hope I fed you enough. While I'm here. So you carry it with you. Like a camel." I can hear the smile in her voice, faint. A baring of teeth. "Maybe that ain't a good way of putting it. Like a well, Jojo. Pull that water up when you need it."

I cough into the blanket, partly from the smell of Mam dying, partly from knowing that she dying; it catches in the back of my throat and I know it's a sob, but my face is in the sheets and nobody can see me cry. Kayla's patting my leg. Her song: silent.

"She hates me," I say.

"No, she love you. She don't know how to show it. And her love for herself and her love for Michael—well, it gets in the way. It confuse her."

I wipe my eyes on the sheets by shaking my head and look up. Kayla climbs in my lap. Mam's looking at me straight on. Her eyelashes ain't never grew back, which makes her eyes look even bigger, and when Mam blinks, I realize we got the same eyes. Her mouth works like she's chewing, and she swallows and grimaces again.

"You ain't never going to have that problem."

While she talking, I want to tell her about the boy. Want to ask her what she thinks I should do about Richie, but I don't want to worry her, don't want to put another thing on her when it's taking everything in her to bear the pain, which I can see now. Like she's floating on her back in an ocean of it. Like her skin's a hull eaten hollow with barnacles, and the pain's seeping through. Filling. Pushing her down and down and down. There's a sound outside the window, and the blades of the box fan cut it as it carries into the room. Chopping it up. Sound like a baby crying. I look out and Richie's passing under the window, letting out one little cry and then gulping in air. And then he's letting out another cry, this one sounds like a cat yowling, and then gulping in air. He touches the bark of each pine tree as he passes up underneath it.

"Mam? After you . . ." I can't bring myself to say it, so I talk around it. Richie moans. "After, where you going to go?" Richie stops and lists. He's staring up at the window, his face like a shattered plate; Casper barks off in the distance, a series of high yips. Richie rubs his neck. Mam looks at me and startles like a horse: for her, this means her eyelids jump.

"Mam?"

"You ain't let that dog get into my garden, did you, Jojo?" she whispers.

"No, ma'am."

"Sounds like he treed a cat."

"Yes, ma'am."

Kayla slides off my lap, walks to the fan, and puts her mouth on it. Every time Richie lets out a little catlike yowl, she hoots back. She laughs as the fan chops it up. Richie gets up, hands still kneading his throat, and walks, crooked and limping, right underneath the window.

"After, Mam," I say. "What happens when you pass away?"

I couldn't bear her being a ghost. Couldn't take her sitting in the kitchen, invisible. Couldn't take seeing Pop walk around her without touching her cheek, without bending to kiss her on her neck. Couldn't bear to see Leonie sit on her without seeing, light up a cigarette, blow smoke rings in the warm, still air. Michael stealing her whisks and spatulas to cook in one of the sheds.

"It's like walking through a door, Jojo."

"But you won't be no ghost, huh, Mam?" I have to ask even though I know the telling hurts her. Even though I feel like speaking's bringing her leaving closer. Death, a great mouth set to swallow.

Richie is rubbing the screen, his hand sliding from side to side. Kayla giggles.

"Can't say for sure. But I don't think so. I think that only happens when the dying's bad. Violent. The old folks always told me that when someone dies in a bad way, sometimes it's so awful even God can't bear to watch, and then half your spirit stays behind and wanders, wanting peace the way a thirsty man seeks water." She frowns: two fishhooks dimpling down. "That ain't my way."

I rub Mam's arm and the skin slides with my finger. Too thin.

"That don't mean I won't be here, Jojo. I'll be on the other side of the door. With everybody else that's gone before. Your uncle Given, my mama and daddy, Pop's mama and daddy."

There's a growl and a hacking bark come from underneath the house, from underneath the floorboards, and I know Casper's back and in the crawl space between the cinder blocks: a black shadow in the dusty dark.

"How?"

"Because we don't walk no straight lines. It's all happening at once. All of it. We all here at once. My mama and daddy and they mamas and daddies." Mam looks to the wall, closes her eyes. "My son."

Richie jerks away from the window and backs up, stumbling like an old man. His arms out in front of him. Casper saying: *Wrong! No smell! Wingless bird. Walking worm. Back!* I stop rubbing. Mam looks back at me like she can see me clear through the pain. Like she looked at me when I was younger and I lied to her when I got caught having a who-can-pee-the-furthest-up-the-wall contest in the boys' bathroom at school.

"You ever seen something like that? Something like a ghost?" Mam wheezes. "Something you thought was strange?"

Richie's climbing the tree like a rope. Gripping the young pine with his insoles, pushing, his hands flat to the feathered bark. Inching up. Swinging his leg around and sitting on a low branch, his arms and legs still wrapped around the trunk. The tree holding him like a baby. He yelps at Casper.

"No, ma'am."

"I ain't never have the talent for it. Seeing the dead. I could read people, read the future or the past in they bodies. Know what was wrong or needed by their songs: in the plants, in the animals, too. But never saw the dead. Wanted it so bad after Given died—"

Richie's yelp slides into a humming. He's singing to Casper, and there are words in it but I can't understand them, like language flipped inside out. A skinned animal: an inverted pelt. I can't help it. I gulp against the feeling I want to throw up all the food that I ever ate. Kayla's rubbing the screen like Richie did, back and forth. Humming.

"No, ma'am."

"But you could. You could have it. The vision."

Mam turns her head to one side, hearing Richie's song. A grimace, like if she could move without pain, she'd be shaking her head no.

"Is there something outside?"

I shake my head for her. Casper whines.

"You sure?"

The blades cut Richie's song. I can feel every wave of his dark crooning on my skin: a bad touch. Leonie slapping my face. Michael punching me in my chest. An older boy named Caleb who sat next to me in the last seat on the bus and put his hand on my lap and squeezed my dick before I elbowed him in the neck and the bus driver wrote me up when Caleb fell into the aisle, choking. All bad.

"No, ma'am," I say. I will not sink her.

Chapter 12

Richie

Riv hugs them even when he's not in the same room with them, even when he's not touching them. The boy, Jojo, and the girl, Kayla. Riv holds them close. He sees that they eat in the morning: oatmeal and sausages. He cuts little slivers of butter and slides them into the steaming insides of the biscuits he mixes and kneads and bakes. The butter melts and oozes out of the sides, and I would give anything to taste bread made with such care: I imagine it moist and crumbly. Kayla smears butter over her face, and Riv laughs at her. Jojo has food at the side of his mouth, and Riv tells him to clean it off. Then they go off to Riv's garden, where they pick strawberries and blackberries and weed until the sun is high. They eat the berries from the bush. I expect to see a winged shadow over them, but there is nothing but this: the garden, green and sweet. Life-giving flowers, ushering forth sweetness from fruit. Jojo sits on his haunches and chews. I bend over him.

"Tell me," I say, "what it taste like."

He ignores me.

"Please."

He swallows, and I can read the answer in his face. *No.* How he holds the deliciousness inside him, a rich secret.

"I want to remember," I say. "Ask Riv. Ask him to tell you."

"Enough," Jojo says, pulling at a weed with a deep root.

"What you say?" Riv asks. He whips the weeds from the soil like knives through cake.

"I done had enough berries," Jojo says. "I'm full." He looks through me and bends to pick at stray grass.

Leonie and Michael leave without walking out to the garden. The red car cranks to life and growls down the road, and they disappear in the tunnel of trees. I think about climbing into the car with them, just to see where they go, but I don't. I follow Jojo and Riv and Kayla instead. I walk in the boy's footsteps, and I watch. I watch the way Riv ushers them around furrows and troughs, how he cooks them beans for dinner, the way he makes sure they are clean when they lie down to sleep. Watching this family grabs me inside, twists, and pulls tight. It hurts. It hurts so much I can't look at it, so I don't. I go outside. The night is cloudy. I want to burrow into the earth, to sleep, but I'm so close. I'm so close, I can hear the sound of the waters the scaly bird will lead me over tumbling with the wind. So I crawl under the house instead, and I lie in the dirt under the living room where they all sleep, making a cot of the earth. And I sing songs without words. The songs come to me out of the same air that brings the sound of the waters: I open my mouth, and I hear the rushing of the waves.

*   *   *

This is what I see:

Across the face of the water, there is land. It is green and hilly, dense with trees, riven by rivers. The rivers flow backward: they begin in the sea and end inland. The air is gold: the gold of sunrise and sunset, perpetually peach. There are homes set atop mountain ranges, in valleys, on beaches. They are vivid blue and dark red, cloudy pink and deepest purple. They are yurts and adobe dwellings and teepees and longhouses and villas. Some of the homes are clustered together in small villages: graceful gatherings of round, steady huts with domed roofs. And there are cities, cities that harbor plazas and canals and buildings bearing minarets and hip and gable roofs and crouching beasts and massive skyscrapers that look as if they should collapse, so weirdly they flower into the sky. Yet they do not.

There are people: tiny and distinct. They fly and walk and float and run. They are alone. They are together. They wander the summits. They swim in the rivers and sea. They walk hand in hand in the parks, in the squares, disappear into the buildings. They are never silent. Ever present is their singing: they don't move their mouths and yet it comes from them. Crooning in the yellow light. It comes from the black earth and the trees and the ever-lit sky. It comes from the water. It is the most beautiful song I have ever heard, but I can't understand a word.

I am gasping when the vision passes. The dark underbelly of River's house looms before me: creaking then silent. I look to my right and see a flash of the water, the rivers, the wilderness, the cities, the people. Then darkness. I look to my left and see that world again, and then it is gone. I claw at the air, but my hands strike nothing; they rend no doorways to that golden isle.

Absence. Isolation. I keen.

When I leave the crawl space as the sun rises, Leonie and Michael are slamming car doors and walking toward the house. The trees are still and silent in the blue dawn light, the air even wetter than the day before. The sun is a hint of shining light through the trees. The sound of the water is strongest now: that other place hovers at the edge of my vision. As they half walk, half stumble together, Leonie looks over her shoulder like someone walks there, on her right, behind her. I dart forward because I see a flash. For a breath, someone is there, someone with a face like Jojo's, lanky and tall like Riv, someone with the same eyes as the saltwater woman who lays in the bed. And then, nothing. Only air. Leonie and Michael stop at the door, hug and murmur, while I circle the spot where I saw the flash. The air feels like needles.

"You need to sleep, sugar baby," Michael says.

"I can't. Not yet," Leonie says.

"Just lay down with me."

"I got something to do."

"Really?"

"I'll be back," Leonie says. They kiss and I turn away. Something about the way Michael grips the back of her neck and Leonie palms his face seems desperate. So desperate and needy it demands privacy. He disappears into the house, and she walks down the side of the road. I cannot help but follow her. We walk single file under the overarching oaks, the cypress, the pines. The road is so old it's almost been beat to gravel. Every so often, there is a house, silent and shut: in some, people speak in low voices, brew coffee, cook eggs. Rabbits and horses and goats graze for their morning feed: some of the horses come to the lips of their yards, raise their heads above their fences, and Leonie brushes their wet noses with her palm as she walks past. The houses come a little closer together. Leonie crosses the street and I see it: a graveyard. The headstones are half-ovals dug into the earth. Some have pictures on them, pictures of the dead once living. She stops in front of a grave nearer the front of the cemetery, where the newly dead are buried, and as she sinks to her knees in front of it, I see the boy I saw over Leonie's shoulder this morning, but now he is etched into marble, and under the picture of his face, a name: Given Blaise Stone. Leonie pulls a cigarette from her pocket and lights it. The smell of it is soot and ash.

"You ain't never here."

Birds are awaking in the trees.

"Would you do it, Given?"

They rustle and turn.

"She's giving up."

They chirp and alight.

"Would you?"

The birds swoop over our heads. They chatter one to the other.

"Would you give her what she wants?"

Leonie is crying now. She ignores the tears, lets them fall

from the blade of her chin to her chest. When they freckle the skin of her collarbone, only then does she wipe them off.

"Maybe I'm too selfish."

A small gray bird lands at the edge of the plot. It needles the earth, twice, feeling for breakfast. Leonie sighs, and it catches and bubbles into a laugh.

"Of course you won't come."

She bends and picks up a stone embedded in the dirt above Given's grave, and she untucks her shirt, holds the hem, and puts the rock into the pocket made by the hanging material. She stands and talks to the air, and the bird hops and flitters away.

"What did I expect?"

Leonie wanders among the headstones, bending and collecting rocks from all the graves, from those just beginning to gather on raw earth, to those at the center and back of the graveyard, where the stones are wind- and water-worn, the names shallow etchings. The birds wheel up in a great flock in the sky, away to find richer earth. When Leonie walks home, the basket made by the front of her shirt is heavy with rocks, and she cries. The long road is quiet. Her tears darken the stone. They are still wet when she walks into the house, past Jojo and Riv and Kayla, still asleep in the living room, into her mother's room. The smell in that room is all salt: ocean and blood. She kneels and lets them tumble out and onto the floor, looks at the saltwater woman, who has startled awake, and says:

"Okay."

The tears and the ocean and the blood could burn a hole through the nose. The saltwater woman, the woman

Leonie crawls toward over the rocks as she says, "Mama, Mama," looks at Leonie with so much understanding and forgiveness and love that I hear the song again; I know that singing. I have heard it from the golden place across the waters. A great mouth opens in me and wails; I am an empty stomach.

The scaly bird lands on the windowsill and caws.

Chapter 13

Jojo

Last night, Richie crawled under the house and sang. I listened to it rise up through the floor, and I couldn't sleep. Pop turned his back to us as he slept and coughed, over and over again. Kayla woke to whimpering every half hour, and I shushed her over the sound of the singing. We all slept late, but Pop has risen by the time I get up from the sofa. Kayla throws her arm over where I slept, and I pull the sheet over her. It's almost noon when I walk out to the yard, to see the boy crouched in the tree outside Mam's window. Somewhere out in the back, I hear Pop's axe swish and thud.

"Come on," I whisper.

I don't look up at the tree when I say it, don't look at the boy inching down, dropping and making no noise, raising no dust. If he was a real boy, the bark would come off in little papery flakes, fall like dry rain. But it doesn't. He stands next to me, curved at the shoulders. He knows I'm talking to him. I lead him across the sun-washed yard and back into the shadows of the woods, where Pop is. A sound like hammering pops and rings in the silence. And again. Pop is beating something. I mean to walk like him: head up, shoulders straight, back a plank, but I find my head down, back curled. All of me drooping. Whenever Pop done told me his and Richie's story, he talked in circles. Telling me the beginning over and over again. Telling me the middle over and over again. Circling the end like a big black buzzard angles around dead animals, possums or armadillos or wild pigs or hit deer, bloating and turning sour in the Mississippi heat.

Pop's banging apart one of the old pens: hitting a corner of it with a sledgehammer until it buckles and folds, already half buried in the dirt. I stop, and Richie walks two steps more and stops. I can't decide whether he is eating the sun or shrugging it off; either way, it's like his shadow is laid over his skin, a dark mask from head to toe, and it walks with him. His hair is the longest I've ever seen it, and it stands up from his head like parasitic moss. Pop swings the hammer down and it cracks, the splinters turned to shards. His sweat is a glaze.

"Termites got in it. Eating it hollow," Pop says. "Won't keep nothing in and nothing out once they done with it."

"You need help?" I ask.

"Kick these boards together," Pop says.

He swings the sledgehammer again, splinters the wood at the joints. I kick the logs to herd them to a pile: where my foot hits, dust rises. Termites spin and flutter through the air, swarming. Their white wings flashing. Pop swings again. Grunts.

"Pop?"

"Yeah."

"You never told me the end to that story."

"What story?"

"About that boy, Richie."

The hammer hits the dirt. Pop never misses. He sniffs and swings the sledgehammer like a golf club, testing its weight. Feeling the swing. A termite lands on my cheek and I swat it off, try not to frown, to keep my face smooth as Pop's.

"What's the last piece I told you?"

"You said he was sick. He'd just got whipped and he was hot and throwing up. You said he said he wanted to go home."

Richie stands untouched by the termites. They waft away from him on an invisible wind. *Find us,* they say. I brush them away with my whole hand, but Pop flinches and flicks them with two fingers.

"That's what I said," Richie says, so low his voice could be the brush of my hand across my face, Pop's finger along his eyebrow.

Pop nods.

"He tried to escape. Well, naw, he ain't try. He did it."

"He broke out?"

Pop swings. The wood cracks and crumbles.

"Yeah," Pop says. He kicks at the wood, but there's no force in it.

"So he went home?"

Pop shakes his head. Looks at me like he's trying to figure out how tall I am, how big my hands, how long my feet. I can wear his shoes now: sometimes when he sends me on errands when it's raining outside, I put on the boots he keeps just inside the back door at the bottom of the pantry. I look at him and raise my eyebrows. Tell him without saying it: *I can hear this. I can listen.*

"Was a gunman named Blue that did it. It was a baseball Sunday; there was visitors. Some good-time girls, some men's wives came. But Blue ain't never had nobody. Called him Blue because he was so dark he shined like a plum in the sun, on the line. But he wasn't right in the head; that's why none of the women would talk to him. Wouldn't take no visits with him. So he caught one of the women inmates out by the outhouses, and dragged her off into a stand." Pop stops, looks back at the house.

"What he do?" I say.

"He raped her," Pop says. "She was a strong woman, hands near as callused as his from all the picking and sewing she did, but she wasn't no match for him. Hit anybody in the head hard enough, it knock them out. Her face—you could barely recognize her. And maybe nothing would have happened to Blue for doing it if she hadn't been the sergeant's wife's favorite. Always the one she called to hang wash and scrub floors or mind the kids. Blue had enough brains to know that. So he left her there, striped skirt up around her head, covering her bloody face, that fabric turning muddy and red. Left her breathing bubbles. To run. But before he could get away good, he found Richie. I don't know where. Whether Richie was around the kitchens or the bathrooms or taking tools from one place to the next, but when Blue lit out, Richie was with him."

"I found them," Richie says. "He was climbing up off her. Big bloody hands. Was one of the strongest gunmen;

he could outpick most everybody. He say to me: *You want a face like hers, boy?* I told him no. And he waved one of them big hands and said: *Come.* Part of me went because I didn't want him to turn my face red like hers. And part of me went because I was sick of that place. Because I wanted to go."

The woods around us are a great dark green tangle: oaks reaching low and wide, vines tangled around trunks and drooping from branches, poison sumac and swamp tupelo and cypress and magnolia growing up around us in a circular wall.

"You went after them?" I ask.

Richie's leaning toward Pop so far that if he were alive, he'd have fell. His jaw works from side to side, his teeth grinding against each other.

"Yes." Pop squeezes the hammer so hard his knuckles whiten, and then he lets his hands loose. He squeezes again, lets his hands loosen.

"Yes," Richie says. "Yes."

A crane cuts the air, gray and pink-kneed, overhead. It doesn't squawk or call. It says nothing.

"What happen?"

Pop measures me again. I push my shoulders back, make sure my chin stays hard.

"Jojo?"

I nod.

"A man like Blue? Is a man like Hogjaw."

Hogjaw: the big, brutal White man who worked with Pop and the dogs. Pop swings and another corner of the pen collapses.

"Got no regard for life. Any life."

Richie opens and closes his mouth. Works his tongue between his teeth. It is as if he is eating air.

"I had to track them."

Swallowing Pop's words.

"Less mind was paid to the women on Sundays. Was five hours before anybody found her, realized Blue and Richie was missing, before the sergeant put it all together," Pop says. "That's enough time to run them fifteen miles to the edge of Parchman. To get back to the free world. The warden yelling at everybody, his clothes wet as if he'd went swimming in them. *A White woman next!* he said."

"It was enough time," Richie says. His voice grating and hollow as a frog's croak. Starved for rain. "He ran so fast. Sometimes I had to follow him by sound. Him talking to hisself the whole time. Not hisself. His mama. Telling her he was coming home. That he wanted her to sing for him. *Sing for your son,* he said. *Sing.*"

The hammer whistles through the air. The termites writhe in their ruined home.

"I wasn't fast enough. He came up on a girl fetching water from a spring. Knocked her down," Pop says. "Ripped her dress clean down the front. She ran home, holding it like that. Little White girl with red hair. Told her daddy some crazy nigger attacked her."

"I stopped him," Richie says. "Hit him with a tree limb. Hard enough to get him off her. Hard enough to get me punched in the face."

"Word was out by then. Richie and Blue had run long

and far enough for the sun to set, and White folks was gathering. All the menfolk. Little boys younger than Richie in overalls hanging by one strap on the backs of pickups. What seemed like a thousand of them. Look like their faces had a red mist on them in the truck lights, but everything else about them look black in the dark: clothes, hair, eyes. I could see it on them: the way every damn one of them seemed to lean forward, eager as hounds to the hunt. And the laughing. They couldn't stop. And I knew that when it came to the two of them, when it came to Blue and Richie, they wasn't going to tell no difference. They was going to see two niggers, two beasts, who had touched a White woman."

Richie has never been so still, so silent. His mouth frozen open. His eyes wide and black. He is balanced on his toes, and he could be made of stone. But every part of Pop moves: his hands as he speaks; his shoulders folding forward as softly as a flower wilting at the hottest part of the day. I've never seen them do that. His face, all the lines of his face, sliding against each other like the fault lines of the great fractured earth. What undergirds it: pain. The sledgehammer fallen.

"I ran them dogs past the fence, past the edge of Parchman, out into the Delta. Through the flat plain, the earth turned to scrub and balded from them black hands. All them black hands. The dirt black as them hands and crumbly. The way it gives under the foot, leaves clear tracks. I followed their tracks, and the dogs followed the smell, through the bristly stands of trees, over them deceitful fields, past the spring and the shacks to more fields, more shacks with

White men and boys gathering and swarming. Moving like one thing. To kill."

Pop ducks his head, wipes his sweat on his shoulder. He stomps his foot and it is like a horse's, warning before it kicks.

"What happen?" I prod.

Pop doesn't look up.

"Warden and sergeants was in cars on the road, following the dogs. Their baying. All them men roaming, had they dogs out, too, and it was a boy who stumble across Blue. He was up a tree in one of them stands to the west. I had to squint at the shouts that came up when they found him. They started firing off they rifles, and the warden and sergeants and trusty shooters rode that way. I heeled my dogs. Waited. Because they wasn't pointed west. They was pointed north, and I knew it was Richie they followed. Wasn't five minutes passed before I saw the bonfire they lit, and I knew what was happening. I knew before I even heard Blue start screaming."

Richie blinks. His fingers splayed like a bird's wings. His blinks start slow, but as Pop talks, they get faster until they're blurred like a hummingbird, and all I see are his eyes, his black eyes, with a thin scrim over them.

"One of the trusties told me later they was cutting pieces of him off. Fingers. Toes. Ears. Nose. And then they started skinning him. That's when I followed the dogs, making them quiet, across that sky turning from blue to black, across them fields, to another stand of trees. And Richie hunched down at the base of one, cupping his black eye. Crying. Nose up, listening to Blue and the crowd."

Richie makes fists, lets them go. Makes fists. Spreads his fingers to wings.

"They was going to do the same to him. Once they got done with Blue. They was going to come for that boy and cut him piece from piece till he was just some bloody, soft, screaming thing, and then they was going to string him up from a tree."

Pop looks at me. Every piece of him aquiver.

"He wasn't nothing but a boy, Jojo. They kill animals better than that."

I nodded again. Richie is winding his arms around himself, hugging tighter and tighter, his arms and fingers growing incredibly long.

"I said: *It's going to be all right, Richie*. He said: *You going to help me? Riv, which way should I go?* I heeled the dogs. Held out my hands to him, light side out. Moved slow. Soothed him. Said: *We gone get you out of this. We gone get you away from here.* Touched his arm: he was burning up. *I'm going home, Riv?* he asked. I squatted down next to him, the dogs steady yipping, and I looked at him. He had baby hair on the edge of his scalp, Jojo. Little fine hair he'd had since he sucked at his mama's tit. *Yes, Richie. I'm a take you home,* I said. And then I took the shank I kept in my boot and I punched it one time into his neck. In the big vein on his right side. Held him till the blood stopped spurting. Him looking at me, mouth open. A child. Tears and snot all over his face. Shocked and scared, until he was still."

Pop speaks into his knees. Richie's head has tilted back until he is looking at the sky, at the great blue wash of it beyond the embrace of the trees. His eyes widen more, and his arms snap out and his legs spread and he doesn't even see me and Pop, but he is looking at everything beyond us, past the miles we drove in that car, past the point where the pine trees turn to field and cotton and just-budding spring trees, past the highways and towns back to the swamps and stands of trees hundreds of years old. At first I think he is singing again, but then I realize it is a whine that rises to a yell that rises to a scream, and the look on his face is horror at what he sees. I squint and barely hear Pop through Richie's keening.

"I laid him down on the ground. Told the dogs to get. They smelled the blood. Tore into him."

Richie roars. Casper is somewhere out on the road, furious, barking. The pigs are squealing. The horse is stamping its pen. Pop is working his hands like he doesn't know how to use them. Like he's not sure what they can do.

"I washed my hands every day, Jojo. But that damn blood ain't never come out. Hold my hands up to my face, I can smell it under my skin. Smelled it when the warden and sergeant came up on us, the dogs yipping and licking blood from they muzzles. They'd torn his throat out, hamstringed him. Smelled it when the warden told me I'd done good. Smelled it the day they let me out on account I'd led the dogs that caught and killed Richie. Smelled it when I finally found his mama after weeks of searching, just so I could tell her Richie was dead and she could look at me with a stone face and shut the door on me. Smelled it when I made it home in the middle of the night, smelled it over the sour smell of the bayou and the salt smell of the sea, smelled it years later when I climbed into bed with Philomène, put my nose in your grandmother's neck, and breathed her in like the scent of her could wash the other away. But it didn't. When Given died, I thought I'd drown in it. Drove me blind, made me so crazy I couldn't speak. Didn't nothing come close to easing it until you came along."

I hold Pop like I hold Kayla. He puts his face in his knees and his back shakes. Both of us bow together as Richie goes darker and darker, until he's a black hole in the middle of the yard, like he done sucked all the light and darkness over them miles, over them years, into him, until he's burning black, and then he isn't. There is soft air and yellow sunlight and drifting pollen where he was, and me and Pop embracing in the grass. The animals are quieting in grunts and snorts and yips. *Thank you*, they say. *Thank you thank you thank you*, they sing.

Chapter 14

Leonie

When I got home with my load of cemetery rocks, Michael left in my car. The weight of the stones in my shirt was heavy, remind me of what it felt like to carry Jojo and Michaela, to bear another human being in my stomach. After I picked up the stones I'd dropped in Mam's room, I bang out the door to find Phantom Given. His head is cocked to the side, and he's looking down the shotgun line of the house, through the living room, through the kitchen, out the back door. He's listening. I stop where I am.

"What?" The word comes out like a little slung dart. Even though I know it must be the dregs of the meth I swallowed, I still feel sober as a lead weight, and here Given is, burnished and tall, in the living room. His mouth is moving like he's repeating something that someone else is saying, and if he could speak, it would be a mumble. Whatever he's hearing, whatever he's mimicking, makes him run to the open doorway of the room, to pause on the threshold of the kitchen, to bow his head and grip the frame. Last time I saw him here, he was living. The blood beating through him like drums. He and Pop had just argued over something, over the Nova or his middling grades or the fact that besides the bow and arrow, he didn't seem to have any passion for anything besides playing football. *You need direction, son,* Pop had said to him. Given had been sitting on the couch, and he watched Pop walk out the back door, slumped down, and winked and whispered at me: *And you need to take the stick out your ass, Pop.*

Given-not-Given's shoulder blades bunch together like fists under his shirt. He shakes his head at me once. Then again at whatever he hears.

"I'm going crazy," I tell myself. "I'm going fucking crazy."

I walk past Given to look out the screen door. Pop and Jojo are hunched down in the backyard, in the dirt by the pigpen, talking. I can't hear anything from this far away, but Given can, and whatever he hears makes his head shake faster and faster, his fist punch noiselessly, once and again, in the molding. It leaves no mark. I expect to feel the brush of his T-shirt against my arm when I walk past, but feel nothing but misty cool. Given's mouth moves, and I can make out what he's saying without words. *Pop,* he mouths. *Oh, Pop.* I squint. It looks like Jojo is rubbing Pop's back. Hugging Pop, and I realize I ain't never seen Pop on the ground before if he wasn't pushing a seed into it or wrestling some animal or pulling up weeds.

A dog bark rips through the creaking kitchen, and Given starts and turns to me, mouths one word, hands open and beckoning me like he could pull an answer from me. *Who?* he mouths. *Who is that?* He runs to the screen door. Casper barks again, a sound that shies up to a panicked yip. Pop seems to be sinking, Jojo holding him up. I don't know this world. Given holds his arms up in front of him like he could block something. I wonder if this vision of my brother is an aftershock of yesterday's high, a shaky meth tremor that comes once, if the massive hit I swallowed has unsewn my body and mind, unseamed me. Given is still there. As the dog's bark rises, Given bleeds. I don't see wounds, but he bleeds anyway, from his neck, from his chest. Where he was shot. He braces himself on the wood frame of the closed screen door, his arms and legs straining. Something is pulling him outside. Pop and Jojo are curled in two, and the dog is still barking, but I don't see nothing, don't see anything until I blink, and like a dark flash at the corner of my eye I see a churning black cloud come to earth in the yard, but then I blink again and it's gone. Given slumps and runs his hands up and down the doorsill; he did this when he was alive, wore the wood of the sills in the house smooth with his rubbing. He freezes and looks at me, and I wish he was alive, was flesh, because I'd kick him. Kick him for not being able to speak. Kick him for seeing whatever it is he sees or hears out in the yard and not sharing that with me. Kick him for being here, now, for taking up space in the waking, sober world, right before me. For knocking the world sideways—birds flying into glass windows, dogs barking until they piss themselves in fear, cows collapsing to their rumps in fields and never rising—still winking and smiling, every dimple and tooth declaring the joke. For dying. Always for that. Given shakes his head again, but this time, slowly—but still, his face blurs. I reach out and step toward him, to push him, maybe, to see if I can feel his brown arms, the calluses on his hands like patches of concrete, but Michaela's cry pierces the air, and he's gone.

Michaela's standing on the sofa, walking from one end of it to another, yelling. Sleep-matted hair, sleep-swollen face. Her little legs clumsy with waking, she trips and falls face-first and mouths the cushion.

"The boy, the black bird," she sobs.

I kneel next to the sofa, pat her hot little back.

"What boy, Michaela?"

"The black bird. The Black boy."

She stands, runs to the arm of the sofa farthest from me, straddles, and slides off.

"He flies!"

She wakes up like that all the time, trailing the blankets of her dreams behind her. She's still sleepy. I catch her under one armpit, swing her up, put her head down on my shoulder.

"Go back to sleep," I say.

When Michaela kicks, her toes are little shovels digging into my belly, trying to break the dirt of the softest part of me. It used to be my walk rocked her to sleep. She dreamed in my womb with sightless blue eyes. Now she flails, smashes my mouth with her hand, and will not let me hold her.

"He want Mam!" she screams, and at that my arms go dead, and Michaela slides down my front, noodle-limp. She lands running, straight to Mama's door, and knocks at it with her little fists. Each little thud married to a breathy whine. Her eyes rolling like a panicked colt's.

"Michaela." I kneel. "Ain't no man trying to take Mama nowhere." Her little knobby knees brush the wood as she hangs from the doorknob, trying to turn with her weight. What I say is mangled truth: no man wants to take Mama, but what she's tasked me to do will usher her away. I move to Michaela on my knees, floorboards grinding my bones, and I wonder at the fear spilling through my chest, scalding-hot grits. I wonder at my short, round toddler with her toes grazing the door, at the future and what it will demand of me. Of her. Michaela's fingers lose their grip on the knob, and I turn it, open it, point at Mama with an upturned palm. "See?"

I am not prepared to see.

Mama hangs half off the bed, half on, her toes on the floor, her legs bound up in sheets, twisted around her, stretched tensile and thin as rope here, wide and voluminous there: Mama caught like a prized sailfish. The one who sails through the air, silver and white, still with the silky feel of the salt water on her: the one who shivers in the sun and fights. It is colder than a spring morning warrants in the room, cold as a November morning, and yet Mama sweats and moans and kicks. Michaela hops into the room, sniffs the air, takes hesitant steps, and reaches to the ceiling. She breathes one little word, again and again.

"Bird," she says.

The room smells like Mama has been turned inside out. Like piss and shit and blood. Like intestines, a heartbeat away from rot. Her eyes are wild. Her arms are pinned in the sheets. Mama struggles to shrug them off.

"Mama?" I say, and my voice seems high and small as Michaela's. "Let me help."

"Too late," Mama says. "Too late, Leonie."

I have to grab her arm hard to free it. My fingers leave shallow ditches in a row in her flesh, my handprint visible on her with every touch. Mama moans. I try to touch lighter, to hurt less, but I can't.

"What you mean?" I say.

Mama is bleeding under the skin. Everywhere my hands touch, there is blood. Trenches in the sand filling with seawater. Underneath: doom.

Mama looks beyond me, to the corner where Michaela has seated herself, still except for the song she is singing as she squints and then glares at Mama. Mama's eyes skitter to my face, up to the ceiling, down at her ruined body. Away, away.

"I heard him," she whispers. "Thought it was a . . ." She pants. "Cat."

"Who, Mama?"

"Ain't never seen them. Sometimes heard them."

"What?"

"Like somebody talking three doors down. In another room."

I free one hand, balled to a fist.

"Said he'd come for me."

All these petals of blood.

"Ain't lè mistè." *No spirit. No God. No mystery.*

On her wrist.

"He lè mò." *The dead.*

Her forearm.

"Young. Full of piss and vinegar."

Rotting flowers.

"Vengeful as a beat dog."

Fruitfulness gone to seed.

"Pulling all the weight of history behind him."

Her breath whines.

"Like a cotton sack full of lead."

She's right.

"But still a boy."

I'm too late.

"Hungry for love."

The cancer done broke her.

"Says he want me to be his mama."

Broke her clean through.

"I always thought—"

Mama claws at my arm as I free her other hand.

"It would be your brother."

I stop.

"The first dead I see . . ."

I can't breathe.

"Would be him."

Given is in the corner of the room, stretched along the seam where the walls join. He looms over Michaela, rigid and fierce as Pop, and for the first time, I am afraid. In life, there was a joke in every line of him, humor that ran along the bones of him, that everyone read in the hang of his shoulders, the shake of his head, his smile. There is none now. The weight of time he never bore in life holds him rigid now, cloaks him somber, whittles him sharp as Pop. He shakes his head, and speaks.

"Not."

Michaela's little song sinks.

"Your."

Mama begins to fight me.

"Mother."

Mama looks beyond me, up to the cracked ceiling, pocked with thousands of little stalactites like the roof of a cave. Pop spent hours dipping a broom in paint and then stabbing the ceiling with the bristles, making circles and loops and swirls, shaping the paint into stars and comets. Mama opens and closes her mouth but makes no sound. I follow her gaze but don't see nothing but the ceiling, that sorry drywall, turning gray from humidity. But Michaela, who whispers her song and waggles her fingers like she does when she sings "Twinkle Twinkle Little Star," does.

"Not." And Given, who speaks, the planes of his face converging and turning sharp as knives, does.

"Your."

And Mama does. She rolls her eyes to the corner of the room where Given looms. She bares her teeth in something like a smile, something like a rictus.

"Mother," Given finishes.

Mama slaps me. Where her hand hit burns. She cuffs me with an open palm on the other side, and my ear throbs with blood. Her right fingers grab my cheek, dig into my eyebrow ridge, and she's holding my face straight, whispering against whatever is above us, at my back, whatever awful thing that's come for her. I hear a whisper above me.

"Come with me, Mama," he says. "Come on."

"No," she says.

Her fingers pull my eyelids up, up, painfully.

"Not my boy," she says.

Feel like she's peeling the skin.

"Given," she breathes.

I yank my head away.

"Baby. Please."

It's the word *baby* that makes me jump off the bed. Because I hear her say it now and I'm her baby again, soft-gummed and wet-eyed and fat, and she is whole and sweet-milked. Her hands fall away from me like husks from corncobs, land just as brittle and dry on the bed before she whips them up, faces them out palms up.

"No, boy. No," Given says.

I sweep the cemetery rocks from the floor where they've fallen, dumping them on the altar to join the rest of it I've already gathered. From the bathroom: cotton balls. From the cupboard: cornmeal. From my trip to the liquor store yesterday: rum.

"Say it," Mama says. She's let her hands fall. "The litany," she says again, and her breath rattles in her throat. She doesn't turn her head to the side, to look at the wall beyond me where Given stands, thrashing against some invisible thing that holds him there. Her mouth opens: a silent wail. Michaela is crying in a way I've never seen her cry before: mouth working, but no sound. There's no time. This moment done ate it all up: the past, the future. Do I say the words? I blink, and up on the ceiling there is a boy, a boy with the face of a toddler. I blink again, sand scouring my eye, and there is nothing.

"Mama," I choke, and it's as weak and wanting as a baby's. "Mommy." My crying and Mama's entreaties and Michaela's wailing and Given's shouting fill the room like a flood, and it must have been as loud outside as it is in here, because Jojo runs in to stand at my elbow and Pop's at the door.

"You got what you came for. Now get," Jojo says.

At first I think he's talking to me, but then he's looking through me and up, and I know who he's talking to. There's strength in his voice, so much that I'm speaking even as I'm crying and pulling Mama up to my heart.

"For Maman Brigitte, Mother of all the Gede. Mistress of the cemetery and mother of all the dead." I breathe hard and it is a ragged sob.

"No, Leonie," says Jojo. "You don't know." He glares up at the ceiling.

"Leonie," Mama chokes.

"Grande Brigitte, Judge. This altar of stones is for you. Accept our offerings," I say. Mama's eyes are steady rolling, steady rolling to the ceiling, where the boy with the smooth face hovered, needy and balled up like a baby.

"Shut up, Leonie. Please," Jojo says. "You don't see."

Mama's eyes steady rolling to the wall where Given has stopped thrashing. They turn to me, beseeching. "Enter," I say.

"Go," Jojo says. He looks up at where the boy flashed. "Ain't no more stories for you here. Nobody owe you nothing here." He raises a hand to Given, and it is as if Jojo has unlocked and opened a gate, because Given pushes through whatever held him.

"You heard my nephew," Given says. "Go, Richie."

I don't see anything, but something must have happened, because Given walks unbothered toward the bed. Pop has slid down the wall, all the upright parts of him crumbling as he looks at Mama, makes himself look at Mama, for once. He's been orbiting her like a moon, sleeping on the sofa with his back to the door, searching the yard and woods for pens and bins and machines to fix so he can repair in the face of what he cannot.

Mama's breath is a jagged wind, coming slower and slower. Her eyes lowered to slits. Her body: ruined and still. Jojo steps out of Given's way. He scoops Michaela, who's crying, "Uncle." Jojo swallows and looks right at Given. Jojo sees him. He recognizes him. He nods, and Given is Given again, only for a breath, because he smiles and there's the joke again in his dimple.

"Nephew," Given says.

Mama's breath slows to a choke. She looks at me, her face twisted.

"Enter. Dance with us," I whisper.

Given's next to the bed, climbing into it, curling around her, saying "Mama," saying, "I come for you, Mama," saying, "I come, Mama," and Mama takes one long, ripping breath, her breath and blood and spirit beating frantic as a moth caught in a spider's web, and then "Shhhh," Given says, "I come with the boat, Mama," and then he moves his hand over her face, from her air-starved chin to her flared nostrils to her eyes, open and open, looking from me to Given to Jojo and Michaela to Pop at the door and then back to Given. Given's hand flutters above her face like he is a groom and Mama is a bride and he has pulled the veil from her head and let it fall back so they can look upon each other with love, clear and sweet as the air between them. Mama bucks and goes still.

Time floods the room in a storm surge.

I wail.

* * *

We cry in chorus. Pop folded over in the door, me with Mama's warm nightgown still in my hands, and Michaela with her face smashed into Jojo's shoulder. But not Jojo. His eyes are shiny but nothing comes from them, not even when he asks:

"What did you say?"

I can't speak. Sorrow is food swallowed too quickly, caught in the throat, making it nearly impossible to breathe.

"Leonie!"

Anger spreads through me: oil over water.

"She asked," I say.

"Naw." Jojo bounces Michaela in his arms, looks at Mama like he's waiting for her to open her eyes, turn her head, say: *Silly Jojo.* "Your words. They let in a river. That's what took her and Uncle Given away."

"Yes." He doesn't understand what it means, to have the first thing you ever done right by your mama be to usher in her gods. To let her go.

Pop is sliding his way up the door to stand. But there's still a curve there at the top of his back: his shoulders a bowl. His head swings on his neck like a pendulum. His throat: broken.

"She did, Jojo." Pop's voice is the only thing about him with some hardness to it: a sheathed knife. "She couldn't bear that pain."

"Mam wouldn't leave us. Not even with Uncle Given."

Jojo gains what Pop's lost of his bearing. First, a brace across his thighs, all the bowlegged softness of his preadolescence dissolved to a granite stance.

"She did," I say.

Then across his chest, which makes his shoulders crow-bar straight.

"She said—" Jojo says.

"It was a mercy, son," Pop says.

And then the headpiece so that the baby face, the last of the milk fat, is steel-still, frozen for war. Only Jojo's eyes peer out, carrying some of the boy in them.

"What you want?" I ask. "To say I'm sorry?"

Those eyes.

"To say I ain't want to?"

I can't control my voice. It whistles, high and whip-thin. There is a rope of fire from my eyes, behind my nose, down my throat, and it coils in a noose in my stomach. Mama is still warm.

"'Cause I ain't. I did what she needed me," I say.

She could be sleeping. I ain't seen her face this smooth, without tension, in years. I want to slap her awake, for asking me to let her go. I want to slap Jojo, for looking at me like I had a choice. And I want to bring Given back from the dead and make him flesh again just so I can slap him, too, for leaving. For taking her. There's too much blank sky where a tree once stood. All wrong. The noose tightens.

"Nothing," Jojo says. "You can't give me nothing."

He looks at Mama when he says it, and I stop smoothing her hair back from her still face. And then he's looking at me and he's hard as Pop and soft as Mama. Censure and pity. I'm a book and he can read every word. I know this. He sees me. He knows it all.

"Girl," Pop says.

And then it stops tight and I am raging, hateful at this world, and I let Mama slide to the mattress and I stand and run at Jojo, who backs away, but he is not quick enough because I am there, and when I hit his face, pain cracks through my palm, pings through my fingers. So I do it again. And I do it again before I realize Michaela's squalling in his arms, scrambling up his chest, trying to get away from me. And Jojo's straight, straight as Pop, all the little boy gone from his eyes: the tide gone out, the sun scorching the residue of water away, leaving hot sand baking to concrete. And Pop's at my side, his body folding over me like a kite falling from the sky as he grabs both of my arms and pulls them together so that my palms touch.

"That's enough," Pop says. "No more, Leonie."

"You don't know," I say. "You don't!" Jojo's rubbing his face into Michaela's little shirt, and I want so much. I want to hit him again and I want to hold him to me and palm his head again like when he was a hairless baby and I want to tell Jojo, *We a family*, and I want to ask him: *What you seen, boy, what you seen?* But I don't do none of that. Instead, I yank away from Pop, walk past Jojo and Michaela, and leave Mama on the bed, her face up to the ceiling, her eyes open, all the warmth gone from out the middle of her. Cold at the heart, time worming its way through her hardening veins.

When Michael comes back, I'm on the porch. He ignores the steps and leaps to where I am sitting. The wood creaks when he lands, and I imagine it crumbling, dry-rotted and warped from the heat, me falling through where I sit on the floor down to the clay earth underneath, that opening up, a hole straight down: an endless well. It is the first hot day of the spring, a foretaste of the damnation that will suffuse the air in the summer, that will make everyone and everything bend.

"Baby?"

"Let's go."

"What? I just got back. I figured we could take the kids up to the river today."

"Mama's gone." I can't stop my voice breaking between the two words. Can't stop the cry that comes out of my mouth instead of the sigh.

Michael sits on the floor next to me, pulls me into his lap: arms, rump, legs, and all, so that I am a great baby, and I slump into him, knowing that he can bear me. Will bear me. I put my nose in his stubble-roughened neck.

"Let's go."

"Shhhh," he murmurs.

"Up to Al's."

Michael knows. He knows what I'm really asking for: the seed at the pulpy heart of the fruit.

"We can just leave."

To get high. To see Given again. Even as I think it, I know he won't come. That wherever he has gone with Mama is final. But the part that Mama looked at in pity across the table, that part hopes.

"We can't," he says.

"Please." The word is small and acid as a burp. It lingers

between us. Michael grimaces as if he can smell the horror and grief in it, all of it distilled to one pungent syllable.

"The kids."

The sky has turned the color of sandy red clay: orange cream. The heat of the day at its heaviest: the insects awoken from their winter slumber. I cannot bear the world.

"I can't," I say, and there are so many other words behind that. *I can't be a mother right now. I can't be a daughter. I can't remember. I can't see. I can't breathe.* And he hears them, because he rolls forward and stands with me, picks me up, and carries me off the porch to the car. He puts me in the passenger seat, closes the door, and climbs behind the wheel. The car shrinks the world to this: me and him in this dome of glass, all the hateful light and dogs shying into ditches and docile cows and crowding trees, the memory of my words, of Mama's gray paper face, of Jojo's and Michaela's reaction to my slaps, of Pop's shrinking, and of Given's second leaving. Our world: an aquarium.

"Just a ride," Michael says.

But I know that if I continue to ask, sour the air of the car with *pleases*, he will drive to Misty's, get her to call her friends up north, call Al, make one last call to Pop to say: *Just a few days.* That he will drive for hours into the black-soiled heart of the state, back toward the cage that held him, drive so far the horizon opens up like a shucked oyster shell. That if I ask, he will go. Because something in him also wants to leave his teary hug with his mother, his fight with his father, my death-crowded household,

behind. We move forward, and the air from the open windows makes the glass shudder, alive as a bed of mollusks
fluttering in the rush of the tide: a shimmer of froth and
sand. The tires catch and spit gravel. We hold hands and
pretend at forgetting.

Chapter 15

Jojo

I sleep in Leonie's bed now. I don't have to worry about her kicking me out of it, waking me up with a punch to the back, because she ain't never here. Not really. She come back every week, stay for two days, and then leave again. Her and Michael sleep on the sofa, both of them fish-thin, slender as two gray sardines, packed just as tight. They don't move when I walk past them out the door in the morning to bring Kayla to the Head Start bus. Some mornings they gone by the time I come back inside for my book bag. The long dent in the sofa the only way I know they was there.

They sleep on the sofa because Pop sleeps in Mam's room now. He got rid of the hospital bed the day we buried her. Dragged it out behind the house, into the woods, and burned it. Told me not to come back there, but I saw the smoke. Heard the flames slapping. Sometimes, at night, after Kayla done fell asleep on my shoulder, so deep her head's heavy as a cantaloupe, I walk to the kitchen to get a glass of water and I hear Pop through the door, hear his voice threading through the keyhole. Once I heard him clear through the wall. First I thought he was praying, but then, from the way his voice whipped up and down, I knew he wasn't. Sound like he was talking to somebody. I asked him the next day, when I got home from school and he was sitting in his usual spot, waiting on the porch with Kayla sitting next to him on the swing.

"Pop?"

He was shelling pecans. He looked up at me, but his hands kept working, kept breaking the shell into shards, prying the meat free. Every other half he'd get, he'd pass it to Kayla, and she'd pop the whole thing in her mouth, smile at me when she chewed.

"Was you talking to somebody last night?"

He paused, half a pecan in his hand. Kayla patted his arm, prodding.

"Pop," she said. "I want it, Pop."

He passed it to her.

"Did Leonie call?" I asked.

"No," he said.

"I should've known," I said, and spat off the porch into the sand. I wished she was there, imagined what it would feel like if I spat right at her. If she'd even notice.

"Don't," Pop said, and went back to shelling. "She's still your mother."

"Michael?" I said.

Pop brushed the bitter dust that rinds the meat from his hands and shook his head, and after that, if I heard him through the door or through the walls, his voice rising like smoke up into the night, I didn't even ask. Because in the swing of his head, the swish, the folding of his wrinkled neck, I saw him lying in the bed in the dark, staring up at the ceiling, looking where she looked when she died, his eyes staring, heard him calling her name, a name I hadn't heard said since before the cancer: *Philomène*. And then: *Phillie*. And then I knew what he was doing when he thought us asleep. Something like praying, but not to God. How he was speaking and asking and searching the craters and the mountains in the ceiling. Searching for Mam. Kayla patted his arm again, but she didn't ask for another pecan. Just rubbed him like Pop was a puppy, flea-itching and half bald, starved for love.

Sometimes, late at night, when I'm listening to Pop search the dark, and Kayla's snoring beside me, I think I understand Leonie. I think I know something about what she feels. That maybe I know a little bit about why she left after Mam died, why she slapped me, why she ran. I feel it in me, too. An itching in my hands. A kicking in my feet. A fluttering in the middle of my chest. An unsettling. Deeper. It turns me awake every time I feel myself slipping. It tosses me like a ball through the air. Around 3 a.m., it lets me drop, and I sleep.

I don't feel it during the day. Mostly. But something about the way the sky turns peach when the sun's on its way down, sinking into the horizon like a rock into water, brings it back. So I take to walking when I know it's coming. But not down the street like my crazy grand-uncle. I walk back through the woods. Follow the trails past Pop's property line, down into the shadowed half-light under the pine trees, where the brown needles spread like a carpet over the red clay earth, and when I walk, it makes no sound.

One day, there's a raccoon pawing at a fallen tree, digging grubs out the trunk. He hisses: *Mine, mine, all mine.* Another day, a large white snake drops onto the path in front of me, falls from a branch of a crooked oak before slithering to the roots and climbing back up the tree to hunt newborn squirrels and weak-beaked, just-hatched birds. The rasp of scales against bark: *The boy floats and wanders. Still stuck.* And the next, a vulture circles overhead, black-feathered and strong, calling: *Here, boy. The way through is here. You have the scale still? Here.* And then that feeling of dissatisfaction, of wormy grief, eases a little, because I know I see what Mam saw. I hear what she heard. In those meetings, she's a little closer. Until I see the boy laying, curled into the roots of a great live oak, looking half-dead and half-sleep, and all ghost.

"Hey," Richie says.

Sometimes I see more than Mam.

"Ugh," I say.

I'm mad as shit. Because when I see his big ears and his arms and legs skinny and brittle as fallen branches, I know part of me been waiting on Mam. Been hoping I'd run into her on one of my walks. And when I see him, part of me know it ain't never going to be Mam, never going to be her sitting on a tree trunk, a rotten stump, waiting for me. That I'm never going to see her or hear Uncle Given call me nephew again.

The wind swoops down into the gloaming, brushes me with a great wing, and rises.

"What you doing here?" I say.

"I'm here," he says. He runs his hand through his hair, and it is still as rain-eaten stone.

"I see that."

"No." Richie reclines against the trunk like it is a great seat. "I thought . . ." He looks toward the trail behind me. Looks toward my house. Makes a sound like breath but doesn't breathe.

"What?"

"I thought once I knew, I could. Cross the waters. Be home. Maybe there, I could"—the word sounds like a ripped rag—"become something else. Maybe, I could. Become. The song."

I am cold.

"I hear it. Sometimes. When the sun. Sets. When the sun. Rises. The song. In snatches. The stars. A record. The sky. A great record. The lives. Of the living. Of those beyond. See it in flashes. The sound. Beyond the waters."

"But?"

"I can't."

"Don't—"

"I can't. Come inside. I tried. Yesterday. There has to be some need, some lack. Like a keyhole. Makes it so I can come in. But after all that—your mam, your uncle. Your mama. I can't. You've"—he makes that breath-sucking sound again—"changed. Ain't no need. Or at least, ain't no need big enough for a key."

A yellow jacket whizzes my neck, wanting to land and suck. I wave it away, and it circles again, until I slap at it, feel the hard little body ping off my palm and ricochet off into the gloom, in search of easier food.

"There's so many," Richie says. His voice is molasses slow. "So many of us," he says. "Hitting. The wrong keys. Wandering against. The song." He sounds tired. He lies down, looks up at me from his bed. His head is bent wrong from the root beneath it, which butts up against his neck. A hard pillow. "Stuck. You seen. The Snake? Did you know?"

I shake my head.

"Me," he drags, "neither. So many crying loose. Lost." His blinks: a cat on the ledge of a nap.

"Now you understand." He closes his eyes. Lets go a bullfrog's croak. "Now you understand life. Now you know. Death." He is quiet as sleep, but he moves. One long brown line, rippling like water. And then I see it. He ascends the tree like the white snake. He undulates along the trunk, to the branches, where he rolls out along one, again in a recline. And the branches are full. They are full with ghosts, two or three, all the way up to the top, to the feathered leaves. There are women and men and boys and girls. Some of them near to babies. They crouch, looking at me. Black and brown and the closest near baby, smoke white. None of them reveal their deaths, but I see it in their eyes, their great black eyes. They perch like birds, but look as people. They speak with their eyes: *He raped me and suffocated me until I died I put my hands up and he shot me eight times she locked me in the shed and starved me to death while I listened to my babies playing with her in the yard they came in my cell in the middle of the night and they hung me they found I could read and they dragged me out to the barn and gouged my eyes before they beat me still I was sick and he said I was an abomination and Jesus say suffer little children so*

let her go and he put me under the water and I couldn't breathe.
Eyes blink as the sun blazes and winks below the forest
line so that the ghosts catch the color, reflect the red. The
sun making scarlet plumage of the clothes they wear: rags
and breeches, T-shirts and tignons, fedoras and hoodies.
Their eyes close and then open as one, looking down on
me, and then up at the sky, as the wind circles them and
moans, their mouths gaping now, the airy rush their song,
the rush: *Yes.*

I stand until there is no sun. I stand until I smell pine
through the salt and sulfur. I stand until the moon rises and
their mouths close and they are a murder of silver crows.
I stand until the forest is a black-knuckled multitude. I
stand until I bend, find a hollow stick, turn to the house,
and whip the air in front of me, away from the dead, to
find Pop, holding Kayla. They shine bright as the ghosts
in the dark.

"We was worried about you," Pop says.

Yes, they hiss.

"You didn't come back," he says. I shrug even though
he can't see it. Kayla squirms.

"Down," she says.

"No," Pop says.

"Down, Pop. Please," she says.

"Let's go," I say. Knowing that tree of ghosts is there
makes the skin on my back burn, like hundreds of ants
are crawling up my spine, seeking tenderness between the
bones to bite. I know the boy is there, watching, waving
like grass in water.

"Please," Kayla says, and Pop lets her slide down.

"No, Kayla," I say.

"Yes," she says, and then she toddles past me, unsteady on the dark ground. She faces the tree, nose up to the air. Head tilted back to see. Her eyes Michael's, her nose Leonie's, the set of her shoulders Pop's, and the way she looks upward, like she is measuring the tree, all Mam. But something about the way she stands, the way she takes all the pieces of everybody and holds them together, is all her. Kayla.

"Go home," she says.

The ghosts shudder, but they do not leave. They sway with open mouths again. Kayla raises one arm in the air, palm up, like she's trying to soothe Casper, but the ghosts don't still, don't rise, don't ascend and disappear. They stay. So Kayla begins to sing, a song of mismatched, half-garbled words, nothing that I can understand. Only the melody, which is low but as loud as the swish and sway of the trees, that cuts their whispering but twines with it at the same time. And the ghosts open their mouths wider and their faces fold at the edges so they look like they're crying, but they can't. And Kayla sings louder. She waves her hand in the air as she sings, and I know it, know the movement, know it's how Leonie rubbed my back, rubbed Kayla's back, when we were frightened of the world. Kayla sings, and the multitude of ghosts lean forward, nodding. They smile with something like relief, something like remembrance, something like ease.

Yes.

Kayla tugs my arm and I lift her up. Pop turns. I follow him as he looks for raccoon and possum and coyote, bends branch after branch as he leads us back to the house. Kayla hums over my shoulder, says "Shhh" like I am the baby and she is the big brother, says "Shhh" like she remembers the sound of the water in Leonie's womb, the sound of all water, and now she sings it.

Home, they say. *Home.*

Acknowledgments

I'd like to thank my editor, Kathy Belden, who always asks necessary questions that lead me to essential answers. I'd be a poorer writer without her, and I'm so grateful she walks with me. I am grateful to her assistant, Sally Howe, who compensates for my absentmindedness and keeps me in order. I would be lost without my agent, Jennifer Lyons, who fights for me continuously, insisting that my work reach a wide audience, and who believed in me from the very rough beginning. Kate Lloyd and Rosaleen Mahorter, my Scribner publicists, are sharp, understanding, and kind, and I appreciate everything they do to help my books thrive. My thanks also go to Nan Graham, who has chosen to champion my work and invest in my career as a writer. I would also like to thank the staff of the Lyceum Agency, who are essential to my books and my word getting out in the world. This is also true of my former publicist and close friend Michelle Blankenship, who introduced much of my work to the reading public and continues to believe in me and care for me.

My department chair at Tulane University, Professor Michael Kuczynski, is generous and thoughtful. Without him and my colleagues at Tulane, I would not have had the time and funding necessary to write this book. The students I've taught at Tulane are exceptional, and I fear they teach me more than I do them. My fellow writers ground, inspire, and challenge me always: Elizabeth Staudt, Natalie Bakopoulos, Sarah Frisch, Justin St. Germain, Stephanie Soileau, Ammi Keller, Harriet Clark, Rob Ehle, J. M. Tyree, and Raymond McDaniels. I adore them, and I could not have written and revised this novel without them.

Finally, I'd like to thank my family: my mother, who loves me and feeds me and hugs me; my father, who teaches me how to be a free spirit; my grandmother Dorothy, who shows me how to tell a good story; my brother, Joshua, who ignites a love that burns as a fire inside of me; my sisters, Nerissa and Charine, who fight with me and for me; my godmother, Gretchen, who makes plants and people blossom; my little brother/cousin Aldon, who remembers all the memories I've forgotten, and who helps me recall them; my cousins Rhett and Jill, who grew up with me then, and grow up with me still; my friend Mark, who helps me pick out furniture and bears me up when I can no longer stand; my friend Mariha, who holds my hand and is determined I not die before I should; my nieces and nephews, who teach me to be silly and give me hope— De'Sean, Kalani, and Joshua D.; my partner, Brandon, who makes me laugh when I need it; my children, who teach me how to be patient, how to love, how to hold, and how to feel joy—Noemie and Brando. In closing, I'd like to thank everyone in my community in DeLisle, Mississippi, who inspire my stories and give me a sense of belonging. I am ever grateful for every one of you.

I love you all.

About the Author

Jesmyn Ward received her MFA from the University of Michigan. She has been a Wallace Stegner Fellow and a John and Renée Grisham Writer in Residence and is currently an associate professor of creative writing at Tulane University. She is the author of the novels *Where the Line Bleeds* and *Salvage the Bones*, which won the 2011 National Book Award and was a finalist for the New York Public Library Young Lions Fiction Award and the Dayton Literary Peace Prize. She is also the editor of the *New York Times* bestselling anthology *The Fire This Time: A New Generation Speaks About Race* and the author of the memoir *Men We Reaped*, which was a finalist for the National Book Critics Circle Award and the Hurston/Wright Legacy Award and won the *Chicago Tribune* Heartland Prize and the Media for a Just Society Award. In 2016, the American Academy of Arts and Letters selected Ward for the Strauss Living award.